Pacifica 2

Pacifica 2

by
Jean-Marc & Randy Lofficier

A Black Coat Press Book

Cover illustration Copyright © 2016 Mike Hoffman
Back cover illustration Copyright © 2016 Stephan Martiniere.

Visit our website at www.blackcoatpress.com

ISBN 978-1-61227-481-2. First Printing. February 2016. Published by Black Coat Press, an imprint of Hollywood Com-
ics.com, LLC, P.O. Box 17270, Encino, CA 91416. All rights
reserved. Except for review purposes, no part of this book may
be reproduced or transmitted in any form or by any means,
electronic or mechanical, including photocopying, recording,
or by any information storage and retrieval system, without
permission in writing from the publisher. The stories and
characters depicted in this novel are entirely fictional. Printed
in the United States of America.

Table of Contents

THE SHADOWMEN

My Life as a Shadowman (2) [1]

The year was 1964. We lived in a house with a rather large garden in the suburbs of Bordeaux. At the end of the garden was an abandoned micro-factory which had once been gutted by fire and ought to have been demolished, because, with hindsight, I now realize it was a deathtrap.

In those simpler times, we just knew it as our playground.

"Our" was myself, of course, age 10, and two of my neighbors: Alain, whose father worked as a mechanic at a local garage, and the Other Alain. Yes, that's how he was known. Even his aunt, who owned the local *bistrot*, where we used to play *baby-foot* (foosball) when it rained, was once heard to call him by that name. There was also Marie-Josée, the Other Alain's sister, but she was a girl, so she won't figure much in this story. And then, there was Dick the Dog, a friendly, sloppy, lazy cross between a Brittany Spaniel and a dachshund.

The game of choice, that season, was Monopoly. Since every reader likely grew up playing that world-famous Parker Bros game, I don't need to go into the kind variations—surely never contemplated by its creator!—that 10-year-olds can create. Suffice it to say that, for some reason, we took an inordinate liking to the brightly-colored bank notes that came with

---

[1] This is the second in a series of occasional remembrances of the author's childhood; the first installment previously appeared in our Vol. 3.

the game, and soon were using them as actual money in what might be termed a tiny parallel economy involving the exchanges of toys, comics, marbles, candy, and other small treasures.

Even Marie-Josée became, peripherally, part of that economy, occasionally using her stash of Monopoly money to purchase items such as beads or trinkets for her dolls, when we had them for sale, having found them in neighborhood dustbins. One might say we were recyclers before the word was invented.

The problem with Monopoly money, however, is that its supply is limited. Some notes were lost; others were destroyed during the heated exchanges that are sometimes part of game play; but most were rapaciously hoarded by their owners who, like Uncle Scrooge in the Disney Comics, were guarded them with the innate ferocity of a starving wolverine.

Purchasing a second Monopoly set might have been a way to suddenly double the money supply, but that would have required answering certain parental questions. "Why do you need a second set when you already have one?" was not an easy one to answer, since "I can't use the money from the first set because I've buried it at the end of the garden" would not, in all likelihood, have been deemed a satisfactory explanation.

I realize I've failed to mention that we had started to bury our loot in various secret places, probably influenced by Disney's *Treasure Island*. Mine, for instance, was buried in a corner of the garden, next to a crop of mint plants. Alain's was buried in a bamboo grove behind his house. As for Marie-Josée, she kept the few notes she had in a small tin can with the rest of her toys. She had stabbed her brother in the hand with a plastic doll's fork when he'd tried to steal them, so he had learned his lesson.

Since getting a second Monopoly set was out of the question, we resorted to the same method used by the Federal Reserve today: we printed our own money supply. Well, not so much *printed* as *drew* it, painstakingly, one note at a time.

In those days, the butcher shop used to wrap their meat in a sort of cellulose, or sulfurized paper, the texture and feel of which somewhat resembled actual bank notes. Being the artist in the group, I was tasked to "recycle" this paper after my mother had thrown it away. I'd clean it, cut it and use colored pencils to draw a batch of freshly-minted *faux* Monopoly notes. In France, the colors were red for the 50,000 francs note, purple for the 10,000 francs notes, and—who cared about the others! We were only interested in the big moolah!

As any economist could have predicted, this uncontrolled inflationary spiral of the money supply only contributed in exacerbating our own perverse behavior. "More!" was the order of the day, and I spent all too many hours drawing new notes—increasingly shabbily as time went by—to satisfy our unbridled rapacity.

I note with sadness that, by that time, we weren't even using the notes to buy or exchange goods. We just wanted to own them, to increase our secret hoards. We had, in effect, become little dragons in a nasty fairy tale.

No one can guess how this madness might have ended if fate hadn't intervened in a rather bizarre and unexpected fashion.

One morning, as I went to the mint plants to add to my secret loot, I discovered—horror of horrors!—that my stash was gone! Vanished! Disappeared! In other words: stolen!

The list of suspects wasn't large. The most obvious one was my soon to be ex-friend Alain, who was a great fan of the Rocambole novels. Rocambole being, amongst other things, a thief, I wondered if Alain hadn't been tempted to imitate his hero to enrich himself at my expense. He denied it, of course, but in a way that I found rather unconvincing.

Needless to say, I stopped producing new money, telling the others the window was closed (in effect) until the robber was apprehended and my money duly returned to me. Ben Bernanke could learn a thing or two from 10-year-olds, if you want my opinion. But I digress...

This stalemate ended quicker than I had expected when, a day or so later, Alain announced that he, too, had been burglarized. His stash in the bamboo grove had been stolen! As he seemed genuinely distraught, I didn't question the veracity of his story and my earlier suspicions vanished.

Questions were asked of our new prime suspect, Marie-Josée—it was a well-known fact that girls were capable of anything—but she told us in no uncertain terms, accompanied by threats of physical violence, that she was innocent.

Then, the Other Alain claimed to have been the victim of the Phantom Thief as well!

It was pretty clear that the investigation wasn't making any progress!

The Other Alain's story, I thought, lacked credibility. The details were vague, and he refused to disclose where he'd buried his stash. So, taking a page from one of my favorite heroes, Arsène Lupin, I decided to use my charm on Marie-Josée to get her to tell me where her brother hid his stash. That failed utterly, but offering to draw her two brand-new 50,000 francs note did not.

Soon, we had proof that the Other Alain had not been the victim of the thief, as he had claimed, since his stash was still there. As a well-deserved punishment, Alain and I confiscated his money, which we split between the two of us. But, at the same, it didn't explain what had happened to our own missing money and who the thief really was. Had the Other Alain been the thief, our money would have been in his stash; it wasn't.

I knew that a hero like Rouletabille would not let himself fall prey to discouragement. He would regroup to think, to do what he called *grabbing logic by its right end...*

If Alain wasn't the thief, and neither was the Other Alain nor his sister, and I certainly wasn't, then who was he? Who had the motive... the opportunity...?

And, suddenly, the truth became obvious. I knew who the thief was!

As I mentioned, the paper I had used to make the bank notes came from the butcher shop. Of course, I had cleaned it before drawing the fake Monopoly designs on it, but it retained its residual meaty odor, if not to a human nose then certainly to...

...Yes! Dick the Dog, totally oblivious of the complexities of the human economic infrastructure, was the thief! He had gone out at night to dig up the meaty-smelling bits of paper which he had then proceeded to chew, spit, and otherwise mangle.

The proof of this was obtained when I found small shreds of what had once been our fortunes in his dirty basket.

After that, somehow, the hoarding of money that we knew were really meat-wrappers, lost its charm. We even stopped playing Monopoly for a long time, although I still today have some of the old Park Bros notes from that very set, which have survived the passage of years; unfortunately, none of the hand-drawn notes survived the jaws of Dick the Dog.

Frankly, I don't think Arsène Lupin or Rouletabille could have done better than I at solving the mystery of the Phantom Thief; and then and there, I swore a sacred oath to someday become a Master Detective. Or a soccer champion. The jury is still out on that one.

First publication:
Tales of the Shadowmen 10, 2013

This short story was written as a sequel (of sorts) to Maurice Leblanc's Arsène Lupin and the Island of the Thirty Coffins. *in which the protagonists compete for the possession of a rare radioactive stone called the "God-Stone"...*

Arsène Lupin: Brighter than the Sun

Note from the Editors: The following document was recently discovered in a heretofore unfiled stash of Maurice Leblanc's personal papers. It was enclosed in envelope marked "Do not open until 50 years after my death." As Leblanc passed away on 6 November 1941, it is only belatedly that we are able to present this historic document to the public for the first time. All the footnotes are by the editors.

Perpignan, 10 March 1941.

Yesterday, I had the unexpected and wonderful surprise of seeing my old friend A.L. again. While his hair is graying, and he is now approaching 70, he remains preternaturally young and vigorous. I have come to wonder if there was not more than he told me about that strange mineral water source he once discovered in the Auvergne.[2]

We spent the evening alternating between joyful reminiscences of his past exploits and commiserating over the sad state of our country these days.

My friend, of course, has been helping the Resistance from behind the scenes, working extensively in the shadows, using his own considerable skills and resources, but also the network of friends and relations he's built during his long ca-

---

[2] Leblanc is referring to the adventure entitled *La Demoiselle aux Yeux Verts* [in English *The Girl With the Green Eyes*, or *Arsène Lupin, Super Sleuth*] published in 1927, in which Lupin investigated the existence of a so-called "Fountain of Youth" dating back to the ancient Roman era.

reer. I hope to be able, one day, to relate some of his recent exploits as Colonel Peer Linnaus, but that, obviously will have to wait for better days.[3]

His latest caper, however, deserves to be recorded right away since, in a strange and unanticipated fashion, it provides a startling conclusion to one of his earlier adventures, which I published under the somewhat fanciful title of *The Island of the Thirty Coffins*.

As everyone interested in science knows, Professor Frédéric Joliot-Curie, a Nobel laureate working at the Collège de France, has been studying the notion of "nuclear fission" for the past two years. The way A.L. explained it to me, such "fission" could be achieved by splitting uranium nuclei, and would release enough energy to make a very powerful bomb indeed which, in the current situation, might be of great interest to the combatants.

The key to controlling this process is to find a "moderator" that would slow down the chain reaction caused by the fission, and Joliot has theorized that "heavy water" could fulfill that role.

"Heavy water," as I learned from A.L., is water that contains deuterium, an isotope of hydrogen. A year ago, the Norwegians, who manufactured some, sent their entire supply— 52 gallons!—to France to keep it away from the Nazis!

Last May, with the German forces advancing on Paris, A.L. devised a plan for Joliot to get the drums of heavy water out of the Collège de France and hide them in the death cells of the prison of Riom, near Clermont-Ferrand—purely as a temporary measure, of course.

---

[3] Sadly, Leblanc never had the opportunity to do so since he passed away eight months later. One such exploit, however, was eventually recounted by Anthony Boucher in " Arsène Lupin vs. Colonel Linnaus" reprinted in *The Many Lives of Arsène Lupin*, Black Coat Press, ISBN 978-1-61227-049-4.

Then, with the help of his friend the Bee Keeper,[4] A.L. made contact with the Earl of Suffolk and Berkshire,[5] a gentleman of fortune if ever there was one, whom he had met earlier in Australia.

Together, they concocted a scheme to use a Scottish coal-carrying steamer stuck in the Bordeaux estuary, the *SS Broompark*, to pick up the heavy water canisters, as well as two nuclear physicists, Lew Kowarski and Hans Halban, and ferry them to Britain.

That happened on June 18 of last year.

A.L. being A.L., he couldn't pass up the opportunity of also spiriting away a small parcel of diamonds that he had taken out of Paris!

More importantly, however, along with the heavy water canisters and the diamonds was a lead-lined box the size of a small coffin that contained the God-Stone. It was accompanied by copies of several letters that Joliot had written beforehand and addressed to physicists Mark Oliphant, a member of a newly-established British uranium committee, and Léo Szilárd, of Columbia University in New York.

The letters recounted the discovery of the God-Stone that A.L. had made on Sarek almost twenty-five years ago, and went on to explain its nature, which Joliot has been secretly studying at the Collège de France where it has been stored since its removal from Sarek.

According to A.L., Joliot has become convinced that the Stone is a very unique and extraordinary sample of "uraninite," containing an unusually high concentration of uranium-235, a substance that could sustain a fission chain reaction and would, therefore, be a crucial component in the manufacturing of a bomb.

A.L. told me that the Earl of Suffolk and Berkshire took the canisters of heavy water first to Wormwood Scrubs prison,

---

[4] Leblanc's nickname for Sherlock Holmes.

[5] Charles Henry George Howard, 20th Earl of Suffolk, 13th Earl of Berkshire (March 2, 1906 – May 12, 1941).

then to Windsor Castle, where they presently reside, but the God-Stone was loaded on board of an American submarine expressly dispatched to pick it up. It is to be taken to a secret location managed by something called the "S-1 Section" of the "National Defense Research Committee."

A.L. does not know what use the ancient Tombstone of the Kings of Bohemia will be to the war effort. Neither do I. I am not, after all, a scientist. However, my friend believes that it may become the building block of that "superbomb" which I mentioned earlier.

A.L. quoted the prophecy of Brother Thomas, that bit of "doggerel" which he had mocked when he had unraveled the secret of Sarek for his friends. He said to me:

"The God-Stone which gives life or death... I have seen too much bloodshed in my life, Maurice, to believe that Man will ever choose the power to give Life over that of creating Death... Yet, I dare hope... Which shall it be? Which shall it be?"

Note from the Editors: *Here ends Maurice Leblanc's hastily scribbled note, attached to the folder containing the manuscript of* The Island of the Thirty Coffins. *With the knowledge of history, we are now able to fill in the blanks by providing further information that neither Lupin nor Leblanc could have known at the time.*

In March 1940, scientists Otto Frisch and Rudolf Peierls had calculated that an atom bomb might need as little as 1 pound of enriched uranium to work. Their memorandum was given to Mark Oliphant, who in turn handed it over to Sir Henry Tizard, and led directly to the creation of the MAUD Committee set up to investigate the feasibility of making an atom bomb. MAUD stood for "Military Application of Uranium Detonation" and was certainly the "newly-established British uranium committee" referred to by Leblanc in his document.

On June 12 of that same year, American President Franklin D. Roosevelt created the National Defense Research

Committee (NDRC), also mentioned by Leblanc, which absorbed the previous "Uranium Committee." We now know that it was this newly-formed NDRC, which took possession of the God-Stone a week later, on June 19, 1940. A coincidence? Perhaps not. Szilárd had very likely informed the White House of the contents of Joliot's letter, and Roosevelt had acted accordingly, ordering NDRC chief, Vannevar Bush, to secure the God-Stone for the Americans.

The following year, the NDRC eventually morphed into the Office of Scientific Research and Development (OSRD). Its most secret department was the S-1 Section or S-1 Uranium Committee mentioned by Leblanc in his note. It is that department which later expanded and became the Manhattan Project.

In August 1941, three months after Leblanc met Lupin—for the last time, as it happened—Mark Oliphant traveled to the United States to push for the development of an atom bomb. His trip was a success and, after the December 1941 Japanese attack on Pearl Harbor, on January 19, 1942, President Roosevelt formally gave the green light to the Manhattan Project.

We now know that the "Little Boy" atom bomb dropped on Hiroshima on August 6, 1945, was made of 64 kilograms (141 lb) of highly-enriched uranium-235.

Official sources state that the enrichment was performed at the Oak Ridge, Tennessee, plant known as Y-12, but that plant only became fully operational in March 1944, and did not begin to send shipments of enriched uranium to Los Alamos until June of that year. Another source of u-235 had to exist in order for Little Boy to be ready on time.

Official records also state that "most of" the uranium necessary for the production of the bomb came from the Shinkolobwe mine, a small town in the Katanga province of Congo, and was made available only thanks to the foresight of the CEO of the High Katanga Mining Union, Edgar Sengier, who had a thousand tons of uranium ore transported to a New York warehouse in 1939—a story which even Colonel Kenneth

Nichols of the Manhattan Project himself describes as "a freak occurrence" in his memoirs.[6]

The truth is that it was the God-Stone of Sarek which provided most of the uranium-235 used in the making of "Little Boy." As it turned out, Arsène Lupin was once again proven right. The blood-drenched saga of the God-Stone finally came to an end when a light brighter than the sun burst upon Hiroshima on August 6, 1945.

First publication:
Arsène Lupin and The Island of the Thirty Coffins, 2014

---

[6] Nichols, K. D. *The Road to Trinity*, pages 44-47 (1987, Morrow, New York).

This story was written as an epilog to Maurice Leblanc's Arsène Lupin: 813, *in part to explain Sherlock Holmes' supposed failure in solving the riddle of 813, and also to reconcile several points left obscure in the novel...*

Arsène Lupin: 642

"6"

From the notebooks of Dr. John H. Watson, written in January 1916, marked "not for publication."

Outside of my friend and distinguished colleague, Monsieur Leblanc, who chronicles Arsène Lupin's adventures, and myself, there are only six people who know the secret of "813."

I remember as if it were yesterday the day of August 12th, 1912. It was a Monday. In the early afternoon, my friend Sherlock Holmes had received a note delivered by messenger advising him that his bother Mycroft wished to see him on an urgent matter at the Reform Club.

When Holmes returned that evening, he was in a foul mood. That, perhaps more than the friendship and trust I knew he felt towards me, prompted him to share with me the essence of his encounter with his brother, despite the fact that all that had been discussed was wrapped in utter secrecy.

Holmes forbade me to write about this matter in the most forceful terms, which is why I did not record our conversation at the time. But today, after receiving a letter from Monsieur Leblanc asking for information about Holmes' visit to Veldenz, I believe that at least the bare facts should be recorded, so that someday, someone might piece together the truth behind the strange affair of "813."

17

To begin with, Mycroft brought Sherlock up to date on what he called the "mad rush towards war" between the great powers of Europe, which he attributed to a web of "malevolent forces," as he put it. Even in England, the "party of war," a cabal of politicians and industrialists, were gaining ground, and Mycroft, who sought to avoid a conflict at any price, felt he was now on the losing side. As he told Sherlock, a number of unpredictable events—a coup in Central Europe, a general strike, an assassination (how right he was!)—could be the match that would light the European tinderbox.

His last, best hope to avert a war was the creation of an independent buffer state between France and Germany—the former Principality of Zweibrücken-Veldenz, once restored to its former preeminence, would serve that purpose. British Intelligence had researched the matter and decided to throw its support behind the efforts of a wealthy South African diamond magnate named Rudolf Kesselbach. Then, the millionaire was murdered in Paris under mysterious circumstances. But, as fate would have it, his killer found a powerful rival in the person of Arsène Lupin—"*him*" or "that Frenchman," as my friend called him.

It turned out that Lupin and his rival competed for the possession of a folio of secret letters and documents that would force Germany to accept the restoration of the Principality of Veldenz. These documents were hidden somewhere in the old castle of Veldenz, and the "813" cryptogram was the key to finding them.

Recently, Lupin's adversary, the mysterious "L. M.," had somehow gained the upper hand. He publicly unmasked Lupin who had been hiding under the alias of Monsieur Lenormand—the Head of the French Sûreté!—and had him arrested.

Holmes was naturally interested by what Mycroft had told him, but could not see how any of this was his business. His brother then proceeded to tell him that his agents in Germany had informed him that the Kaiser's own envoy, Count von Waldemar, was on his way to London to ask for the detective's help in solving the riddle of "813" and locating the missing documents.

My friend was secretly pleased by this sign of recognition of his talents and promised Mycroft that he would have the matter settled in a day or so after arriving in Veldenz. In fact, he already had some notions about the riddle which he was eager to test.

To his great surprise, Mycroft told him that he didn't want him to succeed—*he wanted him to fail!*

Sherlock's brother explained that to find the documents and give them to the Kaiser would crush the dream of creating an independent principality. For the sake of the Kingdom, and European Peace, Holmes' mission was to pretend before the eyes of the world that he had failed to solve the riddle. Of course, secretly, he was to find the documents, make a copy for British Intelligence, and replace them inside their hiding place.

It took all of Mycroft's skills at manipulating his brother—the word is not too strong—and appealing to his better side, to convince him to play this charade.

The unkindest cut was that Mycroft projected that, after Holmes' failed attempt, the Kaiser would have no choice but to turn to Lupin to solve the riddle, and thus free the Frenchman from jail. But, as he explained to Sherlock, who grudgingly saw the truth of his brother's vision, a strong principality controlled by Lupin was still the best guarantor of peace in our times.

As it happened, despite Sherlock's sacrifice, Mycroft's plan crumbled into dust. Zweibrücken-Veldenz never gained its independence and, on June 28, 1914, the bullet fired by Gavrilo Princip in Sarajevo killed Archduke Franz Ferdinand and set Europe ablaze.

There were only six people who ever knew the secret of "813": Mycroft and Sherlock, the Kaiser and Count von Waldemar, Lupin and "L. M.," whose real identity Sherlock deduced soon after his return from Veldenz. None of these six wanted war, and yet, war happened anyway. Something, or someone, had intervened to sabotage Mycroft's plan—but who?

That is, perhaps, the greater mystery of "813."

I hope that setting these few facts down onto paper and sending them to Monsieur Leblanc will perhaps one day help to solve that riddle.

"4"

From the notebooks of Maurice Leblanc, written in March 1916, marked "not for publication."

My esteemed colleague Dr. Watson responded quickly to my request for information about his friend Sherlock Holmes' intervention in Veldenz by sending me the note I attach herewith.

I was fascinated to discover the role that British Intelligence had secretly played in Rudolf Kesselbach's plan, and that Sherlock Holmes had not been as unsuccessful in Veldenz as everyone had been led to believe.

The fact of the matter was that L.M.—Dolores Kesselbach, as we now know—had beaten Lupin to the punch in Veldenz and stolen the documents before he could get to them. The papers later recovered in Léon Massier's possession were, in fact, clever forgeries. Dolores had kept the actual incriminating documents, which could have forced Germany's hand in recognizing Zweibrücken-Veldenz's independence.

During his stay at Bruggen, Lupin was still hoping to marry his daughter to the fake Pierre Leduc, and rule an independent Veldenz from behind the scenes, with Dolores by his side. The unmasking of "L. M." and the tragedies that followed crushed that dream and, it turned out, Mycroft Holmes' secret plan for peace.

Lupin found the authentic documents only after Pierre Leduc/Gérard Baupré's suicide, but by then, it was too late. His spirit broken, his dream shattered, he gave them up willingly to the Kaiser the following spring in Capri.

I will now borrow from my friend Dr. Watson's methodology, and state unambiguously that there were only four people who knew that the letters found in Massier's apartment were fake: Dolores and Massier, of course, who took that secret to their graves, and Lupin and the Kaiser, who never shared the secret with Count von Waldemar and destroyed the documents a few hours after his final encounter with Lupin in Capri.

My own opinion is that, of all three deaths, it was that of Gérard Baupré, an innocent man forcibly enlisted by Lupin to impersonate Pierre Leduc, the rightful heir to Veldenz's throne, that weighed the most heavily on his conscience. Dolores was a monster who deserved her fate; at least, Lupin had spared her the ignominy of the scaffold. As for Massier, he was clearly her accomplice. But Baupré did not deserve his fate. It was his death that made Lupin suicidal and made him surrender the real letters to the Kaiser.

There were, at this final stage of the case, only four people who knew the truth about the Veldenz documents. Two were dead, and neither Lupin nor the Kaiser (who had no clues that the letters he had been given earlier were forgeries until Lupin handed him the real ones) could be suspected of having worked behind the scenes to sabotage the plan of a restored Zweibrücken-Veldenz.

In fine, I am no closer than my friend Dr. Watson in solving the true mystery of "813," which remains as dark and impenetrable as ever.

I will leave these notes in my secret files, hoping that someone, someday, will be able to lift the final veil that still covers this tragic affair.

"2"

In this beginning of the year of Our Lord 1920, as I am about to retire from public life, my master, Colonel Bozzo-Corona, leader of the high council of the brotherhood often known as the "Black Coats," has asked me to consign the main facts of the Affair of "813" for the Brotherhood's archives kept at the Convent of La Merci in Sartène.

There are, after all, only two men alive today that know the entire truth behind this baffling mystery: the Colonel and myself.

The Colonel had first gotten wind of Rudolf Kesselbach's search for Pierre Leduc, and what was at stake— the restoration of the Principality of Zweibrücken-Veldenz as an independent state—through his moles in British Intelligence.

Afterwards, it was child's play to steer the so-called "Lord of Cape Town" towards a private inquiry agent named Barbareux, who secretly belonged to our brotherhood and was not as nearly incompetent as some might have thought. It was easy for him to discover the location of Pierre Leduc, while keeping that information from Kesselbach.

At this point, the Colonel had no desire to stop the "rush to war" that Mycroft Holmes had so cannily detected—quite the contrary, in fact. Our brotherhood owned stock in *Krupp*, *Schneider*, *Vickers*, Thompson, Nobel, Skoda, Lowe, Mannlicher, and virtually every weapon maker on the Continent. We also had financial interests in the stock exchange, which would greatly benefit from a war—and did indeed! War was, therefore, on our agenda, and Kesselbach's dream of a reborn Zweibrücken-Veldenz had to be crushed.

The Colonel gave orders to poison Pierre Leduc in his garret, thinking that his death would nip the whole affair in the bud.

My master, however, had not foreseen the sudden appearance of Arsène Lupin onto the scene. The Colonel had always ordered our brotherhood to stay well clear of Lupin, out of both admiration for his exploits and, to be honest, fear of the retribution that someone like Lupin might inflict upon us.

It turned out that Lupin had infiltrated one of his own men in Barbareux's entourage and came very close to learning of our role in this matter.

It is interesting to note that the most obvious clue that he missed was the fact that Kesselbach was corresponding with someone he called "the Colonel." Lupin mistook this for one of Barbareux's aliases instead of the truth, and forgot all about it. This was to be his most serious mistake.

Lupin, unfortunately, was not deterred by Leduc's death. In his usual, resourceful fashion, he groomed a failed poet, Gérard Baupré, to impersonate the deceased heir to the Veldenz crown. At that point, the Colonel, who had guessed the nature of Kesselbach's widow's personal ambitions, gave her assistance in her fight against Lupin. This eventually resulted in Lupin's arrest.

At that point, the Colonel was planning to eliminate Madame Kesselbach and secure the documents for himself, but the public intervention of Sherlock Holmes, and the return of Lupin onto the scene, put a halt to that scheme. Instead, my master had to watch impotently as Madame Kesselbach stole the documents right from under Lupin's nose.

The Colonel then decided to switch horses in midstream, as it were, and use Lupin to eliminate Madame Kesselbach and her gang. That might have been enough to destroy the prospect of a new Veldenz state, but "might" was not in the Colonel's vocabulary. Lupin had to be broken so that he would abandon his intentions to marry his daughter to the fake Leduc and rule Veldenz.

This is why another "suicide" was hastily arranged. When Lupin returned to Bruggen, he found the fake Leduc hanging from the ceiling. Lupin mistakenly thought the man had killed himself because of his despondency over Dolores's death, and blamed himself for the tragedy, which was exactly what my master desired.

Soon after, Lupin gave the documents back to the Kaiser, putting to rest the Veldenz plan once and for all. Without the Principality's existence, the road to war was well paved. A year later, in Sarajevo, one of our agents put the final touches to my Master's plan.

23

The Colonel's machiavellian intelligence had triumphed over Mycroft Holmes' ingenuity and Arsène Lupin's determination. The Great War could begin. My Master was known to occasionally refer to this as his "greatest affair."

As for myself, I now look forward to my retirement in the calm and comfort I so richly deserve.

Valenglay

First publication:
Arsène Lupin: 813, 2015

The first "Affair of the Necklace" is, of course, the historical case from the 1780s involving Queen Marie-Antoinette and Cardinal de Rohan, which contributed to discredit the French Monarchy before the Revolution. Alexandre Dumas used the story as the basis for his novel The Queen's Necklace *(1849-50), a sequel to* Joseph Balsamo, *in which his version of Cagliostro plays a much greater and more romanticized part. In 1906, Maurice Leblanc used the same necklace as a springboard for a short-story (included in our edition of* Arsène Lupin vs. Countess Cagliostro*) in which young Arsène steals it from the wealthy Dreux-Soubize family. This is the third, and heretofore untold, Affair of the Necklace...*

The Avenger: The Affair of the Necklace Revisited

Paris, 1939

It was the smells that Richard Benson remembered the most. The smells of wood smoke and chestnuts that heralded the early days of winter in Paris.

War had been declared, but other than the bellicose and chauvinistic articles in *L'Echo de France* and *Le Matin*, one never would have guessed it. There were no military operations, the Germans being occupied in the demolition of Poland, while the French felt totally safe behind their impregnable Maginot line.

The journalists had coined a name for it: the "*drôle de guerre*" or "Phoney War," but to someone like Benson, attuned to even the tiniest shift in the zeitgeist, it was but the ominous calm that precedes the furious storm.

The American still remembered the intoxicating smells of freedom and futures unbound that had filled the French capital two years before, during the *Années Folles*, when he had taken his wife, Alice, to a Picasso exhibit at the World's

Fair. They had met the famous painter's paramour, the photographer and poet Dora Maar, who had tried to teach Alice the knife game.

But all that was in the past now. Alice, and their daughter Victoria, were no longer of this world; they existed only as memories, just as tragic to him as Picasso's *Guernica* had been that night, when it had been unveiled.

So much death, so much blood.

And what of him, the survivor? Like the dead soldier in Picasso's painting, he wore the stigma of his martyrdom on his face. He had become a mockery of a man who found succor not in painting bloody visions of a dead horse and a bull, but in the purging of the world's vilest elements.

But it didn't stop the nightmares. Nothing did.

And now, the melancholy smells of Paris had contributed to the loss of another chunk of his past which, like a giant iceberg breaking away from the shelf, would disappear slowly in the impenetrable, murky waters of the past.

Benson chased away the memories and turned into a small street two blocks south of the Luxembourg Gardens. It ended in a cul-de-sac with an imposing building that had known better days. It was an austere bourgeois house that belonged to his friend and business associate, Pierre Duchêne.

Benson had last met the tall, bearded Frenchman in the Congo, where he had been trying to launch an oil company that he wanted Benson to invest in. In the American's opinion, Duchêne was an unusual Frenchman in that he treated the natives with remarkable grace and generosity. This, more than anything else, had convinced him to invest in the venture, and he had never regretted it; since then business had boomed.

Now, Duchêne, unaware of the profound changes that had transformed Benson's life forever, had asked his partner to come to Paris to discuss a "pressing business matter." Filled with curiosity, Benson had cabled his acceptance and date of arrival.

In the declining light of the day, the façade of Duchêne's house exuded a quiet air of finality, as if it was trying to repel an intruder, or at least warn him away. Benson shrugged off the feeling, climbed the five steps of the *perron*, and rang the bell.

A butler appeared and invited the American inside. Monsieur Duchêne, he said, was in the library. Would Monsieur Benson please follow him? Monsieur Benson had no objection.

Guided by the manservant, the American climbed a great marble stairway lined with old-fashioned, dusty oil paintings, which he presumed were a gallery of Duchêne's ancestors. He was then introduced in the library, after which the butler discreetly shut the door behind him. The long room smelled of leather and old books, and was lit only by a desk lamp.

Duchêne, who had been at work sitting behind a large and beautifully carved mahogany desk, rushed to greet his friend.

"Richard. You have come. I am so glad to see you," he declared effusively.

"The same here, Pierre."

"How long has it been? Five years, *non*? Much too long anyway. I've been meaning to come to New York, but you know how it is with business. It is the most demanding of mistresses."

"I wouldn't know."

"*Bien sûr*! I forget. You are married now…"

"Alice and Victoria were killed six months ago…"

Benson generally felt no desire to tell the world the details of the tragedy that had cost Alice and Victoria their lives. So he normally used the white lie of a "tragic plane accident" to ward off even well-meaning inquiries.

The Frenchman's face at once became crestfallen.

"*Mon Dieu*! I didn't know. I am so sorry…"

"But the people who did it paid for their crimes. Their death was avenged."

"That is good," said Duchêne, shaking his head. "That is good indeed."

"Life must go on, as they say. Why did you call me, Pierre?"

"I have the most wonderful business opportunity to present to you Richard. One must act quickly—not too quickly however. It will be best to discuss this in the morning, when our spirits are fresh. Besides, tonight, I have been invited to a most interesting soirée... I thought you might like to join me?"

Benson sighed internally. A Parisian function was just about the last thing he wished to attend. But he perked up when he heard Pierre say:

"...The unveiling of the Queen's Necklace."

The gala was held at the *hôtel particulier* of the Comte and Comtesse de Dreux-Soubise, a stately mansion located in the posh Faubourg Saint-Germain.

The evening was already in full bloom when Duchêne and Benson arrived, dressed in the best of tuxedos. All of Paris' high society was in attendance: businessmen and politicians, archbishops and dons, bankers and generals. Duchêne quickly left Benson to his own devices to go and shake hands with various friends and acquaintances.

Alone and not feeling very social, the American drifted towards the dais where the Necklace was being exhibited, resting on a bed of dark purple velvet in a glass case carefully guarded by two policemen. It was a resplendent piece of jewelry with four heavy tassels, festooned with diamonds, and a smaller piece comprised of even more beautiful, glittering stones arranged in pendants.

"It is a marvelous, *n'est-ce pas*?"

Benson turned and saw a beautiful young woman, with luscious black hair and sapphire blue eyes, dressed in a stunning Schiaparelli gown, standing there, holding a glass of champagne.

"I am your hostess, the Comtesse de Dreux-Soubise," she introduced herself. "And this is my husband, Comte Renaud."

"Richard Benson," the American introduced himself, offering a light *baisemain* to the Comtesse and a slight nod of the head to the older man with a square and rubicund face who had just joined them.

"Glad to meet you, Mister Benson," said the Comte, smiling. "We have already received several offers from your country to exhibit the Necklace. I'm always delighted to do business with Americans. Your people are so, er, straightforward."

"I'm quite sure folks will be lining up for blocks to see it, Monsieur le Comte. So it is Queen Marie-Antoinette's legendary necklace?"

"Only a reconstruction, I'm afraid, but the best we could do under the circumstances. The original was stolen by Jeanne de La Motte in 1785, who dismantled it and sold the stones to British jewelers. I, myself, am descended from the unfortunate Cardinal de Rohan, who had thought to gain the Queen's favor by offering her such a magnificent gift. It's taken my family several generations to put it back together…"

"I had heard it had been stolen again—by the notorious Arsène Lupin?"

The Comte raised an eyebrow at the evocation of what was obviously a painful memory.

"You are well informed, Mister Benson, Yes, that scoundrel Lupin stole it from my late uncle in 1880, but even he eventually felt compelled to return the mounting to us, its rightful owners—a publicity coup, if you ask me. It has taken the Dreux-Soubise another generation and over 30 years to locate and acquire the right kind of stones to restore the Necklace to its original glory."

"I am impressed, Monsieur le Comte," said Benson, truthfully. "I hope you are well insured."

"Such a jewel is more than an heirloom," said the Comte, somewhat haughtily. "It is part and parcel of French History. You cannot put a price on it."

Benson thought that he knew several people in the less savory diamond districts of Antwerp and New York's Nassau

Street who would be eager to do just that, but he decided it was wiser to remain silent.

The Comtesse saw that the Comte had intended his remark to be a light rebuff of the American's honest intentions and stepped in.

"Don't be offended by my husband, Mister Benson," she said in a sweet and compassionate tone. "He is very sensitive when it comes to the Necklace. His uncle was shot by Zigomar when he tried to steal it many years ago. He'd give his life to protect it. I'm sure that, with what happened to your wife, you can understand his feelings?"

Benson nodded. "Of course, it is I who must apologize if I unintentionally gave any offense."

"We shall talk no more of it," said the Comte, back to his jovial self. "I am, in fact, interested in hearing your opinion about the Winstons, Mister Benson..."

QUEEN'S NECKLACE STOLEN!

The *Paris Herald Tribune*'s headline immediately caught Benson's eye as he exited his hotel near the Rue Monge the next morning at around 11 a.m.

He had left the soirée at an appropriately late hour. He had lost sight of Duchêne in the growing excitement of the night, and decided to walk back to his hotel alone. His friend was probably busy gathering more investors for his new business venture—whatever it might be. It was around 2 a.m. when the American had stepped inside his hotel, having enjoyed the long stroll down the Boulevard Saint-Germain.

At once, Benson bought a paper and sat at a café to read the article. Past the usual hyperbole, the facts were as follows: the two policemen making up the daytime watch had come on duty at 6 a.m. and had found the body of one of their colleagues strangled in the tiny bathroom adjacent to the exhibit room, and that of the other guard stabbed near the display case which was, needless to say, empty. The doors of the exhibit room were supposed to have been locked at all times, and since the two policemen could not have killed each other, the only logical conclusion was that someone had come into the room and done the deed.

According to the article, the two policemen were above suspicion, so the notion of them being bribed by an outsider had been quickly dismissed by the police. The thief and murderer had to be someone whom they trusted. The Commissioner in charge of the investigation, Monsieur Gilles, had immediately insisted on talking to the Dreux-Soubise and their staff. But he had met with yet another unexpected discovery: the Comte had disappeared!

The Dreux-Soubise slept in separate bedrooms and the Comtesse reported having said good night to her husband when they had retired for the night at around 3:30 a.m. However, the Comte's bed had not been slept in. Could he have murdered the two policemen and scampered away with his own property? As illogical and insane as it was, it seemed the only possibility.

Benson shook his head in an almost instinctive gesture of denial. He couldn't accept that version of events. Everything in him screamed that there was more to it than what he had just read; there was a darker and more sinister plan at work... But he couldn't figure what it was. He finally decided to let the matter rest for the time being and, since the weather was unusually sunny for the season, walk up to the Luxembourg gardens and his friend Duchêne's house.

The *Paris Herald Tribune* was only a morning paper with a single edition. By the time Benson reached the Luxembourg, the *Matin* had come up with a new edition which shouted (literally in this case, as it was being advertised by a young street vendor):

"COMTE DREUX-SOUBISE ASSASSINÉ!"

Benson's French was more than adequate for reading a newspaper and, a quick purchase and several minutes later, he learned that Commissaire Gilles had been anything but idle. The body of the Comte had been discovered, stuffed in a trunk in a baggage room rarely visited by anyone. What was even more amazing, however, was that all medical signs indicated that Monsieur Dreux-Soubise had been murdered—stabbed, no doubt by the same dagger as the policeman—*no later than 1 a.m!* So it couldn't have been the Comte who had killed the two policemen and stolen the Necklace. More disturbing—*to whom, then, had the Comtesse said good night?*

The writer for *Le Matin* was hysterically blaming, *en masse*, the legendary Fantômas (presumed dead), Belphégor (ditto), Ténébras (ditto) and a host of other criminal masterminds of the past, or their ghosts, but in truth knew nothing for certain, and wrote even less.

One line, however, caught Benson's eye. It was a quote attributed to Commissaire Gilles, a simple statement that said: "It is as if the murderer *had the ability to change faces*."

Benson thought long and hard about this. He was lucky that no one in the French police knew of his presence in the City of Lights. His visible interest in the Necklace the night before and his unusual abilities might have easily branded him as their number one suspect.

What Benson didn't know was that there were other, more sagacious, guardians of the Law in Paris than the police...

Benson took a shortcut through the Luxembourg Gardens. The trees were devoid of leaves, and only the evergreen bushes and the lawns reminded him of past springs in Paris. He saw a white dove flutter by and land gracefully on a skeletal branch. He sighed when he stopped briefly to admire the view of the Pantheon. That, too, evoked other painful memories of Alice. Victoria had played here, launching her small boats in the basin, watching them float slowly away, waiting for her daddy to go recover them in his bare feet...

Shutting the windows of the past, Benson hurried toward Duchêne's house. Something he now remembered from the previous night was puzzling him. A theory of the crime was forming in his mind. His friend might hold the key to the mystery, he thought.

The cul-de-sac was empty, except for a black mastiff rummaging through a trash can, looking for scraps of food.

Once at the house, the American knocked at the door. Twice. Three times. Strangely, no one came to answer.

He tried the handle. The door wasn't locked.

Benson entered the house, which appeared to be deserted. He yelled a couple of times, but got no reply.

Worried, he climbed the stairs with the grace of a jungle cat and proceeded toward the library, where he thought he might find Duchêne.

Stealthily, he opened the door and took a step inside the room.

At that moment, he felt a blow on his skull which was like the explosion of a thousand lights inside his head.

Benson dropped the floor, unconscious.

When he awoke, he was no longer in the library, but inside a small, damp cellar, solidly tied by a rope to an iron ring embedded into the masonry. The ground was wet. Water was seeping from under a square metal gate located at ground level on the wall to his right. Benson easily guessed that if it was raised, water—from the sewers, judging by the smell—would quickly fill the tiny cell and drown its occupant. As it had, in fact, killed the previous occupant, whose foul-smelling and putrefying body, half-eaten by rats, lay discarded on the soil.

Despite the sorry state of the corpse, the American could still identify the unfortunate victim.

Pierre Duchêne.

But if Duchêne had been dead for what looked like at least ten days, who, then, had he met and talked to the day before?

The murderer, of course. The man whom Commissaire Gilles had said, *had the ability to change faces*. The man whom the Comtesse de Dreux-Soubise had said good night to, instead of her husband, who already lay dead in the baggage room. The man who, looking just like the Comte, had had no problem getting the two guards to open the door to let him in—and then, had killed them both savagely.

The door, which was situated on the opposite wall, made of ancient oak and reinforced with iron, suddenly opened with a groan.

Pierre Duchêne walked in, holding a torch—except it wasn't Duchêne, but a ghastly imitation with an unspeakably evil grin on his stolen face.

"I see that you're awake, Mister Benson. Good. It is fitting that you die slowly and painfully," said the murderer.

"Have you come to gloat?" asked the American.

"Actually, no. I'm here to collect samples."

"Samples?"

The man began touching Benson's malleable face, rubbing away the makeup, revealing the pallid complexion beneath.

"Amazing," he muttered. "And this is entirely natural? A consequence of your tragedy? You didn't take any drugs? Undergo any operation?"

"Not as far as I know," said Benson, acidly. "What about you? Because, if I guessed correctly, you and I have the same power. You used yours to impersonate Duchêne, then at the soirée, you murdered the Comte and took his place. From that point on, it was child's play to kill the guards and steal the Necklace."

"Fine detective work. I'm sure you'll be greatly missed," said the man, who had begun to carefully remove skin cells and hairs with small metal instruments and put them into tiny glass vials. "As you surmised, my own condition is entirely artificial..." His face began to shift and change into that of a man in his fifties with almost no chin and a thin, aristocratic nose.

"My real name is Baruch Jorgell," he said, while continuing his macabre task. "I belong to a criminal society called the Red Hand. My abilities are, indeed, the result of a series of operations performed by our master, Dr. Cornelius Kramm, who has rightfully been nicknamed the 'Sculptor of Human

Flesh.' We make a point of keeping tabs of new crime fighters, and when we heard about you and your, er, talent, we decided to kill and impersonate your friend Duchêne in order to lure you to Paris. First, my masters thought you would make an excellent culprit for the Necklace Affair. After all, one of the oldest mottos of our organization is to always *pay the law*. But also, Dr. Cornelius wanted to study you—I mean, your body—to see if we couldn't manufacture more people like you and me. You see, my creation, too, was something of an accident, a successful but wholly unintended side-effect of the operations. But think what a criminal army of faceshifters could achieve... The mind boggles!"

Having finished his grisly task, Jorgell got up and walked to the door.

"I will come and recover your body later. Good-bye, Mister Benson. I hope you're not afraid of rats."

The door shut. Two minutes later, Benson saw the grate slowly being lifted by a cable buried within the wall. The foul smelling waters of the Paris sewers began to invade his cell.

And the rats, too.

Try as he might, Benson could neither break his bonds, nor pull the ring out of the wall. The death trap was centuries old, and had often served its grisly purpose, without fail. Duchêne's body was there to attest it. The American reflected that his crime-fighting career had come to an abrupt end, far sooner than he had anticipated. He knew that he had now fully solved the mystery of the Queen's Necklace robbery, but it was unlikely that he would ever share the truth with anyone.

A more aggressive rodent made a move toward him and Benson used his feet to stomp on it, keeping the others at bay—for the time being.

Suddenly, a massive black form swam through the opening, pushing its way through several rats, the necks of which the creature broke with its powerful jaws. Benson thought he recognized the mastiff he had seen earlier wandering about the cul-de-sac. But what was it doing here...?

Having disposed of the vermin, the dog paddled quickly towards the American and started to chew on his bonds. In seconds, Benson was free. The dog then delivered a powerful lick to his face, creating light ripples in his malleable skin. The Avenger didn't know what say.

"Er, *bon chien*," he finally muttered, petting the animal on the head.

The animal nodded, as if he acknowledged the compliment, and ran to the door. Benson followed him. Jorgell had been so certain of his victim's fate that he hadn't bothered locking it.

In the corridor outside, Benson first turned the metal wheel that controlled the raising and lowering of the gate, then ran swiftly and silently up an ancient flight of stone steps, the black mastiff on his heels.

He arrived in a wine cellar, stepping out of a secret passage hidden behind a movable bottle rack, and, running up another flight of stairs, came out of a small door located on the ground floor under the main marble stairway.

His timing could not have been better, for Jorgell stood on the threshold, with a small suitcase standing next to him, preparing to lock the main door behind him.

When he saw Benson and the dog running towards him, the murderer muttered a curse and swiftly pulled a gun from his pocket. Benson knew that it is only in Hollywood serials that villains missed the hero. He was too far to stop Jorgell, and there was no place to hide in the straight and narrow corridor. The man from the Red Hand would probably hit him with the first shot. He could only hope that it wouldn't be fatal. And that the dog would get him.

Suddenly, just as Jorgell prepared to shoot, a white dove flew in and scratched his face, pecking at his eyes, hurting him, forcing him to instinctively raise his arms to chase the bird away. Several shot were fired. In the air. Harmlessly. Then Jorgell fell with a thud.

Benson had been right.

The dog had gotten him.

The American took the suitcase and opened it. It contained some papers and makeup products, but no necklace, no jewels. He wasn't surprised, because he had a good idea where the Necklace was.

Then, he heard the bells of the neighboring Saint-Sulpice church toll 10 p.m.

"If I hurry, I'll be just in time," said the Avenger.

The night train to Antwerp was scheduled to leave the Gare du Nord at 10:28 p.m. At exactly 10:25 p.m., a man who looked exactly like Pierre Duchêne stepped aboard. He strolled through the first class sleeping car, spoke in whispers to a steward, then proceeded toward a numbered compartment.

He slid the door open and said:

"I'm afraid your trip to Antwerp will have to wait, Madame la Comtesse."

The Comtesse de Dreux-Soubise appeared surprised to see him.

"Jorgell? What are you doing here? You were supposed to take care of the American..."

"I thought it was you, but I needed to be sure," said the Avenger, erasing Duchêne's features from his face and remolding it into his usual likeness.

The Comtesse's eyes grew wide and her jaw dropped slightly as she heard the whistles in the station outside. The train didn't move.

"Yes," confirmed Benson. "Commissaire Gilles' men are already here. Tonight, you will sleep at La Santé. After that..." and he slowly drew his hand across his neck.

The Comtesse fainted.

Benson took a hat box from the baggage rack and opened it. Even under the feeble lights of the train compartment, a myriad sparkles filled the air.

"The Queen's Necklace has been found," murmured the Avenger.

The day after, Benson sat at a café overlooking Notre-Dame, sharing a glass of wine with the mysterious, dark-clad avenger known as Judex. He was a tall man, with dark hair and steel grey eyes, which could become very soft when he felt compassion. He also looked much younger than he ought to have been, but Benson didn't feel it was any of his business to inquire about that.

"Thank you for all the help," he said, pointing at the dove perched on a nearby Colonne Morriss and the black mastiff sleeping peacefully at his master's feet, "and also thank you for trusting in my innocence and letting me finish with my investigation."

"It was quite natural," said Judex. "I never believed for a minute that you could be guilty. I am, however, interested in learning how you exposed the Comtesse so quickly?"

"Easy. When we met, she made a mention of my wife being shot by a gangster. The only person I had told was Duchêne—I mean, Baruch Jorgell. So it came to reason that he must have told her, and she inadvertently let it slip. That proved they were in it together."

"I see," said Judex, nodding slowly. "I predict a bright future for you in our common field of endeavor, Monsieur Benson. Shall we toast to it?"

Judex raised his glass. "To Justice," he said.

"To Justice," replied the Avenger.

The glasses shone briefly in the Parisian sunlight and clinked. Somewhere in Heaven, Alice's spirit smiled.

First publication:
Tales of the Shadowmen 8, 2011

This short story was originally written for a French anthology dedicated to the memory of science fiction writer Jimmy Guieu (1926-2000). The four main protagonists are the heroes of The Brotherhood of the Sword, a short-lived series Guieu had begun in the early 1960s, but quickly abandoned in favor of the far more popular Gilles Novak, a journalist specializing in the investigation of UFOs and other paranormal phenomena. In this story, fiction imitates life, and the aging Brotherhood also passes the baton to its younger successor...

The Brotherhood of the Sword: The End of the Brotherhood

Paris, Spring 1967

Spring had come early that year, and the sun's hot rays flowed freely through the open bay windows and warmed up the richly-furnished three-bedroom apartment located on the Quai Voltaire, on the banks of the Seine.

Jeff Mauroy was sitting comfortably in one of the four leather armchairs of his living-room, a glass of scotch whisky in hand, facing his three friends, Raymond Duchenal, Gilbert Cartier and Robin Alexander.

Three years prior, the four friends had solved a couple of baffling mysteries and, after locating one of the mythical Templars' treasures, had christened themselves the "Brotherhood of the Sword."

"We need to have a serious talk," said Jeff, the leader, in a tone that poorly concealed his irritation, "For some time, frankly speaking, we—the Brotherhood, I mean—have been messing around. It's like we've lost our sense of purpose, we've forgotten our mission..."

An uncomfortable silence reigned in the room.

"Honestly, look at you," Jeff continued. "We haven't had undertaken one single case worthy in the last six months!"

"Well, I've been very busy at the office," said Ray Duchenal, the biologist of the team. "I'm responsible for setting up the biology department of a new organization. It's going to be called the *Bureau International de Prévention Scientifique*. It's going to be huge. We hope to start in three or four years. But it's given me the opportunity to think, Jeff. In the future, missions like ours will best be handled by large organizations of that type. Four men like us, even with the best intentions in the world, and the treasure of the Templars at our disposal, are ill-equipped to save the planet…"

"Wait a minute!" said Jeff, offended. "Don't you forget that only last year, we ensured the protection of the Beffort baby at American Hospital in Neuilly, against the forces of Madame Atomos? And how about Indochina…"

"Indochina was more than twelve years ago, Jeff," said Alex Robin, the youngest of the group, who had begun to gain weight because of his wife Clara's excellent cooking skills. And was now the proud father of two adorable children, Olivier and Philippe. "That's all in the past. You're not young anymore. Do you still climb the five flights of stairs to your apartment two steps at a time?"

"Er, no, I take the elevator now," Jeff Mauroy was forced to admit, in the tone of a child caught with his hand in the candy box.

"And when it comes to fighting for the good cause," said Ray Duchenal, "the secret services don't need us anymore. They have Calone, and Gaunce, and Kovacs, and…"

"And the guys of S.N.I.F.," added Alex.

"OK, OK, but it's still thanks to us that France was able to save the anti-gravitation device of Professor Lancry, don't forget that!" said Jeff.

"Ah, yes, about that…" Gilbert Cartier began. He was a physicist attached to the laboratory of nuclear synthesis of Ivry-sur-Seine.

"What about it?" asked Jeff.

"Well, it seems that it only works at the size of the original model. Once you enlarge it, the anti-G force dissipates. We can, at best, fly a flat iron, but nothing else. And for that, we needed all the energy generated by the Marcoule nuclear plant for two hours."

"It can't be!" said Jeff, with an air of despair.

"It has to do with quantum mechanics," Gilbert murmured, shrugging.

A new silence weighed was in the room, disturbed only by the sound of the ice cubes in Jeff Mauroy's glass, whose hand—probably due to a nervous tic?—had begun to tremble slightly. Then, in a resigned tone, Jeff turned toward Alex:

"We still funded the research of Professor Clairembard on the lost continent of Mu. That's worth something," he said.

Alex Robin, the anthropologist of the Brotherhood, appeared slightly embarrassed, just as his friend Gilbert earlier.

"Professor Clairembard's research... Er... Yes... Well..." he muttered, his eyes trying in vain to avoid those of Jeff. "You know I've never been very good at finances, Jeff... And, well, there were some unexpected setbacks... We lost a bathyscaph..."

"How much did we spend?" asked Jeff, growing somber.

"But the Professor is certain that, this time, he's on the right track..."

"How much did we spend?" Jeff repeated.

Alex leaned over and whispered a figure in Jeff's ear. Having stomached the blow, Jeff asked:

"OK. How much do we have left?"

"After the Clairembard expedition?" asked Alex.

"Yes, after the Clairembard expedition!" Jeff replied, angrily.

"Approximately..."

New whispers.

The electronics engineer, former helicopter pilot and judo black belt, who had never been afraid of anything or anyone, blanched, emptied his glass in one swoop, got up and refilled it. Gil and Ray noted that his tremor was now much more pronounced.

"I've come up with the idea of an investment that would be completely in keeping with the spirit of our mission," Ray began, suddenly. "There's this guy who's been recommended to me by Francis Dalvant, the reporter of *L'Eclair* with whom we worked last March. He knows a colleague who's trying to revive an ailing magazine, but no one wants to lend him a penny..."

"That's ridiculous! Do you see us becoming Press barons?" Jeff threw, his face reddened. "Why not invest in night clubs while you're at it?"

"Don't judge so quickly, Jeff," said Ray, keeping his calm. "This would be a magazine that would help usher mankind into the Age of Aquarius, while maintaining a connection to the past. It would deal seriously with everything the official media ignore: the Templars, UFOs... The guy was turned down by Dassault, who told him that Atlanteans would never buy any of his Mirage planes and, therefore, he wasn't interested. Filipacchi asked him if there were female Templars willing to be photographed in scanty clothes. We're his last chance."

"Hum. And what is it called, that magazine?"

"*Panorama de l'Insolite.* Right now, it isn't worth a penny, but this man has ideas on how to relaunch it. He would make a fantastic editor. I took the liberty of inviting him to come here and present his project in person..."

Ray got up, headed for the door, and opened it.

"My friends, let me introduce you to Monsieur Gilles Novak..."

First publication:
The Mistake of Madame Atomos, 2012

Maurice Leblanc as remarkably discreet about the events that led t the death of Joséphine Balsamo, Countess Cagliostro, in Corsica, as reported by Faustine in The Revenge of Countess Cagliostro *(included in our edition of* Arsène Lupin vs. Countess Cagliostro*). We decided to flesh out these events in an epilog to the book...*

Countess Cagliostro: The Death of Countess Cagliostro

Faustine looked at the young woman who couldn't have been a day over 24. "It's uncanny," she said. "You look just like your grandmother."

"Who are you? I don't understand. I never knew my parents. How could you know my grandmother?..."

"She died to save your life. She asked me to give you this letter. It will explain everything..."

The young woman took the letter and, with a remarkably firm hand, opened it.

My name is Joséphine Balsamo, Countess Cagliostro. I am the "Daughter of Cagliostro," and so are you, my dearest granddaughter.

In a few hours, I will be dead. I plan to drink five drops of the ruby-colored elixir of our ancestor, which will kill me more quickly than the sharpest of daggers. I will give this letter to young Faustine, the only person in the world still loyal to me, with instructions to give it to you if the plans I have made to avenge myself on one of my most hated enemies fail. For it is my fondest wish, dearest granddaughter, that you follow in my footsteps and succeed where I have failed.

Attached to this letter are notes about our family, bank accounts, lovers and foes, and other information which will assist you in the career I hope you will embrace. But if your

43

heart tells you differently, burn these papers and our tradition will die as they are consumed by the flames.

You will first want to know about yourself. I suppose I should start at the beginning. I have had many lovers in my life, but my one true love was a circus contortionist whom I met in Normandy when I was not yet 18. His name was Alexandre Cascabel—Sandre as everyone called him. He was the only good man I ever loved, the one for whom I would have rejected my own inheritance had not a wretched and cruel fate taken him away from me. And, yes, Sandre was your grandfather.

We had a son, whom I named Joseph, after our family's tradition. I entrusted him to be raised by the Cascabels, a kind and loving family of circus performers. I asked them to tell him that I had died along with Sandre, for I didn't want your father to follow my dark path; despite everything else in my life, I wanted him to be an upright citizen, a good man who might find happiness in the peaceful existence of a happily married man, playing with his children in front of the family hearth. But blood will tell...

It was by accident that I found out, much later, that Joseph had become a thief, like his mother. But his carelessness, and his lack of experience, had doomed him. Had he gone after any treasure on Earth, the Moonstone or the Hollow Needle itself, I could have saved him. By then, I had my own criminal organization, my own people... I would have stormed the Gates of Hell itself to save my beautiful Joseph. But the foolish child had stolen the one thing that no criminal on Earth would have dared to touch: The Brigand's Painting.

The events of that fateful night of November 1908 have remained forever seared into my mind. I was in Palermo when I was visited by the Master of the Black Coats and his executioner, who was always called "the Marchef." Some said the Père-à-tous had died in 1842, but that couldn't have been true, since he appeared at regular intervals when the Brotherhood was in trouble. Now, they called him merely the Colonel-Who-Never-Died.

44

Oh, how I still see those monstrous, youthful eyes deeply set in a decrepit, wizened face, the portrait of a centuries-old living mummy, staring at me with inhuman amusement.

"Joséphine, my dove, you have been very naughty," said the Colonel. "No, no, don't bother denying it. I know everything. Your son, that young rapscallion, stole my painting. You know how attached I am to that painting. I know, I know, it's an old man's weakness... and I'm getting old and perhaps a trifle tired, and people take advantage..." Here, the old monster feigned rubbing away a crocodile tear. "What you should have done is immediately bring me back my painting and your son. You understand, examples must be made, lessons should be taught, but I know what rebellious young sons are like..." A ghastly smile spread across his parchment-thin lips as if he remembered a secret known to him alone. "Your Joseph would have been punished, but his life would have been spared. Instead, you tried to help him, covered his tracks, hid my painting somewhere I couldn't find it... That won't do, my angel, that won't do at all."

I said nothing, for I knew that I had already entered the Halls of the Dead. I was doomed, but perhaps I could still save my Joseph. My heart sank even further when I heard the Colonel's next words:

"You tried to send Joseph to South America, which was a foolish thing to do, Joséphine. The young man was delivered to me trussed up like a chicken in less than 48 hours. Now, here is what we're going to do, my dove. Joseph is presently being kept in the caves of Palazzio Monteleone. My Marchef has been working him over for a week now to get him to confess where you hid my painting. He talked, of course. They always do. It was very clever, too. That cave of yours on Monte-Cristo... I recognize your hand in this, my sweet..."

"What will happen to Joseph?" I asked.

"The better question is, what will happen to you, angel. Frankly, I don't think your son is likely to cause me much grief anymore... The strain, you see... The way I see it, an example must be made, as I said. I will give you a choice: you come

45

with me and kill your son with your own hand to put him out of his misery, or my Marchef will continue torturing him, and you as well, with instructions to make you suffer for as long as possible. Thanks to that elixir of yours, your family has strong hearts. I have no doubt yours will last for weeks... That will be my last affair," he added cackling in mock senility.

"What will happen to me if I do as you command?"

"I'm not without compassion, my dove. You will be taken to Sartene, near the Convent of La Merci, and spend the rest of life reading Virgil and trading recipes with the shepherds. You'll soon get used to it, you'll see..."

And this, granddaughter, is how I was made to kill your father, my own son.

My life in Corsica afterward unfolded pretty much the way the Colonel had ordered. I spent a lot of time crying over Joseph's death, but then his fate inspired me to craft my own plans of revenge against those old lovers of mine who had betrayed me, which amused me greatly. The child Faustine, who visited me regularly, must have thought me mad, and perhaps she was correct, for that is what hate and sorrow will do to you. Some of the members of my organization also came to see me once in a while, with the Colonel's permission, no doubt reporting to him everything I did. With the passing of time, I grew used to this new life.

But yesterday, I was visited by Marga, my once loyal second-in-command from the golden days when I ruled my criminal empire. She whispered to me, as if anyone could overhear, that the Colonel had begun to suspect the existence of MY SECRET. She, herself, didn't know what it was, and used all her wiles to make me confide in her, but in vain. I played the madwoman, and she left as empty-handed as she'd come.

Later, young Faustine told me that the new Marchef had been seen in Sartene. Is it all a ruse by the Colonel to force me to reveal MY SECRET, or does he simply plan to have me tortured until I talk? I cannot take the chance. None must learn that I have a granddaughter—that Joseph fathered a girl be-

fore he died. She was well hidden and grew up unaware of her family history.

After I finish this letter, which I will seal and entrust to loyal Faustine, I will drink the elixir and kill myself.

Which may be what the Colonel wishes after all.

Wheels within wheels.

From beyond the grave, I salute you, "Daughter of Cagliostro," my dearest granddaughter. Your destiny is now in your hands.

Joséphine

First publication:
Arsène Lupin vs. Countess Cagliostro, 2010

Following in the footsteps of Talbot Mundy, Louis Jacolliot and Henri Vernes, we chose to conjure up the allure of a magical Tibet-that-never-was in this story that stars Doctor Omega and two other famous doctors from popular fiction...

Doctor Omega: The Three Doctors

Dr. Fu Manchu was hanging spread-eagled on the Wheel of Kali.

Princess Alouh T'ho began the Ultimate Ritual. The Blood Worshippers were gathered around the altar and sang with their mistress.

The Devil Doctor knew that, in a few minutes, the Chinese Princess would drain his blood into the great gold crater resting beneath him. The scarlet gem inside it had once been known as the Heart of Ahriman.

Once the gem was bathed in his blood, his *shen*—no, not just his, but the entire world population's—would be drained, conferring upon the sect life eternal and power beyond compare.

Driven mad by her defeats at the hand of that brazen Frenchman, Leo Saint-Clair, Alouh T'ho cared nothing about even her own Kingdom of China. She had caught the Devil Doctor, her deadliest rival, in a fiendish snare and his death would open a new era for the Everlasting Empress.

Dr. Fu Manchu knew that he was powerless to stop her. His only hope lie with *the others...*

Suddenly, the great bronze doors of the secret temple, located deep beneath Lhasa in a hidden place where few had ever trod, burst open.

Two men stood on the threshold. One was an elderly gentleman dressed in a black frock coat with a scarf around his neck and a rebellious lock of white hair standing up on his forehead. In his hand, he held a small, glowing silver stick; its light pointed unerringly towards the Heart of Ahriman.

The other man was taller, and wore white silk trousers, a satin-lined coat and a turban. His face was elongated by the triangle of a brown mustache and beard. His dark eyes revealed a superior intelligence.

"I bid you—halt!" said the turbaned stranger. "I am Doctor Mystere. You are known to me, Alouh T'ho. Desist from your impious ritual or face annihilation!"

"Doctor Mystere... I've heard of you," said the Chinese Princess, hissing. "Your reputation has reached far beyond India, Rama Rundjee. You are indeed a man to be feared. But you, old man, who are you?"

"Indeed," said the elderly man, smiling. "You may call me Omega, Alouh T'ho, Doctor Omega. I was visiting the famous glass works of Boshan in Shandong when a stranger gave me your message, Doctor," said Omega, this time addressing the captive Fu Manchu. "The trail was long and arduous, and without the help of Doctor Mystere here (The Hindu nodded), we would never have arrived in time..."

"In time?" mocked the Princess. "You are too late to stop me, you infernal meddlers."

"I hope not, because if you complete your ritual, that thing that you call the Heart of Ahriman will create a charged vacuum emboitement that will engulf your entire planet. That jewel really is a pandimensional matrix meant to draw Bose-Einstein condensates from other branes and..."

"Enough, Doctor," said Doctor Mystere. "Your science is beyond mortal understanding. Alouh T'ho, suffice it to say that instead of capturing *atmas*, as you plan to do, you will instead destroy the world."

"Let the world die with me then!" screamed the Princess. "I will not be thwarted again!"

And with a speed that defied belief, her arm lashed out, holding a knife that seemed to come from nowhere. With it, she sliced the throat of the Devil Doctor.

His blood rushed down like a cataract and enveloped the Heart of Ahriman.

Doctor Omega barely had time to press a small button on the side of his silver stick.

Then, the world exploded.

Doctor Mystere was hanging spread-eagled on the Wheel of Kali.

Dorje began the Ultimate Ritual. Those who served the Tibetan mystic were gathered around the altar and sang with their master.

Rama Rundjee knew that, in a few minutes, Dorje would drain his blood into the great gold crater resting beneath him. The scarlet gem inside it had once been known as the Heart of Ahriman.

Once the gem was bathed in his blood, his *atma*—no, not just his, but the entire world population's—would be drained, conferring upon the sect life eternal and power beyond compare.

Driven mad by his defeats at the hand of that brazen American, James Schuyler Grim, Dorje cared nothing about even his own Kingdom of Tibet. He had caught Doctor Mystere, his deadliest rival, in a fiendish snare and his death would open a new era for the Everlasting King of the World.

Doctor Mystere knew that he was powerless to stop Dorje. His only hope lie with *the others*... But what *others*? He felt confusedly that he had forgotten something important... He couldn't quite remember what it was, except for a nagging sense of *déjà vu*...

Suddenly, the great bronze doors of the secret temple, located deep beneath Lhasa in a hidden place where few had ever trod, burst open.

Two men stood on the threshold. One was an elderly gentleman dressed in a black frock coat with a scarf around his neck and a rebellious lock of white hair standing up on his forehead. In his hand, he held a small, glowing silver stick; its light pointed unerringly towards the Heart of Ahriman.

The other was a Chinese man, tall, lean and feline, with a brow like that of Shakespeare—or Satan. He wore gold-embroidered green robes. His face was bare and his striking green eyes revealed a superior intelligence.

"Doctor Fu Manchu! Here!" exclaimed Dorje. "But who is with you...?"

"Indeed," said the elderly man, frowning, "but this isn't quite what I had planned... Obviously, I haven't got it right yet... You, near the altar," he said, addressing Dorje, "let Doctor Mystere go. If you complete your ritual, that thing that you call the Heart of Ahriman will create a charged vacuum emboitement that will engulf your planet. It really is a pandimensional matrix meant to draw Bose-Einstein condensates from other branes and..."

"Don't waste your time, Doctor," said Fu Manchu. "Your science is beyond mortal understanding. That son of a goat herder will never fathom it..."

And, with a speed that defied belief, the Devil Doctor's arm lashed out, throwing a pencil-thin blade that seemed to come from nowhere. The weapon embedded itself in Dorje's throat, slicing the carotid artery.

His blood gushed out like a geyser and fell upon the Heart of Ahriman.

Doctor Omega swore under his breath and barely had time to press a small button in the side of his silver stick.

Then, the world exploded.

Doctor Omega was hanging spread-eagled on the Wheel of Kali.

Ming Tsai Tsou, a.k.a. The Yellow Shadow, began the Ultimate Ritual. The Dacoits of the Shin Tan, gathered around the altar, sang with their master.

Omega knew that, in a few minutes, the Yellow Shadow would drain his blood into the great gold crater resting beneath him. The scarlet gem inside it had once been known as the Heart of Ahriman.

Once the gem was bathed in his blood, his *wathan*—no, not just his, but the entire world population's—would be drained, conferring upon Ming life eternal and power beyond compare.

At least, that's what Ming, driven mad by his defeats at the hand of that brazen Frenchman, Bob Morane, believed. His own time traveling ship had caught the Doctor's *Cosmos* in a fiendish snare—or had it?

Doctor Omega, on the other hand, knew that, this time, everything had gone according to his plan. He only hoped that *the others* wouldn't interfere...

He was to be disappointed.

Suddenly, the great bronze doors of the secret temple, located deep beneath Lhasa in a hidden place where few had ever trod, burst open.

Two men stood on the threshold. One was a Chinese man, tall, lean and feline, with a brow like that of Shakespeare—or Satan. He wore gold- embroidered green robes. His face was bare and his striking green eyes revealed a superior intelligence.

The other wore white silk trousers, a satin-lined coat, and a turban. His face was elongated by the triangle of a brown mustache and beard. His dark eyes also revealed a superior intelligence.

"I bid you—halt!" said the turbaned stranger. "I am Doctor Mystere. You are known to me, Ming Tsai Tsou. Desist from your impious ritual or face annihilation!"

"Doctor Mystere... I've heard of you," said the Yellow Shadow, smiling. "Your reputation has reached far beyond India, Rama Rundjee. You are indeed a man to be feared. And I see that you travel in the company of my old associate, whom I once knew as Dr. Natas. How fare you, Fu Manchu?"

"Quite well, thank you, Ming. I fear that you have something that belong to me," he added, pointing at the Heart of Ahriman.

"You and I share the same goals," said the Mongol. "Restoring the values of the Celestial Empire and ridding this benighted planet of the corruption of western influence. Why don't you combine your powers with mine instead of siding with that interloper?"

"You speak of peace, Ming Tsai Tsou," said Doctor Mystere, his hand raised, preparing to strike with one of his mysterious, but always deadly, weapons. "But you leave only death in your wake. If power is required tonight, you will not find Doctor Mystere's wanting..."

"May I say something first?" said Doctor Omega.

Ming turned around. His face rarely expressed surprise, but, this time, he couldn't prevent his amber-colored eyes from registering total astonishment at seeing the Doctor nimbly step down from the Wheel of Kali, rubbing his wrists.

"But... How..? Who...?"

"Indeed," said Doctor Omega, smiling. "I could see that, with the arrival of these two meddlers, there was a chance that you might not complete the ritual, and, frankly, I don't want to do this a fourth time..."

The three others looked at him uncomprehendingly.

Doctor Omega pulled a small, glowing silver stick from his pocket.

"That thing that you call the Heart of Ahriman will create a charged vacuum emboitement that will engulf your planet. It really is a pandimensional matrix meant to draw Bose-Einstein condensates from other branes..."

"Enough, Doctor," said Doctor Mystere. "Your science is beyond mortal understanding."

"No, I understand what he is saying," said the Yellow Shadow, frowning. "It seems that I made a rare miscalculation. Please go on, Doctor..."

"You see, my body isn't quite like yours, and my blood has certain properties..."

And with a speed that defied belief, the Doctor used his silver stick to slice open his left hand.

Before the wound closed, miraculously, several drops of blood fell upon the Heart of Ahriman.

Doctor Omega smiled and put the silver stick back in his pocket.

Then, there was a flash but, this time, the world did not explode.

When things returned to normal, only two men stood in the now-empty temple: Doctor Omega and Doctor Mystere. The altar was empty. The Heart of Ahriman was gone.

"I don't know what you did, Doctor," said Rama Rundjee, rubbing his temples, "but I have a splitting headache."

"A small side-effect of the temporal convergence," said Doctor Omega. "It will soon go away. As for what I did, Men have long been far too careless with the Heart of Ahriman. It was like leaving a lighter unattended in a powder keg. The Heart is an artifact created a long time ago by my people; only one of us, only our blood, could render it harmless."

"But is it gone now?"

"I assume Doctor Fu Manchu took it. The other fellow struck me as far too scientifically savvy to entertain using it ever again."

"But what if Fu Manchu could somehow find a way to restore its powers?"

The Doctor smiled and pulled the Heart from under his jacket

"I'll find a supernova somewhere and dump it in its vicinity."

"But if you have the real Heart of Ahriman, what then did Fu Manchu steal?"

In an undisclosed location, the Devil Doctor threw a red crystalline object against a wall where it shattered into thousands of harmless shards.

On one of them, one could read the tiny inscription: *Made by the Boshan Glassworks, Shandong, China.*

First publication:
Doctor Omega and the Shadowmen, 2011

This is a satirical tale that was originally penned for the program book of a U.S.-based Doctor Who *convention. It draws its inspiration from various memories of Hollywood story conferences and pitch meetings. Cassandra Troy, the Doctor's companion, is the heroine of a science fiction comics story by the undersigned, drawn by the great Gerald Forton, that was meant to be a pilot for a graphic novel that never sold...*

Doctor Omega: Doctor Omega and the Producers

"We appear to have landed, Doctor," remarked Cassandra Troy.

The elderly gentleman with a rebellious tuft of white hair looked around as if events were, for once, overtaking him.

"Landed? Ah, yes. That would have happened when I restored the ancillary power to the *Cosmos*. I flicked all the switches at random. Like flipping *I-ching* coins... Well, let's find out where we are, shall we?"

A brief look at the scanner told the Doctor and Cassandra that the *Cosmos* had taken them back to Earth.

"What a surprise," sighed the Doctor. "The Mother of All Cosmic Catastrophes!"

"But, Doctor, we're in America. California. The 1980s. I did a paper on California once!" said Cassandra.

The door of the *Cosmos* slid open and they stepped outside. The *Cosmos* had rematerialized in what, at first glance, appeared to be a grungy industrial park. There were blank, anonymous-looking warehouses, separated by dull, tar-covered alleys.

Suddenly, the towering figure of an Electroman rose to confront them...

"Boy, it's hot inside that suit!" said the Electroman.

Cassandra had never seen the Doctor so completely taken by surprise before. He looked genuinely confused as the lumbering silver giant took off his head to reveal the jovial, if sweaty, face of an ordinary mortal beneath.

"You're here for the movie, aren't you?" asked the ex-Electroman, unaware of the effect he had just had on the Doctor.

"What?"

The word triggered something in Cassandra's memory. Suddenly, she knew where they were.

"A movie, Doctor," she exclaimed. "We're in Hollywood!"

Roland DuBay—Rollie to his friends—was a professional movie extra, a bona fide, dues-paying member of SAG and half-a-dozen other unions. He had been a U.S. cavalry officer in *Geronimo II* (shot in the third scene), a drug-crazed terrorist in *Die Hard V* (blown to smithereens in the middle of act 2) and even one of the Wicked Witch's child-stealing monkeys in Woody Allen's remake of *The Wizard of Oz*. But what he hated the most were sci-fi pictures, because it was always so damned hot inside the suits.

Still, he thought, *bills gotta be paid, Melissa has to be kept in the Valley lifestyle she's grown accustomed to, and the kid's gonna be going to college one day. Not to mention that the electric Ocelot needs new plugs.*

Meaning that Rollie DuBay needed the job badly, and if this was what it took to get it, he was prepared to be the best Electrogoon ever to lumber across a Hollywood set.

Not one to let an opportunity pass—he had gotten the job of the Flying Monkey in the *Oz* picture by reading Mia Farrow's best-seller beforehand—Rollie realized at once, with the unique feeding instinct that only actors and predators share, that the funny-looking elderly stranger in the black frock coat might be his ticket into the picture.

"*Doctor?*" he said. "I'd heard they wanted to cast a big-name star. Someone like Robin Williams or Danny DeVito. But I can see why they went with you. Neat threads. It always helps to dress the part. That's why I borrowed this suit from Props. But they're so darn hot. Too much insulation."

Now that he had a firm grasp on the situation, the Doctor was back to being his unflappable self.

"Well, you look the part, and I do have some experience in the matter," he said firmly.

"Thanks," Rollie replied. "But do you think you could put in a good word for me with Mr. Bialystock? I'd really like to be in this picture."

"Mr. Bialystock?"

"You know, the producer."

"Yes, of course. Silly of me. I don't see why not," said Doctor Omega. "Take us to your, er, producer."

"Glad to. Follow me."

Rollie DuBay put his electro-helmet back, thanking the muses for bringing him together with the two strangers. While lumbering forward, he thought, *The little guy must be one of these Famous Foreign Actors from one of these foreign films Tom and Annie like to watch on* Bravo... Tom and Annie were his neighbors, a university professor and a high school teacher. Rollie, himself, preferred the Moron Channel and hated anything that sounded even remotely foreign. *The bird must be his entourage. Hey, she's kinda cute in that leather outfit.*

Unaware of Rollie's mercenary thoughts, Doctor Omega and Cassandra Troy followed the extra along the studio's alleys, crossing paths with a variety of people dressed in diverse costumes and uniforms. No one paid any attention to them.

"They must be making a movie about you, Doctor," said Cassandra.

"Oh, dear. Then it is a good idea to take a little look around. I was here once before. Can't say that I cared much for it. I mostly remember a lot of running around. A sense of great chaos and disorder..."

"A sense of great chaos and disorder" was precisely the state of mind of Janice, the blonde receptionist who was desperately trying to make sense of the messages left for her boss, Mr. Bialystock, taken during her lunch break by an intern.

Suddenly, she saw a lumbering metal giant walking into the bungalow, followed by an old man and a tall red-head girl in a skimpy leather outfit. She sighed. No, definitely, today wasn't her day...

"Jhani Ista Bialustin?" said Rollie.

Actually, what he had said was, *Janice, is Mister Bialystock in?* but the electro-helmet had not been designed for speaking parts.

Janice started to reach towards the can of mace she kept under her desk just in case. The week before, an extra from *Dances with Werewolves* had bitten a receptionist, and she was not going to take any chances.

Rollie fathomed at once what was going on and removed his helmet. He had learned early on his career to ingratiate himself with the studio Cerberuses that secretaries and receptionists were.

"It's me, Rollie," he said. "These folks are friends of Mr. Bialystock."

Janice, who had been hired only two weeks earlier, had no idea who was a friend of the producer or not. The authoritative manner in which the small stranger (*Obviously a famous Foreign Actor,* she thought) was studying the framed posters of Bialystock's previous pictures, *Springtime for Hitler*, *Honey I've Shrunk My Tits* and *Beverly Hills Robonuns II*, convinced her that he was indeed *someone*, instead of being merely *anyone*.

"Mr. Bialystock isn't here yet, but I'm expecting him any minute. Why don't you wait for him in the conference room with the other foreign gentleman," she said, pointing towards an open door.

"We'll be happy to," said Doctor Omega with a courteous nod of the head. Followed by Cassandra and Rollie, who wasn't going to let his meal ticket out of sight if he could avoid it, they walked into the room.

"Doctor! You! Here!"

The person who had been waiting in the room was a small, blond man, with a deceptively angelic face, who looked a lot younger than he really was. Although he was dressed in a nattily-tailored blue suit, something about his bearing suggested a military man.

"Lieutenant Langelot!"

"Captain, now, I'm afraid."

The two men shook hands, obviously and genuinely happy to see each other. The Doctor introduced Langelot to Roland ("Please call me Rollie") DuBay and Cassandra, who came from the Year 586 of the Terran Hegemony, far in the future.

"This is quite a surprise, Doctor," said the Captain from the Service National d'Information Fonctionelle (SNIF for short), one of France's top military intelligence service. "You're just about the last person on Earth I'd expected to see at this hearing."

"Hearing? I'm not sure what you're referring to, Captain. I thought this was a movie. Please tell me more."

"You're not here for the hearing? But then how?... Ah, I should know better than to ask. You've always had the knack of showing up whenever you're needed the most. Although, to be frank, this is not quite in the same league as the threats we used to fight."

"Isn't it, Captain?" replied the Doctor. "And what is the threat this time? Vampires? Electromen? Mr. T?"

"Worse, Doctor. Lawyers. Hollywood lawyers."

"Ouch," grimaced Doctor Omega, amused by his friend's gloomy face.

"It's not a joke, Doctor. SNIF's reputation is at stake. Yours, too."

"How can that be?"

"The people who run this studio, Miracle Pictures it's called, are making a picture about SNIF's glory days. They're calling it *Is Paris Boring?* The producer is a madman! Anyway, even though the Élysée eventually decided to cooperate with the project—it was either that, or let him do a hatchet job on us—my direct superiors felt that Mr. Bialystock was approaching the project in, shall we say, a very cavalier fashion. So they requested, as a condition for their cooperation, that SNIF be allowed to have a consultant on the set, with the right of script approval. Needless to say, Bialystock fought tooth and nail against the idea, but he was out-voted by the Studio brass who felt it was too good an opportunity to let pass. And that, Doctor, is how I came to be in this wretched place."

"Come now, Captain, surely a trip down memory lane can't be that painful?"

"If only that were the case, Doctor," sighed Langelot, "but ever since I arrived, it's been one row after another with Bialystock. The man is impossible. He decided to have some crazy Belgian play me—Jean-Claude Van Dumb or something like that. A great Q rating he said—as if a Q rating had ever defeated a Hormovar! And, as if that weren't enough, now there's this damn lawsuit. The BIDI has objected to the way it is depicted in the film. They feel that they're being portrayed as a bunch of ruthless villains led by a power-hungry madwoman."

"So?"

"They say it's damaging their reputation."

"But that's exactly who they are."

"If I've learned one thing here, Doctor, it's that truth has nothing to do with motion pictures. The BIDI is a big defense contractor now. Their president is Madame Schasch's own son, Anton, and a hearing has been set to resolve the issue. That's what I assumed you were here for, you being there at this time..."

"No, this is the first I've heard about any of it, but I'll be glad to give SNIF a hand, Captain. For the sake of the truth, of course."

Most of the Doctor's and the French Captain's conversation had flown over Rollie's head, but the actor had managed to grasp an important fact or two, such as, *If the small fella isn't an actor, but the real thing, then he must have some kind of creative approval deal. If I stick with him, I'm a shoo-in.*

This current of speculative thought was interrupted by Janice

"Max, er, Mr. Bialystock's back. He'll see you now," she said.

"Come, Doctor," said Langelot. "Let me take you to meet my arch-enemy."

"??"

"The producer, of course."

A few minutes later, the Doctor and his growing entourage walked into a plush office.

Such is the power of entourage that the word had begun to spread around Miracle Studios that a FFA (Famous Foreign Actor) was taking a meeting with Max Bialystock. Worried producers were making discrete inquiries to nervous agents, while deal memos for a remake of *Gigi* were being unearthed from the drawers of legal departments and dusted off. Fortunately, the Doctor remained blissfully unaware of this flurry of activity on his behalf.

Bialystock himself was a portly man with a strange haircut and a hyper kinetic attitude. He was presently on the telephone but gestured to everyone to sit down. Finally, he hung up and addressed Langelot.

"Great news, kid, I've got my extra $3 mil. We can blow up the Eiffel Tower!"

"But we didn't blow up the Eiffel Tower," said Langelot with genuine frustration.

"I know, but you need a big pay-off. This is a big budget picture, kid. The audience wants to see big things. We can't just end the show with half-a-dozen electroguys being discombobulated in a warehouse."

"But that's the way it happened."

"So what? I'm giving them the way it should have happened. Why should you care, anyway? It means a bigger part for Jean-Claude and the little fellow..." Suddenly, the producer's eyes noticed the Doctor at last and lit up. "You must be Doctor Omega!"

The Doctor nodded enthusiastically while smiling from ear to ear. Bialystock got up and began pumping Omega's hand.

"I'm thrilled to meet you. I've been pushing for Robin to play you from day one, but the Studio won't come up to his percentage of the gross. Now that I've seen you, I know my instinct was right. It's got to be Robin."

Maybe I can get a speaking part this time, thought Rollie. *I'll need to change agents then.*

Bialystock rushed back to his desk and pushed a button on the intercom.

"Janice. Send a memo to the Studio head! I've gotta have Robin. It doesn't matter what it costs." Then, without a break, he asked the Doctor, "What do you think of my idea for the ending? Do you agree with the kid?"

"No, I don't agree with the kid," grinned Doctor Omega. "I wish we could have blown up the Eiffel Tower too. I never liked what Gustave did."

"Oh no, not you too, Doctor," sighed Langelot, raising his eyes. *This is it*, thought the Captain. *He's gone Hollywood.*

At that moment, Janice walked into the room.

"The hearing is scheduled to start in half-an-hour, Mr. Bialystock. The lawyers are waiting for you in Conference Room 4."

"Guess we should get a move on, then," said Bialystock. He suddenly noticed Cassandra and Rollie's lumbering figure. "Who are all these people?" he inquired.

"Friends of mine," said the Doctor.

The producer cast a puzzled look towards Rollie, who grinned.

"Ah. Well. Oh, fine. Come on, all of you," he said, waving them along.

A few minutes later, Bialystock, Langelot, Doctor Omega and his still-growing entourage walked into a plush conference room. In its center was a long black marble table. A dozen lawyers in business suits sat around it, representing the marshaled forces of Miracle Studios' legal department. Langelot introduced Doctor Omega as "SNIF's then-scientific advisor," accompanied by his assistants. No one thought of questioning the Doctor, Cassandra or Rollie's strange attires. Being lawyers, they merely assumed that everyone who was not a lawyer was a kook.

"I assume you're here to corroborate what the Captain has already told us?" asked a well-tanned, middle-aged man named Rosenberg, the head of Miracle's legal team.

"Essentially, yes," said Doctor Omega.

"Terrific. We can use an extra witness. The other party has been very aggressively claiming that we're defaming the character of their late chairwoman and founder..."

Before Rosenberg could continue, a secretary opened the door and let in another half-dozen participants: the BIDI lawyers, who went to sit down at the opposite end of the black table. A grey-faced man named Wharton, obviously the senior attorney, began speaking.

"The Bureau International de Documentation Industrielle, or BIDI, is an important and respected organization, with an impeccable record. We have no intention of allowing the name of our late chairwoman and founder, Madame Angelique Schasch, to be slandered. The woman was a humanitarian, and no one will say otherwise. This 'Electromen' business is nonsense. We have files in our archives that will clearly establish that SNIF fabricated the entire thing for its own, political reasons. To sum up, I'm afraid that the script, as it stands now, is totally inacceptable. Unless all mention of the BIDI and Madame Schasch are deleted in their entirety, we shall have no option but to continue with our lawsuit."

"See you in court then, you stiff-necked, sheep-schtupping, Nazi-sucking shyster!" erupted Bialystock, who had quickly reached his boiling point.

"Now, now, Mr. Bialystock, please calm down," said Rosenberg. "Those words are uncalled for. Especially that bit about the sheep." He then turned towards Wharton, and continued smoothly. "We have commissioned a revised screenplay—at considerable expense to Miracle Studios, I might add. We're confident that it more than adequately deals with your objections by removing several possibly questionable scenes..."

At that point, there was a loud *harrumph* noise from Bialystock, who raised his eyes to the ceiling and shook his head, but Rosenberg pointedly ignored the producer's glaring disapproval.

"We at Miracle," Rosenberg continued, "feel that the film now presents a balanced version of the events in question, and does not in any way defame the management of your company."

One of Rosenberg's assistants handed several copies of the revised script to the BIDI attorneys, who began studying it as one.

"SNIF just wants to make themselves look as if they were doing something other than sitting on their duffs, sucking up the French taxpayers' money," remarked a younger BIDI attorney, with a face which the Doctor thought bore an appropriate resemblance to that of a weasel.

"How dare you!" shouted Langelot, slamming his fist on the table. "Your vaunted Madame Schasch was a dangerous, power-hungry maniac, and if we're all sitting here in this room today, it is only because SNIF was able to stop her! Several brave and decent men died during that mission, and you have no right to sully their memory with your lies!"

"More likely, they shot themselves during one of your ill-conceived training exercises. We should add civilian endangerment to our charges," snickered the weasely lawyer.

This time, the Captain stood up, almost sending his chair reeling backward. But Rosenberg, grabbed him by the arm before he could vent his wrath upon the arrogant lawyer. "Captain, please. I'm sure we can straighten this whole thing out to everyone's satisfaction. Sit down. Have a glass of Perrier."

He snapped his fingers and one of his assistants ran out of the room, quickly returning with a glass of sparkling water.

Please, God, don't blow my chances now, begged Rollie silently.

There was a long, painful silence while the BIDI attorneys reviewed the revised script. Finally, Wharton raised his eyes.

"Pending a more detailed review, this would indeed appear to be adequate," he said.

There was an audible sigh on the Miracle side of the table.

"Of course," the attorney continued, "it must be made more obvious to the casual viewer that this character... this 'Doctor Omega'... is the real villain of the piece. He is the one who clearly entrapped Madame Schasch and besmirched the good name of the BIDI..."

"*What?!*"

This time, it was the Doctor's turn to jump to his feet. His face was red, and if looks could kill, Wharton would have been reduced to a small pile of ashes on his chair.

"May the Vahks feed on your bones, you Phtooz-infested maggot. I'll bring the Curse of Kheoba on you and your Hobbal-brained lawfirm..."

"Shut up, Doctor, or I'll personally see to it that you never work in this town again!" shouted Rosenberg, finally losing his composure. Then, turning towards Wharton, the attorney added with a tired smile, "I believe we have a deal..."

Rollie DuBay smiled.

Things were going to be all right after all.

First publication:
Doctor Omega and the Shadowmen, 2011

Like many French aficionados of my generation, I did not dis-cover Fantômas through the original novels of Pierre Souvestre & Marcel Allain (although these were still widely available in the 1960s), but through the somewhat cheesy but colorful, extravagant and humorous trilogy of films directed by André Hunebelle, starring the legendary Jean Marais (from Beauty and the Beast*) in the twin roles of Fantômas and jour-nalist Fandor, and the comedic superstar Louis de Funès as the bumbling policeman Juve. While a parodic travesty of the original stories, those films still managed to preserve the myth of Fantômas and instill awe and fear at the sight of the green-masked villain, who was certainly anything but funny. It is to them that this story is dedicated...*

Fantômas: The Sincerest Form of Flattery

Monaco, 1964

The man woke up.

He blinked. Twice. He could barely make out his sur-roundings beyond the simple fact that he was in a bed, in a white room. It was sparsely furnished, with only functional furniture: a chair, a formica table, a small sink and the narrow bed in which he lay. *A medical room*, he thought. There was a small, slit-like window. He noticed at once that the glass was reinforced.

He got out of bed and walked to the window in his pa-jamas. Outside was a park. *Not much to be learned from that.*

Then, he went to the door, which of course was locked. There was a square window, also of reinforced glass. He could see a corridor, white walls, green linoleum floors, and, just at the edge of his field of vision, a wheelchair parked against a wall. *A private clinic*, he guessed.

He sat on the chair and performed the set of mental and physical exercises he did on a daily basis to remain at his best. He felt oddly tired, as if he had just been running a marathon. *How long have I been here?* he thought. *And where is "here?" Have I been injured?*

His neck hurt. *Maybe I have whiplash.*

The man looked at his reflection in the small mirror above the sink and suddenly remembered who he was.

He was Diabolik.

Diabolik's last memory was of the accident.

He reran the events through his head, as if he was running a film in reverse. The casino. The corniche overlooking the Mediterranean. The sparkling lights of Nice behind him. A king's ransom in diamonds safely stored in the Jaguar's glove compartment. The car, hugging every bend in the road, obeying its driver like a tame panther. And, at the end of the road, Eva, waiting for him in their getaway plane...

The black helicopter had come out of nowhere, oddly silent (*a new model? to be checked later*), spitting a hail of bullets from its twin machine guns. Diabolik had swerved, managing to avoid the enemy's fire, but a stray bullet had shredded a tire, causing the car to career out of control, running over the edge of the cliff and falling straight into the sea.

That was all he remembered. Nothing more.

He returned to the door and banged on it several times, calling out. Almost at once, he heard a voice saying: "Doctor Garrick! Monsieur Valmont is awake!"

There was a flurry of steps and a man dressed in a white coat unlocked the door and entered. He was somewhat portly and Diabolik thought that, with his jowls and kindly eyes, he looked like the French actor Michel Simon.

"Good afternoon, Monsieur Valmont," said the man, extending his hand. "I'm Doctor Garrick. You have caused us a lot of worry, you know..."

Diabolik shook the doctor's hand. It was oily, almost greasy, but deceptively firm underneath.

"Where am I?" he asked.

The Doctor shook his head.

"Yes, yes... The neurologist said you might suffer from some memory lapses, after your... your... er..."

Somehow, Eva must have rescued me and left me in the care of these people, thought Diabolik. *Obviously, she can't have told them the truth. They must think the car went over the cliff in an accident. Better play along until she shows up...*

"My accident?"

The doctor's eyes grew wider while his face suddenly expressed deep concern.

"No, no, Monsieur Valmont," he said, very softly. "Facing up to the truth is the first step towards your recovery. There was no accident. You tried to commit suicide... To hang yourself."

Automatically, Diabolik reached for his throat with his hand, *and he felt the bruises on his neck.*

"If your son hadn't come home unexpectedly, you would have died," continued the kindly Doctor. "Now let me examine you." He pulled an ophthalmoscope from his pocket.

Diabolik grabbed the man's wrist and saw him wince, so strong was his grip.

"What do you mean, *my son*?"

The doctor's face looked increasingly concerned.

"Your son Carlo, Monsieur Valmont... Don't you remember?" Then he added to himself, muttering under his breath, "Heavens! This is bad!"

Diabolik let go of the Doctor and forced himself to count down slowly from ten to zero. *I don't understand what's happening. Is this man playing some kind of game? I have to find out more...*

"You're right, Doctor," he said with what he hoped was a sincere smile. "My memory is still playing tricks on me. Tell me what you know. I'm sure it will help me remember."

The Doctor smiled again, although Diabolik could tell that he didn't totally believe him, but probably saw no harm in doing what his patient requested. While he performed the eye exam, he said:

"You're Horace Ralph Valmont; you're married to Anna and you have two children, Carlo, 18, and Francesca, 16. You work at the Depository Bank of Zurich here in Monaco. Something to do with Mergers & Acquisitions, I believe... Now, what I'm going to tell you next is very hush-hush... Your wife was terribly concerned about your safety, which is why she booked you into my private clinic... Apparently, your son..."

"Carlo?"

"Yes, Carlo, owed money to the Mafia... A pretty large sum, I understand... You were working on an important deal, with several bidders, including one connected to the Sicilians... They blackmailed you to push things though in exchange for forgiving Carlo's debts... You did it, because you had no choice... But your boss, Signore Ginko, who hates you, found out about it... He was going to report you, have you arrested and sent to jail... The Sicilians, of course, wouldn't like that... So, understandably, you chose the quickest way out... I'm sorry."

"You mean, I hung myself?"

"Yes, but Carlo, who was supposed to be away with friends, came home early and found you. He saved your life, Monsieur Valmont. Your wife immediately had you transported here. You remained nearly comatose for three weeks. Frankly, some of my colleagues were starting to give up on you, but I said, wait, he'll pull through, you see..."

This isn't possible. I'm not Horace Valmont. I'm... Diabolik.

"Now that you're better, we're going to move you to a more comfortable room. And I'll call Anna to tell her that you're awake. No doubt she'll want to visit you soon... But you must take it easy, you understand?"

In the course of the next five days, Doctor Garrick introduced Diabolik to his wife, Anna, a middle-aged, mousy-looking brown-haired woman with a chubby face, a non-entity; Carlo, his duly contrite son, whom he could tell right away would never amount to anything and would break his mother's heart; and Francesca, his daughter, 16 going on 25, wearing clothes that made her look like the cheap tramp she was likely fated to become.

He learned that his nemesis, Ginko, his boss at the Monaco branch of the Depository Bank of Zurich, had hounded him ceaselessly, denied him a promotion and purposefully kept him under his thumb to do all the drudge work—that is, until the day of the scandal.

Diabolik asked to spend time in the clinic's library and combed through the newspapers and old magazines kept there, searching for a trace of his criminal exploits—anywhere, but none were to be found. On the other hand, there was a small press article in the bank's internal reporting that the trusted and reliable Horace Valmont had fallen victim to a domestic accident (*fallen off a ladder while changing a light bulb! Even that cover story was transparently lame—like the rest of his presumed life*)

Could it all be true? Could he be this mediocre bank employee, frustrated in a dead end job, with an utterly dreary family, who, in what he thought would be the last moments of his life, had constructed a glamorous scenario—one where he was strong, free, rich and powerful, bold and handsome, with the stunning Eva Kent for his lover, always triumphing over the plodding Ginko, his natural inferior?

Or was "Horace Valmont" the fictional scenario, an elaborate conspiracy meant to drive him out of his mind?

There was only one way to find out.

Diabolik took his wallet from the inside pocket of his jacket, hanging in the closet, and fished out an electronic pass in the name Horace Valmont from the Monaco branch of the Depository Bank of Zurich.

There he would find the answer.

Doctor Garrick had not objected to the visit. On the contrary, he told Diabolik—Horace Valmont—that finding himself back in familiar surroundings might stir his memories. As far as the good doctor knew, Diabolik was still suffering from a bout of amnesia.

Once inside the building, Diabolik had gone straight to the elevator that would take him down to the vault. His electronic pass had sent the cabin down, and enabled him to open the several gates of titanium bars that stood between him and his goal.

Safe deposit box number 9.

At last, he stood before the blank metal wall, with ten indentations.

The box could only be opened with his retinal pattern and the print of his ring finger.

Diabolik stared at the tiny scanner while applying the surface of the fourth digit of his right hand to the ultrasensitive plate.

If he was really Diabolik, and not the insipid Horace Valmont, the vault would release the box and, inside, he would find what he remembered storing there: a small gun, ten passports in various names and countries, and 20 bearers bond drawn on a Liechtenstein bank for an amount totaling $100 million—one fifth of his treasure, the rest kept in other safety deposit boxes in other banks known to him alone.

He heard a discreet whirring sound. *Excellent!* he thought. The silver metal box slowly slid out on invisible railing. Diabolik breathed a sigh of relief.

He grabbed the box and opened it. The gun was there; so were the passports.

The bonds were gone

Suddenly, he heard a laugh behind him, except it wasn't that exactly, but more like the low growl of a tiger—if a tiger could laugh.

He turned around and saw that the eerie laugh came from Doctor Garrick, who was presently pulling off the lifelike mask that had been his face. Diabolik couldn't help admiring the rubber-like syntheflesh which was undoubtedly superior to his own products.

Beneath it was another mask—a pale, green face, with barely sculpted features; naked, brutal, emotionless; the only thing alive in it were the two steel grey blue eyes shining with incredible intelligence and malice, and occasionally a flash of humor—the macabre wit of the torturer taking delight in his victim's pain.

"Do you know who you are now?"

"Yes; I am Diabolik."

"Excellent. My job is done then. You're cured."

"You took my money. Knowing who I am, you still dared to steal from me. Are you insane?"

"Ah, yes. I thought you might want an explanation. Very well. That gun is totally harmless by the way. Unlike mine... You'd do well to listen to me..."

"Who are you?" asked Diabolik.

"Fantômas," replied the man in the green mask.

"That's impossible. Were he still alive today, Fantômas would be almost 100!"

"And yet here I am. Because of you, one might say, you and all the others. Fantômas in Mexico, in Argentina, Kriminal, Killing, Satanik... The world today seems awash in Fantômases. At first, I planned to kill you all, one by one... You don't know how close you came to death when I shot your car on the corniche... But then, I came up with another plan... I decided to... tax my imitators."

"What do you mean?"

"I told myself: Make them pay—pay a tax on the right to be Fantômas—the right to live really. So I set up the clinic and the persona of kindly Doctor Garrick. I took your retinal pattern and fingerprints during the initial exam. After that, I needed a few days to get in here, which explains our little mind game... From my study of you, I knew you wouldn't be fooled for very long. But I wanted to have this chance to explain myself to you."

"Where do we go from here?"

"You go on being Diabolik, just as before. I still have many others of your colleagues to visit. Unless you prefer another kind of resolution?"

Diabolik looked at the man who called himself Fantômas. For the first time in his life, he truly felt that the issue of a combat would be... uncertain. It was a new sensation and he didn't like it.

"You can have this victory Fantômas—if that is who you are," he finally said. "But never cross my path again. Never touch even a hair of any of my friends. Never let your shadow fall across any of my interests, or else, I swear I will kill you, no matter how strong you are."

"I would expect no less of you, Diabolik."

And before Diabolik could utter another word, Fantômas had stepped out into the corridor, leaving behind him the mask of Doctor Garrick. When Diabolik rushed out to look for him, he was gone. The titanium bars, the electronic elevator, none of that seemed to have mattered. He had vanished like a wraith on the first ray of dawn.

Fantômas was true to his word. He and Diabolik never crossed paths again.

On the secret grapevine exclusive to the world's top criminals, Diabolik heard that others had been similarly taken in by someone claiming to be Fantômas—then no more was heard of him. It seemed that the first and greatest Lord of Terror had returned to oblivion.

But in his dark heart, Diabolik knew that, one day, Fantômas would return.

First publication:
Tales of the Shadowmen 7, 2011

The ultimate goal of any story published in Tales of the Shadowmen *is to, not change, but deepen the appreciation the reader has for the characters being pastiched. For example, one can hardly imagine the Nyctalope without taking for granted the new elements added to his biography by Roman Leary or Emmanuel Gorlier; the same could be said of Fantômas, Arsène Lupin, Doc Savage/Ardan, Doctor Who/Omega, or even The Little Prince, whose "more real than real" exploits have been chronicled in our pages. In a similar fashion, one hope that, after reading the following story, the reader will never look at the classic French New Wave films of the 1960s* Alphaville *and* Last Year in Marienbad *in quite the same way...*

Jerry Cornelius: J.C. in Alphaville

Jerry: "I promised them nothing less than the Millennium."
Beesley: "I'm afraid we'll have to put back the Millennium for a while."

Michael Moorcock. *A Cure for Cancer*.

Berlin, 1944: The Men Who Would Be Gods

They were four. Four brilliant men. Four evil men. They already had more wealth and power than most men on Earth, but they wanted more. They wanted their own world to shape and rule to their heart's desire.

They wanted to be gods.

They secretly shepherded Adolf Hitler's meteoritic rise to power, because they recognized in him a bit of themselves, and they thought he might make it possible for them to achieve their dreams.

They were wrong

Misshapen Rotwang was the architect whose visionary madness inspired Albert Speer and Leni Riefenstahl; he was the necromancer who had sent Heinrich Himmler's *Ahnenerbe* looking for the Spear of Destiny and the Holy Grail in Montserrat and Rennes-le-Château.

Leonard Orlok, last scion of an ancient and dark dynasty, was a mathematician who worked with Leonard Zuse on the design of the Z series of binary electrically driven mechanical calculators, before creating the world's first thinking machine, the Alpha-10.

"M," a tall, gaunt, sinister physicist, was the younger brother of the notorious crime-lord Mabuse; like him, he ruled over an invisible empire of gamblers and whores at the heart of Berlin, playing bizarre variations of the Game of Nim with satanic abandon for the souls of his victims.

The last of the four was dwarfish Ohisver Müller, an apikoric Jew and an alchemist, who was privy to the secrets of Rabbi Loew and Ramon de Tarrega. Some claimed he could animate clay and make gold, and had masterminded the Wall Street *krach* of 1929 which, ultimately, had secured power for the Nazis.

The Four had put their trust in Hitler, but their madness eventually infected the Führer, and his dream of a 1000-Year Reich died a miserable death in the Russian winter of 1943.

The Four easily managed to avoid the *Götterdämmerung* of 1945. Not for them the shameful benches of Nuremberg, or the hangman's noose! Rotwang went to Pasadena, California, changed his name to Blicero, but still worked on his crazy dreams. Orlok relocated to France, changed his name to Von Braun, and continued designing thinking machines. M escaped to Argentina, changed his name to Morel, and became a writer of some repute. And Ohisver Müller fled to Turkey, didn't have to change his name and continued to despoil life much as he had before.

But, at night, when the mundane duties of their days had been discharged, the Four still dreamed of being gods.

Natasha Von Braun had just turned 14. She smiled because she was happy. To celebrate her birthday, her father had invited three friends from his days in Berlin that she wasn't supposed to talk about.

They had brought their own children, including little Maria, who was the same age as she was.

The four of them played in the *pinède* behind the property. The white-walled house, which was now known to the locals as *"la maison de l'Allemand,"* had been built on the hillside of the picturesque village of Rennes-le-Château, in Southern France, in the shadow of the Tour Magdalène, the folly built by Father Béranger Saunière in the 19th century.

While the children played hide and seek in the woods, the Four, having enjoyed the delicious lunch cooked by an elderly local woman, went out on the stone terrace and, sitting under multi-colored parasols, began to discuss what had brought them all together again.

"I take it that you've finally succeeded, Orlok?" said the beefy, ruddy-skinned man with piercing black eyes and long slick hair pulled back in a pony tail.

"Please, don't call me Orlok, Rotwang," said Natasha's father. "My name is now Von Braun. Leonard Von Braun. But, yes, I believe that success is within our grasp."

"And my name is now Dominus Blicero, don't you forget it, but we remain who we are. In this company, I shall continue to call you Orlok, and you can continue to call me Rotwang. Now, you will forgive my skepticism, because you have made such claims before."

Ohisver Müller, a small, wizened man—almost a homunculus—whose features were strangely ageless and whose almost colorless eyes sparkled with infinite cunning, jumped in:

"Rotwang is right. It is hard to erase the memories of our failure at Germelshausen."

76

"It was not Orlok's fault if we failed at Germelshausen," said the fourth member of the cabal, a tall, gaunt, saturnine man, usually known only by his initial, M. "We weren't ready yet."

"I have sunk a huge amount of money into this operation..." began Müller.

"We have all contributed equally," interrupted Rotwang. "Don't forget it was I who killed Otto Rahn after he found the Spear of Destiny, and lied to Himmler about it."

"And I who delivered a true copy of the *Legamaton*," added Müller.

Orlok-Von Braun made a pacifying gesture with his hands.

"Gentlemen, gentlemen! The reason we failed at Germelshausen is that we didn't have the raw computing power necessary to create order out of chaos. Now, with my new Alpha-60 machine, and M's equations, we can fabricate our own pocket realities in the Outlands, those dregs of creation existing on the edge of the multiverse. With the Spear of Destiny, the primordial energy that remains there can be shaped according to our own desires to bring about the very worlds we wish to bring into existence.

"For a long time, we have each wished for our own perfect world, what Hitler promised us, but failed to deliver. But now, the time is right, my friends. The Conjunction of a Million Spheres is almost upon us. The Pattern of Amber has been desecrated. The Infinite Earths are in Crisis. The Gunslingers of Gilead are no more, and Wampus has fought his last battle on Labyrinth. The world is turning. We have the dreams, and now, we have the power to will them into existence..."

"Metropolis," whispered Rotwang.

"Müllertown," said Müller.

"Marienbad," muttered M.

"...And my own Alphaville," finished Von Braun.

"You come highly recommended, Herr Cornelius," said the tall, cadaverous, white-haired old German dressed in an old-fashioned grey suit, of the type worn by bankers before the Great War.

The interview room was painted in drab yellow and brown. The paint had flaked off in a few places, leading Jerry to reflect that the Castle had seen better days. It was lit by two single 40 watt bulbs, barely bright enough to cast shadows. A simple oak table separated the two men. In the Castle, it was late winter afternoon all the time.

"We aim to please, Mr. Klamm," replied Jerry Cornelius, a tall, androgynous, dark-haired young Englishman dressed in the latest and brightest Carnaby Street fashion.

The English Assassin lit up an *Acapulco Gold* cigarette and looked for an ashtray. From somewhere behind him, Herr Erlanger, Klamm's non-descript secretary, brought him one.

"Our common friend, Fräulein Persson, advised us that you were the best man for the job, and I'm now inclined to agree with her," said Klamm, perusing a brittle sheet of yellowed onion-skin paper which Jerry presumed was a letter of recommendation from Mrs. P.

"What is the job exactly? Your secretary here was disappointingly vague when he approached me," asked Jerry, indicating Erlanger, who had returned to stand silently near the door.

"Yes, I gave strict instructions to Herr Erlanger to be the soul of discretion," answered Klamm. "It is not good when too many people know of our business, as I am sure you will agree. Now, what do you know of the Outlands, Herr Cornelius?"

"What I've picked up here and there, mostly. They're bits of 'what was' mixed up with 'what might bes' located on the edge of creation, right?"

"We at the Castle prefer our definitions to be more scientifically exact, but I commend you for your excellent grasp of our problem."

"What problem?" inquired Jerry, who still didn't understand what the officious German wanted from him.

"The problem is, as you've accurately stated, the 'what-might-bes,' Herr Cornelius. Too many of them can disrupt the structure of the multiverse..."

"I thought Chaos was taking care of that?" interrupted Jerry.

"A common misconception, I'm afraid. Both Chaos and Law are in accord with each other. There is always a Balance, as you well know. But the Outlands are outside the multiverse. The Balance exerts no power there. However, as long as they remain, shall we say, on the periphery of things, no one bothers about them. But when they start encroaching onto reality and disturb the equilibrium, then we have to..."

" 'We?' "

This time, Klamm ignored the interruption and continued:

"... prune the excrescent or superfluous manifestations."

"I see. So that's why you need me—to, er, 'prune' a bit of excrescent creation which threatens you. I can do the job all right, Mr. Klamm, but I'm going to need more details. A lot more details."

"Have no fear, Herr Cornelius, you will be adequately briefed... The excrescence we're talking about was formed just about ten years ago... His creator, Leonard Von Orlok, *alias* Leonard Von Braun, brought it into existence—and others just like it—right out of the stuff of creation itself. He called it Alphaville. It now threatens to expand and invade the rest of the multiverse. We have already dispatched several agents through the Outlands. One of them is waiting for you there."

"For me?"

"Didn't you understand? That is what we want you to do, Herr Cornelius," said Klamm. "Find Alphaville—and destroy it.

Alphaville

"*I'm very well, thank you, not at all*," responded the parking attendant in an emotionless, mechanical tone when Jerry handed him the key to his Lotus Seven.

The English Assassin had parked near the Grand Omega Minus Square. He was now dressed in a leather bomber jacket and wore a long, white silk scarf.

Stepping outside the parking garage, Jerry reflected that Alphaville looked like Paris reimagined by Albert Speer, and inhabited by extras from a Leni Riefenstahl movie. It was a glamorous, but depressing sight.

"Mr. Cornelius?"

A beefy man with dark hair and the look of a beaten dog, dressed in a rumpled dark suit under a trenchcoat, had appeared as if out of nowhere.

"My name is Henry Dickson. I work for the Castle."

"Henry Dickson? I knew your father."

"Everyone does," sighed the detective.

"I'm eager to hear your report," said Jerry. "Shall we find a place to have a drink?"

"There are no cafés in Alphaville," replied Dickson, glumly.

"No bars? No pubs? What do people here do for fun?"

"They don't."

"Don't?"

"Have fun," explained Dickson. "Come to my hotel room. I think I still have a bottle of Loch Lomond left from my last trip to the Outlands."

Dickson's hotel room at the Bunker Palace Hotel was as sad and rumpled as the detective. It consisted of a bed, a nightstand, a dresser, a small desk and a chair, all white. It was lit by a fluorescent tube that managed to be both too bright, and yet not bright enough, depending on where one was sitting.

Once inside, Dickson found the bottle of scotch in the drawer of the night stand. Its label wasn't Loch Lomond but ZAT 77. Jerry made a face.

"It's that or tap water," said Dickson, getting two glasses.

"To your health then," said Jerry, grabbing one of the glasses.

Jerry settled on the formica and vinyl chair, while Dickson sat on the edge of the bed.

"I think I've managed to get what we need," finally said the detective.

"I'm listening," said the English assassin.

"Von Braun—Orlok—lied to his partners. Well, not lied, maybe oversold them... He didn't tell them the whole truth..."

"Which was?"

"To create a place like this..." Dickson made a circle with his hand to encompass all that was around them. "...you need more than a super-computer, no matter how advanced it is. Alpha-60 might have laid out the plans for Alphaville, and the other cities, it might even sustain them, but it didn't create them."

"Who did then?"

"A Prince of Hell, Duke Murmur, with whom the Four entered into a compact. In exchange for a prize, Murmur did what the Fallen do best: create this mockery of life, this soulless travesty of all that's holy."

"Have you identified what that prize was?"

"Yes, I have."

"So, what is it?"

"It is not a what, but a who."

"I don't understand."

"Are you familiar with Dostoyevsky's *Brother Karamazov*, Mr. Cornelius?"

"I read it a long time ago."

"In it, Ivan Karamazov asserts that neither truth nor harmony—meaning utopia—is worth the suffering of a child."

"I still don't follow you."

"Karamazov was wrong. Utopia is precisely worth the suffering of a child. Like his vampire ancestors, Orlok has taken the life of a child—his child—to create his personal utopia."

"Natasha?"

Natasha Von Braun had turned 24. The fact didn't matter to her, because she was dead inside. To everyone, she appeared to be a stunningly beautiful dark-haired woman, but her empty eyes told another story, for they revealed the absence of her soul.

The inhabitants of Alphaville had been made, or conditioned, by Alpha-60 to be automatons, productive social units. Natasha's life, however, had winked out of existence ten years earlier, when Duke Murmur of Hell had snatched her soul. If she remembered at all what had happened that day in Rennes-le-Château, it was like the experience of a librarian pulling out an index card from a book and looking at the information printed on it. The memory of her spiritual death was just one more bit of information that had been catalogued in her mind, but remained unfelt.

Using the *Legamaton*, or *Key of Solomon*, the Four had summoned Duke Murmur and traded the souls of their own children for their precious utopias. As Dostoyevsky had sensed, it was with the tears of a child that worlds were created.

Outwardly, Natasha Von Braun seemed alive, but inside, she was dead. She moved about Alphaville like a diligent ant through an anthill, with a purpose, but without a soul. She went shopping, she dined out, she attended functions organized by Alpha-60, and did everything required of her without the least emotion.

Sometimes, she even went to the movies.

Jerry Cornelius had been surprised to discover they had movies in Alphaville. He thought the medium too fanciful to be allowed to even exist in Leonard Orlok's model city. He was wrong.

"Sometimes reality is too complex for oral communication," had declared Alpha-60. "But film embodies it in a form which enables it to be spread all over the world."

So he and Henry Dickson had gone to see *Tarzan vs. IBM* at the Grand Rex. To tell the truth, it was a bit different from what Jerry had expected. Tarzan—the villain of the piece—was a slobbering, raging, barely articulate man-ape spreading anarchy in excremental fashion—quite literally, throwing poop at the world, while IBM—Integrated Basic Man—was the perfectly well-adjusted and socially productive superhero who managed to stop the beast, thanks to the application of General Semantics.

The audience was polite, laughing and applauding in a controlled fashion at all the appropriate moments.

All in all, it was a terrible way to spend an evening, thought Jerry. He wouldn't have agreed to go if Dickson hadn't been able to secure two seats next to Natasha Von Braun's.

Jerry pulled out his needle gun.

I walk down these corridors, through these halls, these galleries, in this structure of another century, this enormous, luxurious, baroque, lugubrious hotel, where corridors succeed endless corridors, thought Jerry Cornelius, as he carried Natasha's inert body to his room in the Bunker Palace Hotel.

After the kidnapping, he and Dickson had split up. The detective had gone to prepare the next step of their mission, while Jerry had taken the girl to his car and driven to a safe place, a room that Dickson had booked in advance at the Bunker Palace Hotel.

Soon, Natasha began to regain consciousness. She half sat up on the couch and gazed at her kidnapper with profound amazement, as if she understood nothing of what she saw.

With a slow, gentle gesture, she brushed her hair back from her forehead and blinked her eyes, dazzled by the room's bright lights. She was trying to get her thoughts together and was looking for words to express them.

"Didn't we meet at that hotel in Marienbad last year?" she asked.

"I don't think so," said Jerry. "I've never been to the Outlands before."

In Alphaville, if you watched a movie, the movie also watched you. The kidnapping of Natasha Von Braun had been monitored and analyzed by Alpha-60.

The image of Jerry Cornelius, however, did not compute. Each frame of the film showed a different man: an albino, a negative man, a dark-skinned warrior, a golden boy... Alpha-60 could not make sense of it and filed it for further evaluation. But the image of Henry Dickson was crystal clear. He could be seen. Tracked. Captured.

And so he was.

The problem with the new breed of humanity that Alpha-60 had brought up, thought Leonard Orlok, was that they didn't make for good interrogators.

To question Henry Dickson, he had had to ask Rotwang to send one of his own assistants: a congenial man with an endearing smile called Jack Lint. A torturer's torturer, as it were.

"I don't expect you to die, Mr. Dickson, I expect you to talk," said Jack Lint.

"But I've already told you everything I know," begged Henry Dickson, strapped into a mechanical chair that might have been designed by Gaudi. There were electrodes poking in and out of his skull, cups attached to various parts of his chest, and even soft tendrils squeezing his eyeballs. He didn't like to think about what was happening below the belt. "Jerry Cornelius has gone back into the Outlands with the girl," he added. "I don't know where."

"You're lying. But it doesn't matter. Say your lie again and again. Alpha-60 is very patient. He will be recording it and checking every minute variation in your narrative. If there is anything more, he'll detect it."

"But there's nothing more!"

"Tut-tut—if there is even a slight tremolo in your voice, it might prove a clue to some nugget of deeper truth that you don't wish to keep hidden from us. My machines will keep your larynx properly humidified and pump anti-sleeping drugs into your body. It is only if you stop talking that that horrible pain will return. We don't want that, do we?"

"..."

"Do we, Mr. Dickson?"

"No..."

"Then let's start talking."

By an amazing coincidence, "Then let's start talking," were precisely the words Jerry had just said to Natasha. The English assassin had uncovered the sign of the demon Murmur, Archduke of Hell, in charge of 30 infernal legions, on Natasha's right breast. He was not an exorcist, generally preferring to reason with demons rather than expel them forcibly. Besides, in a case like this one, he didn't think force would prevail. He had an idea, but talking was required.

"What do you want?" replied Natasha Von Braun in a voice that was a couple of octaves lower than normal, and seemed to resonate strangely around the room. *It was Murmur's voice, not hers*, thought Jerry

"Just talk, nothing more," said Jerry.

"What about?"

Jerry pretended to consider their options.

"Let's put our cards on the table: you know who I am, and what my mission is..."

"A mission doomed to fail."

"Possibly. But what if I convinced you to leave this woman of your own free will?"

"That is absurd," said the Demon Lord.

"I could make you a better offer..."

"What do you mean?"

"How does the exorcism ritual go, '*Strike terror, Lord, into the Beast now laying waste your vineyard*?' Well, this Alphaville is not a terribly exciting vineyard now, is it?"

"..."

"Hardly worth an Archduke of Hell's time, if you ask me," continued Jerry. "You must be rather bored here. I know I would be. Come on, admit it, Your Lordship, you *are* bored."

"Perhaps," said Murmur, with some reluctance. "A little. What do you offer?"

"You made a bad deal, but you don't have to be bound to it for eternity. Let's be frank: when it comes to creating pocket dystopias, Orlok and his friends are pikers. Metropolis is basically about crushing the workers and building taller buildings. Müllertown is capitalism gone amok, runaway speculation and insane Ponzi schemes. M's dream of Marienbad has created a society of apathetic super-rich stuck on the same groove for how long? And this Alphaville here is the worst of all: imperial dreams with mindless drones and an unlimited supply of microchips. Not bad, but what if you could get all of the above in a single package—better and bigger?"

"I'm listening."

"You know that I belong to the Guild of Temporal Adventures," continued Jerry. "I've got just the place for you and your reprobate friends: America. Fifty years from now. Turn left at the Millennium and when you see the Towers come down, you've arrived. Trust me; you'll be like a bug in a rug!"

"Hmm... I know the time period of which you speak... You make a compelling case."

"Don't I?"

"I would like to seal our pact," said Murmur.

"What do you have in mind?" said Jerry, with a slight frown. Bargaining with demons—especially Archdukes of Hell—always contained a small margin of uncertainty, sometimes too close for comfort.

Natasha grabbed his white silk scarf, pulled his face down to hers and sensuously kissed him on the lips.

Jerry relaxed and smiled.

"I see. Love is what makes the worlds go round, eh?"

"Not love. This mortal doesn't know the meaning of the word anymore than I. Just sex."

"Sex is good enough for me," said Jerry, taking off his leather jacket.

The Castle, a week later

"Our next agent has already been assigned, Mrs. Persson," said Herr Klamm. "A Mr. Lemmy Caution. One lump or two?"

Mrs. Persson reflected that she had never tasted tea that was so dishwaterish, except once in Moscow under Gorbachev, but she refrained from saying so.

"Two, please. Mr. Caution is an excellent choice, Herr Klamm."

"I believe so. When Natasha Von Braun discovers love, Alphaville will be destroyed. It's only a matter of time."

"It is always a matter of time. How is the rest of your, er, pruning campaign going?"

"Very well, I'm happy to report. In Metropolis, Rotwang has relocated the demon that inhabited Maria into a mechanical creature of his invention, but I'm confident things will fall apart soon. Our agent Pierre Brok has just brought about the fall of Müllertown, and X is doing the same to Marienbad."

"What about Mr. Cornelius? I understand he was gone when Alpha-60's men arrived at the hotel."

"Truthfully, we don't know what happened to him. But it's highly likely that Duke Murmur just dropped him off somewhere else in the Outlands."

"Well, in that case, he'll find his way back. I doubt there is anyone or anything that can truly faze Mr. Cornelius."

Elsewhere in the Outlands

Jerry woke up. Murmur was gone, but strangely enough, the Demon Duke's seal which had been on Natasha's breast, had been transferred to him during their lovemaking.

He didn't know what it meant. He would worry about it later.

A fat little man with a pointed hat was looking at him with deep suspicion in his piggish eyes.

"*Merdre!*" said Père Ubu! "Come and see what the cat just dragged in, Mère Ubu!"

First publication:
Tales of the Shadowmen 6, 2010

Dennis Power imagined that the secret origins of Judex went as far back as the Dawn of Time itself. In this story devoted to a character that is as surely as archetypal and timeless as any other, we journey to Earth's farthest future...

Judex: The Earth Abideth Forever

A billion years in the future stood the city of Diaspar. Humanity had long since left Earth for the stars, and those who had chosen to remain behind stayed forever immured within its great walls.

In Diaspar, the Central Computer created bodies in which those people lived, and stored their minds at the end of their allotted lifespans, before recreating them to live again, and again.

From time to time, a Unique awoke, one who had had no previous lives. They were anomalies. Most were harmless eccentrics or bold pioneers capable of opening much needed new vistas in an otherwise unchanging pattern; only a few, a very few, were truly dangerous.

Danker was one of them.

But Yarlan Zey, the genius who had built the Central Computer, had had the foresight to predict even this, and had devised a cure.

As Danker wrapped his hands around his girlfriend's neck and began to squeeze, in a secret vault, deep within the Central Computer, a switch moved, seemingly of its own accord.

Judex awoke.

First publication:
The Shadow of Judex, 2013

Most people are familiar with Edmond Rostand's play, which popularized and forever defined the character of Cyrano de Bergerac; fewer, however, know of L'Aiglon *(The Eaglet), his 1900 play in which the great Sarah Bernhardt played the tragic part of Franz, Duke of Reichstadt, Napoleon's son, kept prisoner in the Austrian Palace of Schönbrunn after the French Emperor's downfall...*

Lecoq: Christmas at Schönbrunn

Paris, 1860 / Schönbrunn, 1828

In a large canopy bed, sweating and groaning beneath the covers, lay Père Tabaret, the *bon vivant* of the Rue Saint-Lazare, better known as *Papa Tire-au-Clair* by the agents of the French Sûreté.

Seeing him, one could understand how his neighbors had never had the slightest suspicion about his amateur police work. No one with his looks would ever be credited with superior intelligence. With his receding hairline and his immense ears, his obnoxiously turned-up nose, his tiny eyes and big lips, Père Tabaret looked like an idiot—a rich idiot at that.

It was true that, if examined closely, his resemblance to a hunting dog, whose instincts and aptitudes he shared, was remarkable. When he went down the street, impudent urchins turned around to yell: "Fetch!" He laughed at this scorn, and even took pleasure in adding to his silly appearance, making even more striking the saying that "he is not truly intelligent he who does not appear to be so."

Seeing the young policeman, whom he knew well, enter his bedroom, Père Tabaret's eyes lit up.

"Good morning, Lecoq, my boy," he said. "I'm glad you still remember your poor old *Papa* from time to time!"

Lecoq was about 26, beardless, pale, with extremely red lips and an abundance of wavy black hair. He was short, but well-proportioned, and each of his movements showed unusual strength. There was nothing remarkable about his appearance, except for his eyes, which either sparkled brilliantly or grew extremely dull, according to his mood.

"I found something that I thought would be of interest to you, Papa," said Lecoq, "knowing your fondness for history, I mean."

"Ah! Ah!"

Lecoq pulled a notebook out of his pocket. The paper was yellow and the brown leather binding dirty. "This is something I recently found in a chest belonging to my father."

"You don't mean...?"

"No, not my adoptive parents," said the young policeman. "May they rest forever with the angels—my real father, he who was known as Lecoq de la Periere."

"I remember him well," said Tabaret. "I had to piece together the events surrounding his death in 1842 for those dimwitted folks at the Rue de Jesusalem. They are so easily confused... Certainly, anything chronicled by that fearsome rogue is bound to be of considerable interest."

"Indeed! There is one passage in particular, *Papa*, for which I would like your opinion. It takes place in 1828 in Schönbrunn ..."

Lecoq's Diary:

Is it a coincidence that the Austrian Emperor chose to confine his 14-year old grand-son Franz to the same apartments that his father, Napoleon, occupied twice; once after Austerlitz and once before Wagram?

The castle has 1500 rooms. My master, the Colonel, does not believe in coincidences, He thinks that Emperor Francis of Austria, or rather his *éminence grise*, the wily Prince Metternich, would never leave such a thing to chance. No, it is not a coincidence—they sought to humiliate the boy by making his father's quarters his prison—but it will serve us well in the days to come. Metternich will regret this final last slap to Napoleon's face!

Born Prince Imperial, King of Rome and Prince of Parma, the youth is now known simply as Duke of Reichstadt. He never sees his mother, his only company being that of his preceptors, all carefully hand-picked by Metternich himself: Count Districhstein, who teaches him the classics; Monsieur de Foresti, military tactics; Everard, English; von Prokesch-Osten, fencing; Nyberg, dancing... and Metternich himself, history.

What irony! Prince von Metternich teaching history to the son of Napoleon Bonaparte!

The Colonel and I arrived at the inn in Vienna in late November, giving ourselves a month to prepare. We posed as dry goods salesmen and, indeed, did good business while we were there. The Emperor's secret police were quickly reassured as to who we were and quickly stopped investigating us.

The first step in our mission was to reactivate some of the contacts Henri de Belcamp had set up in amongst the local *Rosenkreuz* in 1813. A few of them were servants at the Castle and it soon became natural for them to spend an evening drinking beer in the smoke-filled backroom of the inn.

As was the tradition, the Emperor's Court celebrated Christmas at Schönbrunn. Following the recent custom, a tall conifer tree was cut from the slopes of Schneeberg and set up in the Great Hall, decorated with bags of sweets, toys, oranges, stuffed birds, small sparkling bells of gold and silver, and multi-colored garlands.

The Emperor's intimate circle of friends and family, field-marshals in shiny uniforms, and ladies in munificent gowns, added to the joyous atmosphere of the season.

Emperor Francis made a point of including young Franz in the festivities; it was, after all, the one time in the year when the young recluse was authorized, nay, encouraged, to mingle with others. It was also a reward for his good results with his studies.

One of the Colonel's spies had reported to us that the Emperor had expressed concern about young Franz's interest in Cesar's *Gallic Wars*, fearing that the child would draw a connection between the Roman Emperor's military genius and his own father's. He instructed Districhstein to divert his studies to Horace and Tacitus instead.

As for history, as taught by Metternich, it focused on the high feats of Franz's ancestors—on his mother's side, of course: the Emperors of the Holy Germanic Roman Empire, not "the other Emperor!"

Franz was thus, in everyone's eyes, a perfect, young, loyal German.

The first time I laid eyes on the boy was the night of December 24. The Colonel and I had used a secret passage to gain entrance to the Prince's apartments.

When I saw him, he wore the standard white uniform of an Austrian cavalry commander. His skin was unusually pale and his lips lacked color His wavy blond hair, which he had inherited from his mother, fell to his shoulders Only the eyes seemed alive in that tragic face, even though it seemed as if he was trying hard to extinguish their flame.

He walked towards us at a serene pace, a figure of melancholy.

Did he remember the great radiant palace of the Tuileries, where he had spent his early years? The tricolored flag of his homeland? One could not tell, but I suspect that he did.

And what did he remember about his father, this fearsome man whose very name was never ever uttered in his presence? A man about whom no one dared ask any questions? These were heavy burdens for a child.

Earlier that day, the Colonel had bribed one of the servants to leave a present on Franz's nightstand.

It was a tiny Christmas tree, no more than a few inches tall, a mockery compared to the giant tree filling Schönbrunn's Great Hall. But that tiny tree—no more than a branch, in truth—was decorated with tiny blue, white and red *cocardes*, and a small roll of blue paper was tied to its "trunk."

Franz had surely unrolled the paper: it wasn't a letter, but a portrait, more akin to an *image d'Epinal* than a well-crafted masterpiece, with its bright colors and simple lines. It depicted a man wearing a black tricorn, a great grey coat over a military uniform. He stood at the head of a row of French soldiers bearing a French flag. In the sky flew an Eagle under a radiant sun.

There was only one word under the portrait: NAPOLE-ON.

And now, Franz had come to meet the man who had triumphed over the resources of one of the mightiest empires on Earth to deliver him that portrait: Colonel Bozzo-Corona.

"Do not fear, my child," said the Colonel. He took Franz's hand in his, and deposited a light kiss on it.

"Who are you?" asked the Prince. "Why have you come here?"

"I have come to tell you about your father, Monseigneur," said the Colonel. "And also to tell you of France, and the millions of people who have remained faithful to his memory."

"My father! France!"

"I have traveled 5000 leagues to bring you this branch taken from the Garden of the Tuileries, a piece of boxwood identical to millions kept in the hearths of those still faithful to the name Napoleon."

"The Tuileries… Napoleon…" repeated the youth, obviously trying to place an image over those names he remembered from his childhood.

"There are, Monseigneur, millions of men and women in France who think of you, believe in you, and would gladly give their lives for you. There is a tradition that, on Christmas' eve, the sky opens and the angels come down to Earth to bring joy and God's blessings to the children of men. I didn't want you to be the only one forgotten in this season. I'm not sent by

God, of course!" Here, the Colonel allowed himself a small chuckle. "If my associate and I were able to come to you, it is only because of a secret passage set up by your father when he stayed in these very apartments. We seized the opportunity of tonight's festivities to reach you safely."

"You knew my father? What was he like?"

"I played merely a modest part in his ascension. Cesar, whom I'm told you admire, was but a dwarf compared to your father. He was the Emperor, a lord worshiped or feared by over 80 million people. Yet, he died alone, seven years ago, on a windswept rock lost in the middle of the Atlantic, just as trapped as you are here. One of my associates tried to rescue him, but in vain. Napoleon died after five years of painful agony, his eyes fixed on your portrait, and when his sun finally set, there were millions in France who screamed out their pain. Now, their faith has been transferred to you. Your name alone causes the powerful men of this world to quake in fear—ask your grandfather.

"But France is prideful. She wants someone who will seize her, conquer her despite all obstacles; she does not want to be courted politely by someone resigned to follow the edicts of Fate, without ambition or passion. Now, Monseigneur, the time has come for me to ask you what I came here to ask on behalf of those millions: Will you follow us? Will you take this secret passage that your father himself had built, leave this prison and come back with us?

"I have millions dedicated to your restoration, more money than God himself could count, resources that you can hardly suspect. If you come with me, your Empire will be even mightier than your father's. I have men in England that will destroy the perfidious Albion from within, conspirators in Russia that will pave the way for you... Your Empire will reach from Ireland to the Urals... The decision is yours."

"And...?" asked Père Tabaret.

"Nothing," replied Lecoq. "The entry stops there. There is a brief note recording their return to France on December

95

27, but nothing at all about what happened that night in Schönbrunn. The only thing we know for certain is that Franz chose to not follow the Colonel and make a bid for a Second Empire."

"Hm-hm. And what do you think happened?"

"Myself, I think the will of the Imperial child had already been thoroughly broken by that bastard Metternich and his preceptors. He was scared by the brilliant, but dangerous future that the Colonel had laid out before him."

"Possible, possible, but I don't agree. What? You look as if you've fallen from the clouds, my boy," said Tabaret. "Do you think your *Papa* is trying to *tell you a salad*?" [lie]

"No, certainly not, but…"

"Be quiet! You're surprised because you don't know the first thing about history. You need to be educated on this point if you don't want to remain an idiot like Gévrol for the rest of your days. Now, would you please take down from my bookshelf, over there, on the right, the big folio edition by Mathieu Auguste Geffroy…"

Lecoq quickly obeyed and, as soon as Tabaret had the book, he began to flip through it rapidly, until:

"Ah! Here it is! Listen well, my boy! '*After 1828, the surveillance around the Duke of Reichstadt was tripled. No Frenchman was authorized to see him. Even poet Joseph Mery, who had traveled to Schönbrunn to present the Prince with a heroic poem written about Napoleon's Egyptian Campaign was denied admission and could only see the young man from the opposite end of the Imperial theater, sitting alone in a darkened loge. Some say the Duke was poisoned; others that he died of tuberculosis on July 22, 1832. The day he died, a thunderbolt destroyed one of the bronze eagles decorating the castle's gates. And Germany breathed a collective sigh of relief.*'

"Now, if fear or despair, as you believe, had motivated the Prince to refuse the Colonel's offer, why would the Austrian Emperor have tripled the security around him? The only answer is, far from being a broken man, the young Duke had, instead, inherited his father's iron will and determination. The Emperor realized this and became mortally afraid his captive would change his mind."

"I don't understand," said Lecoq.

"Clearly, there is another explanation for your father's account. Instead, Franz saw all too well what the Second Empire the Colonel offered him would bring. The wars, the devastation, the deaths and worse of all, the triumph, the iron heel of a French tyrant grinding the Old World beneath his boot. The Old World, I say? More, perhaps. With no England to challenge him, no Russia to crush his armies, with the power of the Black Coats behind him, perhaps a smarter and more flexible Napoleon might have easily become Master of the World. And that is what, in his considerable wisdom, the Duke rejected."

"But how could he know...? How could he be sure...? A mere boy of 14... Unless..."

"Ha-ha! Unless someone *showed* him, you mean?" said Tabaret, smiling.

"That's impossible..." whispered Lecoq.

"No. Merely *improbable*... You must learn to distinguish between the two, my boy. Tell me, what was the name of the Prince's English teacher?"

"Everard. I couldn't find much information about him."

"If what I suspect is true, you won't find any. I met a Manse Everard, once... A most charming English gentleman... Let me tell you a story about him..."

Memo: From Time Patrol Agent (Unattached) Manse Everard to Colonel Graigh.
Operation Caged Bird successful. Divergent Second Empire timeline eliminated. Colonel Bozzo-Corona will bear watching.

First publication:
Tales of the Shadowmen 10, 2013

This present-day story features the Italian comic-book hero Martin Mystère (created by writer Alfredo Castelli), who previously met Colonel Bozzo, the seemingly immortal godfather of Paul Féval's Black Coats, in the story we co-plotted with Alfredo for the Almanacco del Mistero 2012. *It also foreshadows the events of our forthcoming novel,* The Return of the Nyctalope, *published in 2013...*

The Nyctalope: The Ides of Mars

for Alfredo Castelli

Los Angeles, 2012

The sky was the color of rust, and so was the sand beneath his feet.

Martin Mystère looked up and saw a white dot, barely larger than the size of a nickel, up in the sky. The landscape around him was hilly, desertic, totally barren. He knew at once where he stood because he had often looked at the photographs with awe.

He was on Mars—and specifically, near the Columbia Hills.

But if he was truly on Mars, how could he still be alive? Breathing?

He lifted a foot off the ground and took a tentative step forward. The surface gravity on Mars should have been only 38% of that of Earth. So if he wasn't really on Mars, then, where was he?

He didn't have time to ponder this mystery because he heard a small cough coming from behind him.

An old man, leaning on a cane, had mysteriously appeared. He was tall, with a wizened yet still strong face, long white hair and dark eyes that were full of a strange energy. He was dressed in a black frock coat reminiscent of late 19th century fashion. Next to him, holding a ridiculous umbrella, as if to shield the old man from the dangers of the hostile environment, stood a huge, burly man with a short beard and closely cut hair.

Martin recognized them both at once.

"Colonel Bozzo-Corona and the Marchef," he said.

Colonel Bozzo-Corona was the preternaturally ancient godfather of a criminal empire once known as the Brotherhood of Mercy, or the Black Coats, which was now operating under the name of BlackSpear Holdings. Martin had met him and his associates only a few months before.

"Good afternoon, Professor Mystère," said the Colonel. "As you have undoubtedly surmised, you are not on Mars itself, but on a very accurate holographic simulacrum built from NASA's very own data. My lovely associate, the Countess de Clare, could tell you exactly how it works—she is our science specialist—but I'm afraid I can't."

"Where are we, I mean, really?" asked Martin.

The Colonel shook his head. "I'm sorry I can't tell you that either, Professor, but I can tell you *why* you are here."

Martin smiled. "That's a start I suppose. I'm listening."

The Colonel pointed with his cane towards a pair of tracks in the rusty sand, heading up a small hill a hundred or so yards away.

"Do you see these tracks? They're made by one of the NASA's two Martian rovers—*Spirit*. You may have heard of it?"

"Yes, of course. It was damaged by the Martian winter and stopped broadcasting in March of last year."

"Ah. That's what the US Government told everyone, but *Spirit* is, in fact, doing fine and still broadcasting images."

"I don't understand," said Martin, genuinely perplexed. "Why...?"

"Let's follow the tracks to the other side of that hill, and you will have the answer to your question, Professor, although I doubt it will satisfy you."

Treading on the sand-which-wasn't-there, Martin Mystère, Colonel Bozzo-Corona and his bodyguard walked up the simulated Martian hill. Martin couldn't help but notice that the Colonel was not winded in the least when they reached the summit.

There, in front of him, he saw *Spirit*—and the ruins of the city.

When he got off the Air France flight at LAX, Los Angeles' international airport, the Nyctalope knew that he didn't have much time to act—a couple of days at the most, if his information was correct.

Avoiding the curiosity of Homeland Security was easy. His papers, conveniently updated by the French intelligence department which occasionally employed his services, could withstand even the harshest scrutiny. They didn't even have to change his name, just his birth year, as there were too few people alive today who remembered the name of Leo Saint-Clair.

He hailed a yellow cab and gave his destination: a discreet hotel in La Cañada. As the taxi negotiated its way onto the 405 freeway, Leo reminisced about the last time he had been in California. It was in 1949 and 1950... There had been that incident in the desert involving an ancient Martian capsule... Then, he had had to stop John Parsons from building a rocket to Mars... He had to kill Parsons and the Martian, whom had once been a man called Damprich, but had posed as the entity "Bartzabel." Disaster had barely been avoided. Earth had again been saved, without anyone being aware of it.

Now only one Martian remained, intent as ever to destroy Humanity.

But not if Leo acted in time.

For once in his life, Martin Mystère could not believe his eyes. It was astonishing enough to discover an ancient city on Mars, spread before him, partly buried beneath the sands of the red planet, but the ruins didn't even look alien.

He had expected golden spires, strange alien shapes, perhaps a decadent and crumbling architecture, straight out of Ray Bradbury's or Leigh Brackett's imaginations. But instead what he saw could have been designed by Gustave Eiffel. It was clearly of Earth manufacture.

He ran down the hill, careful not to stumble, followed by Colonel Bozzo-Corona.

Martin approached the first girder and saw some writing on it: *Fabriqué par les Aciéries Schneider – Le Creusot.*

"French? *French??*" he exclaimed. Then he turned towards the Colonel and, pointing at the ruins, shouted: "Is this another of your tricks, Bozzo?"

The Colonel made a calming gesture with his hand. "No trick, I promise you, Professor. This is a totally faithful simulacrum of the same corresponding spot on Mars, which has been secretly studied by the Americans since *Spirit* stumbled on it last March. Of course, they don't know what I know..."

He chuckled, a dry sound like two bones knocking each other, something which Martin found extremely annoying.

"And what do you know?"

"You are a lover of mysteries, Professor Mystère," replied the Colonel, not responding directly to Martin's question. "There is perhaps no one on Earth who knows more about the secret history of our planet than you. And yet, this, perhaps the greatest secret our world has ever known, has totally escaped your notice until now. Strange, isn't it?"

"I research the past, Colonel, not science fiction stories," said Martin, curtly.

"Ah, but this started in the past... A long, long time ago, in fact... You are aware, undoubtedly, that our planet was visited by extra-terrestrial beings several times during its pre-cataclysmic days?"

"Yes, of course. There are conflicting legends, myths about the Elohim who walked on Earth and married the Daughters of Man..."

"Suffice it to say that at least some of these beings came from the fourth planet of our Solar System, when it was still inhabited by powerful civilizations... Whoever they were, no one knows for sure, but they were, for the most part, evil, and left deep scars in our collective psyche... Whether in the West, China or India, Mars, Mangala, Yinghuo, came to symbolize the Enemy of Earth... The god Ares was often depicted as a villain, and today is still, even in your comic-books... Its color red came to represent blood, violence, aggression..."

"An interesting theory."

"More than a theory, Professor, for myths aren't the only things the Ancient Martians left behind on our planet; they also left some of their technology—I guess you might call it 'rocket science,' although it didn't involve the combustion of propellants, like our own primitive spacecrafts."

"How do you know all this?"

"Because some of their technology was found in the Gobi desert in what appears to be an ancient spaceport, by Kiang-Ho of the Golden Belt, a mad Mongol who was defeated by Rama Rundjee, the man nicknamed Doctor Mystère, after whom you yourself are named. This is where I became involved..."

"You?"

"I was interested in space technology even before that discovery, because I had read the works of Messieurs Verne and Wells, and I foresaw a day when Man might be driven to go out in space and explore other worlds..."

"You mean, plunder and loot?"

"Please, Professor! I also invested heavily in the Conquest of the American West. Manifest Destiny is what made your country the greatest in the world. I similarly believe it is man's destiny to subjugate the Heavens. Doctor Mystère, I knew, would crush that Mongol upstart, once alerted to his mad plans of world conquest, and so he did, leaving me to hire one of his assistants, a man named Oxus, whose research I then financed. Oxus gathered a group of like-minded men around him, which he christened the Fifteen. A few years later, they established the first human colony on Mars..."

"You're kidding me?"

"I am not. Unfortunately, one of the Fifteen, Koynos, fell in love with the beautiful Xavière de Ciserat, who at the time was fianced to the notorious French explorer Leo Saint-Clair. Koynos kidnapped Xavière and took her to Mars. Somehow, Leo found a way to follow them. What happened after that is not entirely clear. Koynos died. Leo reclaimed Xavière and eventually wrestled the control of the colony away from Oxus. Then, some kind of catastrophe struck. They all died—but for one—and every trace of Man's first organized venture into Outer space was expunged from the records of Human History."

"But why?"

"That's what I want you to find out, Professor Mystère."

From his hotel window, the Nyctalope had a perfect view over the 210 freeway and the Jet Propulsion Laboratory, supposedly of Pasadena even though it was really located on neighboring land belonging to the incorporated city of La Cañada Flintridge.

The last Martian had succeeded in avoiding him for almost a century now, but tonight, their long standoff would come to an end.

Leo's mind returned to 1917 and the tragic events that had precipitated the death of the Martian colony.

The Ancient Martians had not perished. Sensing the slow, agonizing death of their world, losing its atmosphere, turning into a barren desert, they had mutated into a microorganism, a collective intelligence, buried in the sands, waiting, waiting...

Waiting for the day of the Earthmen...

For the technology they had left behind on Earth was but the sweet bait of a lethal trap.

When Oxus and the Fifteen had set foot on Mars and built their colony, the organism had struck and stealthily invaded the bodies of the humans, lodging itself inside their hearts, from which it could command its host, after having destroyed anything that made him or her human.

It wasn't a simple task. Many had died; others had succumbed to a sort of genocidal madness. Those who had not been possessed were killed by others, who had expired in turn.

During the Martian onslaught, Leo had lost Xavière, by then his wife, and their two children. It was a tragedy which he still felt today, a century later, with just as much pain as he had experienced then.

One man, however, had proved invulnerable to the alien attack: he, Leo Saint-Clair, because of the accident of fate which had conferred upon him that damnable artificial heart that also made him immortal. He had experienced a bout of temporary madness, but had quickly recovered.

Against the Nyctalope, the Martians themselves could not prevail.

Three Martians—for they were no longer humans—only three—had managed to escape, fleeing back to Earth in one of the rockets built by the Fifteen with Martian technology. They had gone to Earth, hoping against all odds to either return with more victims, or bring Martian seeds to our world. Either way, their success would spell doom for Earth.

But the Nyctalope had followed, a wrathful angel bent on vengeance, determined to save Earth from the Martian menace.

He had killed the first Martian—once a man named Jolivet—in 1932, pursuing him all the way back to Mars and destroying his ship.

The second Martian—Damprich—had tried to manipulate Parsons, in 1950, to build another rocketship to Mars, and Leo had killed them both too. There remained only one Martian, who had been behind many attempts at enticing Men to travel to the Red Planet. Leo had been forced to assume the role of the "Great Galactic Ghoul," destroying or causing the failure of more than 10 launches towards the Red Planet, and preventing five of the missions which had land on Mars from transmitting their data back to Earth.

But his Martian enemy was nothing if not patient, and resourceful. The latest mission, christened *Curiosity*, included, unbeknownst to the public, a plan to bring Martian soil samples back to Earth. The deadly microorganisms would at last be released on our planet where, in its oxygen-rich atmosphere, they would proliferate. Most of the population would die; the rest would become Martians.

That could not—would not—happen. Leo would see to it.

It was his destiny.

"Wait a minute," said Martin Mystère. "I know the story you're telling me. I read it when I was a kid. It's *Le Mystère des XV* by a French writer... Jean de La Hire. That Leo Saint-Clair—the man you're talking about, it's his hero... The Nyctalope!"

Colonel Bozzo-Corona pretended to poke at some sand with his cane.

"Like many famous persons, the Nyctalope had his biographer. Holmes had Watson, Rocambole, Ponson du Terrail, Greystoke, Burroughs, and even I had that *feuilletoniste* Féval, until I was obliged to silence him... La Hire embellished some of the Nyctalope's exploits, of course, and made up stories when Monsieur Saint-Clair did not deign tell him what really happened. If you remember *Le Mystère des XV*, you will recall that it has no proper ending. Why? Because Saint-Clair did not tell La Hire what had really happened on Mars. So he just made things up."

"And what did happen on Mars?"

"That is precisely what I want to know.

"I take it the Nyctalope was the one man whom you mentioned who survived the death of the colony?"

"—and managed to return to Earth, yes."

"But surely, for a man such as you, with all your power, your organization, it would have been child's play to…"

"…To capture, even kill Leo Saint-Clair?" interrupted the Colonel. "Yes, I guess I could have. But no one in over a century has ever defeated that Devil of a man, and I haven't reached my age by taking unnecessary risks… Besides, I know I couldn't have broken him and made him talk, whereas he will confide in you."

"In me? Why me?"

The Colonel's gaze became veiled, absent, as if he was peering into another time. Martin Mystère could almost see the tendrils of the past breaking through and trying to grasp him and pull him back into the mists of History.

"I knew your ancestor Rémy d'Arx very well, you know… Everything he learned about my organization, he found out by talking—and listening. He had the same gift as you do: the ability to elicit confidence… My gift is to make and protect secrets; yours is to expose them and learn the truth. You are the greatest truth-seeker of our age, Professor Mystère. If anyone can learn the Nyctalope's secret, it is you."

Buying a gun in Los Angeles was ridiculously easy. Leo had found what he needed right away on Del Mar: a Lorcin L-380, purchased for $100. It was a fairly well-made gun. It had pretty good heft and balance, although the craftsmanship was poor, and some of the materials and internal parts would not hold up, but for the short-term, it was an adequate weapon and would kill his target just as quickly as a .45.

He then had stalked the Martian until the Invader had gone, alone, into the multi-storied JPL car park. Leo knew that killing his foe would not be enough; he also had to destroy her *Curiosity* project—or at least, the secret part of it. But he had played "Galactic Ghoul" before and was confident that he would. What mattered was to put an end to this cat-and-mouse game once and for all.

With a few, quick moves, he shut off the electricity in the car park, which was suddenly plunged into total darkness. The

Nyctalope had chosen his night well: there was no Moon up in the sky, and the lights from the outside street lamps only outlined the edges of each floor, but provided no light inside.

Of course, the Nyctalope did not need lights!

Stealthily, moving like one of those great jungle cats he had hunted in the past, Leo neared his prey. The Martian kept moving towards its car undisturbed as if it, too, was nyctalopic. Leo pointed his gun and fired a shot.

The bullet hit the Martian squarely in the back. The creature fell to the ground; its legs twitched, then it remained still.

Leo sighed. It was all over, at last.

He took a step forward, planning to take the body to the station wagon he had rented earlier and parked in the car park, intending to bury it in the Mojave Desert. It was the least he could do, he thought.

As he bent forward, the bullet hit him in the chest.

Martin Mystère was not a Nyctalope, but anticipating some kind of situation like this, he had borrowed a pair of night vision goggles from Colonel Bozzo-Corona.

He had awakened in the backseat of a limousine driven by the Marchef. The Colonel had told him they were now in Los Angeles, driving towards Pasadena where BlackSpear's agents had spotted the Nyctalope. The rest was up to Martin.

Before he left the limousine, the Colonel had handed Martin a disposable cell phone, to contact him, a set of keys to a Dodge parked nearby, and a gun, which Martin had refused. Instead, Martin had asked for the goggles, which the Marchef had pulled out of the trunk.

Then Martin had discreetly tailed the Nyctalope, until he saw him getting shot in the car park.

Leo Saint-Clair fell to his knees, clutching his chest. His opponent stood up, casually removing a bullet from the bullet proof jacket hidden under her coat.

Until then, Martin had not had a clear view of Leo's prey, but now he saw that she was a tall, stunningly beautiful woman with long, black hair. Her face was somehow ageless, but her dark eyes were full of ancient malice.

She delivered a kick of her foot to the Nyctalope, who was still moving, and breathing raucously.

"This time, you have lost, Leo Saint-Clair," she said. "The only way to get rid of you for good was to draw you into this elaborate trap. I knew you could not miss this opportunity. I have only one regret: that you will not live to see my world rise again out of the ashes of yours, your species replaced by mine..."

The woman now aimed her gun at the Nyctalope's head.

Martin pulled his own stun gun and fired a paralyzing bolt at her.

The woman stopped, then turned and saw Martin. Moving slowly, as if in slow motion, she advanced towards him, raising her hand to point her gun at him.

Martin had never seen his stun gun fail before but then the woman had just identified herself as not human. Could she be—a Martian? he wondered.

He fired another stun blast, without any better results. In a matter of seconds, the Alien would shoot him. He had to run.

Martin jumped to take cover behind a car when he heard the shot. Surprisingly, he didn't see the bullet fly by and hit the concrete column behind which he had stood.

He bent forward to take a peek.

The left side of the woman's head had just exploded. Though his goggles, Martin saw a phosphorus-bright corolla of blood burst from her broken skull and splatter around.

The Nyctalope, leaning on one knee, his gun firmly in his hand, had just fired the fatal shot.

Martin rushed from behind the car he had used for shelter. Leo was getting back on his feet.

"We need to get you to a hospital," said Martin. "You took a bullet in the chest."

"My circulatory system has already repaired itself," said the Nyctalope. "I'll get the bullet removed later. Thank you

108

for saving my life…" Then he took a long, hard look at Martin. "I've seen you somewhere…" he added.

"I'm Martin Mystère. I…"

"Ah yes. I've seen your program on TV. Perfect. You're just the man I wanted to see…"The Nyctalope pulled a small spiral-bound notebook from one of his pockets. "Give this to Colonel Bozzo. It will tell him everything he wants to know—and warn him about Mars."

"Colonel Bozzo? How did you know that I…?"

"Don't you work for him?"

"Not exactly, no, but…"

The Nyctalope forced the notebook into Martin's hand.

"Give this to him. And tell him that Man will conquer the Heavens—just, not his kind of Man. I've taken steps already."

"I don't understand," said Martin.

"He will," replied the Nyctalope, with a grim smile. "Now help me load this body into that station wagon there… I'll go and bury it in the desert."

"Don't you think we should leave it here for the police? Or the scientists perhaps?"

"No," said the Nyctalope, opening the station wagon. Martin helped him pull the body inside. "Besides, she deserved better than that."

"She?" asked Martin.

The Nyctalope sat behind the wheel and turned the key in the ignition. The vehicle started right away.

"Once, she was Xavière de Ciserat. My wife."

As the station wagon drove away in the darkness, Martin Mystère understood why no one in over a century had ever defeated that Devil of a man.

First publication:
Night of the Nyctalope, 2012

The character of the Phantom Angel—in reality, Sleeping Beauty, awakened by Doc Ardan in the 1920s, as told in "The Reluctant Princess" in Pacifica 1*—returns in this story in which Randy tells the origins of a spear we found hidden in the attic of our 19th century house, using this real-life anecdote as a springboard to spin a new yarn featuring the dynamic heroine...*

The Phantom Angel: The Spear of Destiny

Chalabre, The 1920s

"Maître Sainclair, I need your help."

The young woman, once known as "Sleeping Beauty," but known as the "Phantom Angel" ever since she had been released from a magic spell by Doctor Francis Ardan, was sitting in the comfortable office of Gaston Sainclair, the well-known Parisian attorney.

"Our mutual friend, Rouletabille, from the *Société Secrète des Aventuriers*, told me you were the best person for the job," she continued.

"I'm flattered, Mademoiselle L'Ange," Sainclair answered, "but certainly you of all people don't need the aid of a stodgy old solicitor like me."

"*Au contraire*, Maître. You are precisely the person I need. Let me explain and you'll soon understand why. As you know, since Francis awoke me from my spell, and I realized that women could have a life of their own in this brave, new world, I have dedicated myself to helping those in need."

"And you've made quite a good job of it, Mademoiselle!"

"Thank you, Maître. I have been rather pleased with the results of my little escapades...

"At any rate, I recently helped a young woman named Sylvie Mac Dhul who was being horribly mistreated by her evil stepmother. I discovered since then that this woman was none other than the master criminal known as Belphégor.

"Belphégor didn't seem to appreciate my efforts on Sylvie's behalf and has made it her mission in life to destroy me.

"I have to admit that I have rather been enjoying the conflict, as one does a good match of chess. But now, I have found something wondrous that must be kept hidden from her."

Sainclair interrupted the Angel:

"Certainly you don't need someone with my poor talents to help you with something like that?"

"But your talents are precisely what I need, Maître! I have located what I believe is the Spear of Destiny, buried in the tomb of Saint-Louis, and Belphégor wants nothing more than to get her hands on it. I need to hide it in a place where she will never think to look."

"And how am I to help you with that?"

"Hidden things have a way of being found; don't you think? I've always thought, therefore, that hiding them in plain sight was the wisest course of action. Yes, I could easily take the Spear to a secret cave, or bury it deep beneath the ground, but I know Belphégor; neither of those options will stop her."

"So," said the lawyer, now intrigued in spite of his qualms, "where *do* you think it should be hidden?"

"I think a small house in a country village would be ideal. Belphégor would never think of looking in a place that is so mundane and beyond her experience. But I can't be the one to either find or purchase such a house, or she'll know. So, my dear Maître Sainclair, I need you to act on my behalf and find a place where the Spear can be kept in safety."

"I can do that, of course, but do you have any idea of where you want me to look for this house?"

"As a matter of fact, I do. You know that I was born in the Pyrenées. I have kept a fondness for the region, even though I now live here in Paris, and I think I should like the house to be somewhere there, perhaps in the foothills…"

"I know the perfect village, my dear!" said Sainclair excitedly. "It's an old bastide village that is neither too small, nor too grand. It's set right in the intersection of three rivers, but is a bit off the beaten path, so doesn't attract a lot of attention. I'm sure I can find you something appropriate there."

"And what is this place called, Maître?"

"Chalabre, Mademoiselle."

"Chabrol?"

"No, Chalabre."

"I like the sound of that. Please go as soon as you are able, Maître. I'll feel much more relaxed once the Spear is out of Paris."

Sainclair took the night train to Toulouse, then on the morning, after a good breakfast, continued his journey to Bram, then switched to catch the line going to Lavelanet, and finally arrived in Chalabre in the late afternoon. While not a metropolis, it was a bustling town of several thousand residents, most of whom were employed in the local shoe and textile factories.

The original city walls had been knocked down barely a century earlier, and new, bourgeois homes had been built on their ruins. It was one of these that he was lucky enough to find available for purchase.

The house, located on Cours Colbert, charmed him with its quirky construction: each room was on a separate half-floor, so that there were no corridors linking the rooms, simply a central staircase from which each floor blossomed like the petals of a very large flower. He offered the owner his asking price; very reasonable Sainclair thought, for a house of this size, and asked the local Notary for the final papers to be signed as soon as it could be arranged.

On the appointed day, the Phantom Angel disguised herself as much as possible and joined Sainclair on the train. A long, thin, well-wrapped parcel had been placed in the luggage compartment.

When the train pulled into Toulouse, the luggage attendant was found unconscious in the car; the parcel was missing. A lithe figure, dressed in black from head to toe, jumped off the train before it had full stopped and ran down the platform; it was carrying the parcel!

Sainclair and the Angel were told the sad news. Sainclair was devastated, but the Angel laughed light-heartedly.

"Mademoiselle! This is tragic! Why aren't you upset?" asked the lawyer in shock.

"Why, Maître Sainclair! Belphégor has just stolen an ordinary spear of African origin; a simple souvenir made for gullible tourists. The *real* Spear of Destiny is waiting for us in Chalabre at the office of the Notary. As soon as we sign the documents and receive the keys, it will be safely stored in the attic, where no one is likely to find it for 100 years!"

First publication:
Tales of the Shadowmen 6, 2010

This story was written for Meteor House's wonderful collection The Worlds of Philip José Farmer 2: Of Dust and Soul, *and is a prequel to Farmer's first* World of Tiers *novel.*

Robert Wolff: The Wolff that One Hears...

> "Then let us start as soon as it is light tomorrow,
> if we can. The wolf that one hears is worse
> than the orc that one fears."
> Boromir.
> J.R.R. Tolkien
> *The Fellowship of the Ring.*

Like many stories, this one began with a dog.

A dog named "Robot."

(You can't make up details like that!)

It started on September 8, 1940, near the peaceful village of Montignac, in the lush and green Périgord region of Western France. At the time, people there lived a life of quiet, but very real, desperation. France had signed a humiliating Armistice with Nazi Germany in June of that year. Yes, Montignac considered itself lucky not to be in the occupied part of the country, but in truth, the crushing blow of the recent defeat, combined with the dismal aspects of everyday life under the meretricious Petain régime, weighed heavily on every soul.

But perhaps not on Robot's, for he was merely a dog, a handsome setter-terrier mix with a smooth, long brown coat, who remained steadfastly oblivious to his humans' miseries. Robot continued to enjoy his daily routine of running in the hills, digging holes, running some more, chasing after voles and little furry animals, and did I mention the running?

All that he did in the company of his young master, 18-year-old Marcel Ravidat.

Tall and strong, Marcel had been apprenticed as a mechanic to the local Citroen garage. His boss thought him gifted with tools, having a good comprehension of engines, and knew his future would be bright—after the War. (Everything in those days was measured by "After the War.")

Rather shy, but good-hearted, Marcel had been nicknamed the "Convict" by the villagers, not because of any blemish on his character—far from it!—but because of his flattering resemblance to the actor Harry Baur, who had played the burly Jean Valjean in the film version of *Les Misérables*, which had screened with considerable success at the local theater a year before.

Once, the verdant hills surrounding Montignac had been planted with grapes, but the *phylloxera* epidemic of 1880 had killed them all, and the locals had chosen to replace them with pines. Then, the pines had been cut down and nature had eventually reclaimed the land, which had returned to wilderness.

Robot liked the wild; it suited him just fine.

That afternoon, Marcel noticed his dog digging more madly and obsessively than usual at the bottom of an excavation. It was a big hole in the ground that had been caused by the uprooting of an old pine that had been struck by lightning.

"What is it, Robot?" said the young man, understandably curious about his dog's manic behavior.

Marcel stepped into the excavation, expecting to find a nest of voles, or perhaps a dead, half-buried bird, the latter being considered a supreme delicacy by Robot. But instead, at the bottom of the excavation, he saw nothing but a hole. Not just a hole, but something that was quite out of place in such an ordinary bit of rural scenery. It was about ten inches in diameter, but deep, and dark, *very dark*.

It looks like a vent hole from Hell, Marcel couldn't help thinking.

The young man gathered a few pebbles and dropped them into the hole, then listened. It took a long, long time for them to hit bottom.

There was something down there.

Marcel was nothing if not enterprising, and he had, as the French put it, *de la suite dans les idées*, or follow through. Therefore, he returned four days later, without Robot, this time, but accompanied by three strapping young friends, Georges, Simon and Jacques, all under 17. They were equipped with small pick axes, and they quickly enlarged the hole enough to let Marcel descend into the pit at the end of a rope, carrying an oil lamp.

And there, Marcel discovered an extraordinary, magical underworld of caves, lakes, stalactites and stalagmites—and fabulous paintings.

Marcel Ravidat had just discovered the prehistoric wonders of the Caves of Lascaux!

Things flash forward to the early 50s, when Germany and France had become allies, but Western Europe trembled under the threat of the Cold War—and mutually assured nuclear destruction. Lascaux had been opened to the public "after the War" in 1948 and, for the first time, the contents of those wonderful caves were being probed, poked, catalogued and investigated by serious and dedicated scientists.

No one was more serious and dedicated that François Bordes, a burly man, barely 30, with short-cropped hair and a square face who looked as if it had been chiseled out of stone. Monsieur Bordes was a native of the region, and shared the good common sense and salt of the Earth nature of the local peasantry. His parents had scrimped and saved to send him to the University at Bordeaux, and he was working on his doctorate thesis on *Les limons quaternaires*, but had lost none of his genuine attachment for his region and its traditions.

Sometimes, at night, he looked at the sky and wondered—not about the next day's weather, like his fellow Périgordins—but about the cosmos, and in that he was different from them. Remember this, as it will be important later.

As we become acquainted with Monsieur Bordes, we discover him, assisted by an intern from the University, busy selecting and cataloguing tiny samples of rock, wood and coal. Once assembled, he would take this collection to the University of Chicago, where the famous physical chemist Willard Libby had just developed a method for radiocarbon dating. There was much argument at Lascaux between those scientists who thought that the paintings were from the earlier portion of the Upper Paleolithic, and those who favored later years. It was hoped that the new carbon-14 process would settle the controversy once and for all.

As befitted such a delicate scientific task, an eerie silence reigned in the caves, only broken by the scraping and chipping sounds of the tiny geological tools and sample gathering. But, suddenly, there was an ominous sound, not unlike the crack of a whip. The kind of sound no scientist ever wants to hear at his workplace.

"Monsieur Bordes..." stammered the intern.

"What is it, Jérôme?"

"I'm sorry. It just came out in my hands... It fell out by itself, I swear..."

François Bordes saw that the young man was holding a hefty chunk of rock in his hand. This was almost vandalism, since the samples were supposed to be very small. Reports would have to be written; explanations provided. There would be a long night ahead of him. He prepared to berate his young assistant accordingly, when he noticed *something* protruding from the stone.

Something which had no business being inside a rock.

It was a small piece of metal, the corner of something embedded inside the rock, as if the stone had formed around it like a cyst.

Bordes put his finger to it and gently touched the tiny pyramidal point protruding from the rock. It was indeed metal. The archeologist was familiar with crystals and metal ores and the wonderfully pure geometric shapes they could often take, but he had never seen anything like this. It looked... manufactured.

"Should I call the supervisor?" asked Jérôme the intern, oblivious to Bordes' concerns and far more preoccupied by the fate of his internship if his act of "vandalism" were to be discovered.

"No," said Bordes after a minute of reflection. "This requires more study and analysis. I'll take it to the lab. I think we're finished here for the day."

François Bordes was a pipe smoker. It helped him relax and, more importantly, it helped him think. He had smoked pipe after pipe for several hours, while grappling over what to do about his discovery.

First, he had used his geological tools to delicately expose a little more of the metal artifact inside the rock. But instead of providing answers, this operation had only raised more questions.

The exposed section of the artifact was now an inch wide and half-an-inch thick. It looked like a small metal tablet, perhaps four by five inches in total, judging from the size of the rock. Bordes could not identify the nature of the metal with the equipment at his disposal in Montignac. But what he had literally unearthed had shaken him deeply.

There were rows after rows of microscopic characters engraved with uncanny precision on one side of the tablet!

Bordes had spent a lot of time thinking about that discovery. He could have stopped there and waited for the morning to gather a team of scientists. That would have been the right course of action. But then, they would have taken the tablet to Bordeaux, perhaps even to Paris, and Bordes would have received a cordial but insincere handshake, and his role in the discovery would not guarantee him even a modest footnote in the future academic publications that would no doubt be written.

The man who sometimes looked at the night skies and wondered, finally made up his mind. He sighed and, with a heavy heart, took his rock hammer and brought it down on the rock.

This, at least, he thought, would buy him the footnote.

The stone broke into two, sharp fragments, plus some smaller shards of rock, and released the tablet within. As Bordes had surmised, it was about four by five inches, made of some kind of dark green metal, and engraved with about a hundred lines of tiny characters.

The archeologist cleaned the tablet with a brush and took a magnifying glass to study the markings.

He did not recognize the characters. They looked a little like proto-Basque carvings, but they weren't proto-Basque; if they had been, he would have been able to identify at least a few signs, even though ancient languages were not his specialty.

He went to his reference shelf and returned with a book by Professor Aristide Clairembard, a renowned archeologist from the Collège de France, who had written many authoritative articles about the languages of "lost civilizations," such as Mû and Atlantis. Clairembard was presently on Easter Island, looking for Mûvian remains.

After an hour of study and meticulous comparisons, Bordes found some similarities between certain characters on the tablet and samples recorded in Iceland by Professor Lidenbrock in the 19th century. Clairembard, who was always generous with praise, stated that only one man had been able—and then, only partially—to decipher those writings, a brilliant American Professor of Ancient Languages at the University of Illinois at Busiris named Robert Wolff.

Bordes smiled. Since he had to go to Chicago to deliver the samples for carbon-dating by Professor Libby, it seemed like fate. After all, Busiris was virtually next door...

A month later, François Bordes found himself crossing the threshold of the University of Illinois. It was the week after Thanksgiving and the archeologist, well acquainted with the subtle currents of academic life, could sense that everyone was already preparing for the holidays.

A rugged man in his fifties, with sharp, grey eyes that seemed to reach deep into one's very soul, was waiting for him at the appointed time and place, just outside Carmody Hall. Bordes thought that he looked a little like the actor Cary Grant, but then, many Americans reminded him of Cary Grant, who wasn't even born in America.

"Professor Wolff?" he said hesitantly.

"Monsieur Bordes," responded the man warmly, extending his hand. "You're right on time. Who said Frenchmen are always late?"

"Someone who doesn't like France?" replied Bordes, with a smile.

"Well said! Actually, one of your compatriots said it just the other day, when he showed up late for a lecture."

"Really?"

"Yes. We have a distinguished visitor from your country. Doctor Oscar Le Rouge from the Collège de France. He arrived last week to give a lecture on pre-Akkadian languages."

"I'm afraid that's quite out of my specialty. I wouldn't know anything about it."

"But it is in mine. Le Rouge has quite a few interesting theories. His lecture was truly fascinating. But come with me, I'll introduce you..."

Wolff pushed open the doors of the lecture hall and invited Bordes inside. There was a small gathering of teachers and students talking, or rather listening in awe to a tall, large and well-built man, with flamboyant, red hair.

"Doctor Le Rouge," said Wolff, pushing his way through the small crowd, "there's someone you should meet—from your native country, no less. François Bordes, one of the archeologists working at the Lascaux site."

Le Rouge had a pleasant, rugged face, the type of handsome face that Madison Avenue loved to use, because women found it irresistible, and yet men did not feel threatened by it. He spoke with a hint of an accent that might have been French, but then, might not have been. His smile was warm and genuinely friendly. Bordes knew that he should have liked the man, and yet something deep inside him screamed to not trust him.

"Docteur Le Rouge," he said, shaking the hand proffered to him.

"*Monsieur Bordes, c'est un plaisir, non, plutôt un honneur pour moi...* But out of courtesy for our hosts, let's continue in English. How is your English?"

"I manage," said Bordes, still reluctant to let himself be drawn in by the man's geniality.

"Monsieur Bordes is too modest," interjected Wolff. "We've spoken on the telephone many times and he's quite fluent."

"Ah yes, I remember you mentioning it before, Professor Wolff," said Le Rouge. "Something to do with some archaic writing, possibly Nippurian I believe?"

"That's what I hope to find out," said Wolff. "Monsieur Bordes has brought the tablet with him, and I plan to carefully transcribe every sign starting tomorrow."

"I see. Are you planning to stay in Busiris, Monsieur Bordes?"

"Alas, no. This is only a side-trip for me. I'm really here is to have all the Lascaux samples carbon-dated by Professor Libby in Chicago."

"I see," repeated Le Rouge. For some unfathomable reason, Bordes felt that the other Frenchman was not pleased with the news; it was as if he had just told someone his cat, then his dog had died.

"Well, then, I wish you good luck," said Le Rouge, offering his hand, indicating that the conversation was over. "I will be most eager to read your findings when you publish them."

Bordes thought about an article with his name on it appearing in the *Bulletin de l'Institut Français d'Archéologie*. What recognition. What notoriety.

By the time he pulled out of his *rêverie*, Le Rouge had walked away with his entourage.

"Well, Professor Wolff," he said, "it is time for you to take a look at this tablet."

It was mid-December. François Bordes felt the beginning of winter's bite as the cold winds of the season roared across the campus of the University of Illinois at Busiris. He looked at the sky as any Périgordin would have done, and while the climate in this region was unfamiliar to him, he could almost smell the storm approaching.

Raising the fur-lined collar of his leather jacket, the archeologist accelerated his pace and briskly walked the ten blocks to the indoor shooting range where he had been told he could meet Wolff.

Once inside, he took off his jacket and shook as if, somehow, he could get rid of the penetrating cold that had managed to seep through it. Rubbing his hands, he walked towards the shooting gallery. With its dark wood-lined walls and soft red carpet, the range was a welcome refuge from the outside. For the first time since he had left Chicago, Bordes felt truly relaxed.

He almost glided over the three small steps that took him to the shooting gallery. There, he saw Wolff methodically unloading a Winchester precisely into the center of a target.

"Good afternoon, Professor Wolff," he shouted.

Wolff put down the rifle and smiled at the sight of the newcomer.

"Monsieur Bordes! I didn't expect to see you back from Chicago so soon. How was your trip?"

"Very successful, thank you." The Frenchman looked at the target and the narrow grouping of bullets in its center and whistled in admiration. "You are quite a shot, Professor Wolff..."

"Robert, please. Would you like to try?" the American said, pointing at the rifle on the counter.

Bordes made a self-deprecating grin.

"I'm afraid I've only shot quails and wild boars in the Périgord. We're not like you, cowboys!"

Wolff laughed.

"You are exactly like us, cowboys, François! I've heard tales of the exploits of your *maquisards* during the War. Now, if I were to ask you to shoot the elephant gun I keep in my office, that would be something else, of course... Anyway, what brings you back to Busiris so soon?"

"I had to come back to see you, Robert, because, well, something rather unusual has turned up..."

"Let me guess?" said Wolff. "It's about the tablet, isn't it?"

Bordes nodded. During his previous visit, he had left the tablet with Wolff, to be deciphered, taking just a few scrapings for the carbon dating tests.

"I've finished the transcription and I took it to our computer lab," continued Wolff. "They've just received a new ENIAC computer. I think it will take at least that much to crack it. But the first results have been promising, and I'm confident that..."

"No, it's not that. I don't doubt your abilities as a linguist," interrupted the Frenchman. "There's no better expert in Ancient Languages than you, Robert. But, you see, the carbon dating turned up something very strange..."

"I see. What did they find?"

"That's where it gets odd. The rock surrounding the table is, of course, very old, as you would expect from that area. Tertiary. Around 50 million years, give or take. But the tablet itself... It's no older than 10,000 years."

"That can't be."

"You see my puzzlement. How can a 10,000 years-old artifact be entirely contained inside a 50 million year-old rock. That's impossible. One of the two has got to be a fake. And yet, I saw that sample being removed with my own eyes... I cracked the rock open myself..."

"Are you sure it's not an elaborate prank by one of your students? They do that all the time here, too. Why, recently, one of our grad students has taken to running on the rooftops at night disguised as a gargoyle... Sooner or later, the campus police will catch him, of course—just as you'll catch your practical joker."

Bordes looked unconvinced.

"A practical joker capable of devising an ancient language that has even you sweating bullets, Robert? Is that really possible?"

Wolff considered the question for a moment, and shook his head. "I admit you've got a point, François. No one could forge those markings, not to mention the fact that I still don't know how they were actually engraved... I tell you what— let's go and take another look at that tablet. It's in the safe in my office..."

Wolff stepped into his office. It was a small room, by university standards, but cozy, with a nice view of the campus—a prized achievement, for which Wolff had had to fight for years. It was furnished with a sturdy mahogany desk, presently half-hidden under a pile of student papers waiting to be graded, two metal filing cabinets, and a handsome oak bookcase. A collection of Colts, Remingtons and other guns hung over it. Bordes followed his colleague and went to sit in one of the two leather chairs facing the desk.

Wolff took a look around the room, then froze.

"François, *someone*'s been in here," he said suddenly.

"How can you tell, Robert?" asked the Frenchman, looking skeptical. "You've told me yourself you locked your office when you went down to the range, and the key has not left your pocket since."

"I tell you, *someone*'s been in here," repeated Wolff.

He pointed towards a travel bag sitting on top of the filing cabinets.

"See that bag? It was closed before, but it no longer is. No, I tell you again, *someone* was in here—while I was at the range."

"Have you checked the safe?"

"The tablet!"

Wolff rushed to a small portable safe sitting on the bottom shelf of the bookcase between two piles of books in Ancient Greek.

"It looks undisturbed, but we'll soon find out..."

With a few flips of the fingers, he turned the tumblers and the safe opened with a click. Inside were some documents, money, a passport, but—no tablet!

"The tablet's gone!"

"But who could have taken it? And why?" asked Bordes, crestfallen.

Wolff slammed the safe shut, then paced about the room.

"Who knew you'd left it here?" he asked.

"Well, there's Professor Libby in Chicago and his team, but their integrity is beyond question."

"I agree. Anyone else? Did you make a copy of the markings?"

"I did send a rubbing to Professor Clairembard, but he's on Easter Island, on the other side of the world. How could he...?"

"Clairembard, you say? Hmm... That might be a clue... I have an idea. All may not yet be lost. But before we take action, we need to make some preparations..."

The weather had gone from bad to worse, if that was even possible. The storm that François Bordes had predicted had arrived, and gales of frigid rain, melted snow really, hit the university with unabated violence. Fortunately, there was virtually no one around to suffer the wrath of the elements, everyone having long before sought refuge inside.

The University's computer sciences lab, located in a modest, one-story brick and glass building, was ordinarily closed for the night, but Wolff had a key and everyone was used to seeing him work late, when he could grab some free time on the computer to help him decipher the latest cuneiforms from Iran or pre-Minoan writings from Crete.

The rain was falling hard on the skylight just above the desk where Wolff sat; its surface was lit only by a goose neck lamp. He got up, grabbed a print-out from the jaws of the ENIAC and returned to sit at the desk. He spread the pages of the original transcription he had made of the tablet's microscopic characters and compared them, one line at a time, with the contents of the print out. Behind him, the ENIAC continued chattering, spewing out more data and drowning out the sounds of the gale.

After he finished reading the print out, Wolff remained pensive for a minute, then returned to the computer, took the next batches of pages, and again went back to the desk for more comparisons.

Suddenly, he heard a noise coming from the skylight; it sounded like a pet scratching at the door to let his master know that he wants in, but when he looked up and peered into the darkness, he saw nothing and heard only the wind.

Wolff checked his watch. It was now past midnight. Perhaps his intuition had been wrong. Perhaps....

Suddenly, he heard another sound, this time from behind him. It was the click of the door. Someone had entered the room and closed the door behind him. Wolff smiled. He had been right after all. The man removed a large hat, soaked by the rain, revealing a reddish mop of hair. He then took off his dripping coat and hung it on a stand by the door.

"Professor Wolff," the newcomer said. "What are you doing here on a night like this...?"

"I could ask you the same thing, Doctor Le Rouge," said Wolff, purposefully not extending his hand. "What is our distinguished visiting professor doing hanging around this humble abode at this time of the night?"

"Research for a paper I plan to write..." responded Le Rouge evasively, sounding slightly annoyed.

"If you want the computer to yourself, I'm almost done with it," said Wolff, gathering his papers.

"May I see?..." asked Le Rouge, barely hiding his eagerness.

"Certainly," Wolff replied, handing him the sheath of papers. But, as he got up from behind the desk, he dropped them and the papers fell and spilled across the green linoleum floor.

"Oh, how clumsy of me! I apologize," said Wolff. "Could you give me a hand?"

"Of course."

Wolff began picking up the sheets of papers from the floor and handing them to Le Rouge, who straightened them, stacked them, and eventually handed the pile back to Wolff, after leafing through it.

"Any insight, Doctor Le Rouge?" asked Wolff, frowning lightly as if to better study his opponent.

"No, of course not," replied Le Rouge, in all appearance sincere. "How could I?"

"But I understand that you've worked with your fellow countryman from the Collège de France, Professor Clairembard, the only man to have found samples of Mûvian writings. Some of those signs should at least be familiar to you?"

"No, I'm afraid it's all gobbledygook to me. I admire your ability to make sense of it all, Professor Wolff. Have you managed to decipher any of it?"

"Yes, some. But that is not the most interesting thing that I found…"

"Ah?" said Le Rouge, falsely casual.

"Yes. You see, Doctor Le Rouge, these papers are written in an alphabet that no one as yet can identify. Its very origins are a mystery and its significance seems to mostly belong in the realm of myths…"

"I don't see what you're getting at…"

"You will. When I dropped these papers, on purpose, I confess, they were all mixed up. You will note than none of the pages are numbered. Yet, when I gave them to you, one by one, you sorted them out—unconsciously, I presume—and handed them back to me in the right order. So I ask myself: how is Doctor Le Rouge, a man who professes total ignorance of the contents of this document, nevertheless able to read it fluently, far more than I who spent ten days assisted by this wonder of modern technology (Wolff waved towards the computer) studying it assiduously?"

There was a long silence. Wolff was waiting for Le Rouge to respond, but no answer was forthcoming. He saw the fires of uncontrollable rage and wounded pride burn and grow within the eyes of the man who called himself Le Rouge but who—he was now certain—was *someone else*.

Strangely, at that moment, he felt an odd kinship, a strange rapport with this mysterious visitor, and he saw in the other man's eyes that he felt it too. But Le Rouge's own moment of uncertainty was short-lived, consumed by the unleashed fury that engulfed him in seconds.

"Mislik! To me!" he shouted to the sky, managing to overpower the sounds of the storm. "Mislik! I, your creator, am calling you!"

The skylight suddenly broke into a million shards with a shattering sound of broken glass and metal, letting in the gale and the raging rain. A monstrous being made of stone, a living gargoyle, with fiery eyes of electric blue, jumped into the lab. Wolff briefly remembered the reports about a practical joker gallivanting on the rooftops dressed as a gargoyle and smiled wistfully. He also recalled that such reports had coincided with the visit of Doctor Le Rouge—and the first call of François Bordes.

"You have learned a secret that doesn't belong to you, Professor Wolff," spat Le Rouge, grabbing his coat and making for the door. "A secret of the Lords that belongs to no human. Mislik, kill him and destroy this place. Nothing must remain of it!"

Le Rouge then stepped through the door and vanished into the night.

The Mislik, surprisingly fast for a creature made of stone, lumbered towards Wolff. Its deadly purpose was all too evidently clear.

"François! Think of it as just another wild boar from your Périgord!" shouted Wolff.

François Bordes came out from behind the ENIAC, where he had been hiding, and fired Wolff's elephant gun. Twice.

The Mislik shattered, exploded into a thousand pieces, but at the same time, spreading a lava-like substance, which began to set fire to everything it touched. Bordes thought it looked like Grecian fire. In a matter of minutes, the lab had turned into an inferno. Luckily, the two scientists were able to escape before it was entirely consumed by the flames and burned to the ground.

"Well, this is it then," said Wolff.

"What do you mean?"

"No more tablet, my transcription, the punched cards, the print-out... all gone. We have nothing. And if you want my advice," he added, hearing the sound of the fire engine in the distance, but getting closer, "we're probably better off leaving and forgetting this ever happened."

But they didn't forget, of course. Ever.

After he had returned to France, François Bordes launched a discrete investigation into Doctor Le Rouge. Professor Clairembard remembered him only as a recent acquaintance he had made at the Collège de France. His credentials were impeccable—but all false. No traces of him could be found anywhere. It was as if he had never existed.

The French archeologist never solved the mystery of how a 10,000 year-old tablet could have been found inside a 50 million year-old piece of rock. He finally convinced himself that the tablet was indeed a fake, but never looked at the skies and the world around him in quite the same way.

A few years later, he became a science fiction writer of some stature under the nom-de-plume of Francis Carsac. In his first novel, *Ceux de Nulle Part* (Those from Nowhere), he wrote about aliens who could make new stars and fought creatures made of stone, which he called "Misliks."

As for Robert Wolff, over the next few months, he experienced a spate of strange, colorful, exotic dreams, filled with creatures of legend, and a world that looked like a wedding cake. But he never seemed to remember those dreams when he woke up, and soon, they went away.

The only one who remained truly at peace was Robot, who lie peacefully under the lush and green hills of Périgord, buried one sad morning by his young master, having lived a long, happy and well-filled life of running in the hills, digging holes, running some more, chasing after voles (and did I mention the running?), and never knew how close he had come to exposing one of the secrets of the Lords.

First publication:
The Worlds of Philip José Farmer 2: *Of Dust and Soul,* 2011

There is little need to explain Alf, *a sitcom created by Paul Fusco and Tom Patchett and broadcast from1986 to1990. This script was written in 1987.*

SCRIPTS

Alf: *Alf's Halloween Adventure*

ACT ONE

FADE IN:

<u>INT. TANNER LIVING ROOM - DAY (Alf, Willie, Kate, Brian, Lynn)</u>
(ALF IS SITTING ON ONE END OF THE COUCH WITH HIS USUAL LITTER OF FOOD BAGS. HE IS CRUNCH-ING NOISILY ON THINGS. WILLIE IS AT THE OTHER END, TRYING TO READ OVER THE SOUND OF THE TELEVISION, WHICH IS PLAYING AN EPISODE OF THE BOB NEWHART SHOW - LOUDLY. KATE IS AT THE TABLE WITH HER SEWING MACHINE AROUND WHICH ARE VARIOUS BITS OF ORANGE, FURRY CLOTH)

TELEVISION (V.O.) (VOICE OF CAROL KESTER) Bob, you guys have got to give me a raise...

ALF (TALKING TO THE SET) Come on, Carol, go for it! All you've got to do is make up a good, convincing story. Those guys are just a bunch of soft-hearted chumps. Someone like that always falls for a good line. C'mon, show some crea-tivity here!

(WILLIE LOOKS UP FROM HIS BOOK AND STARES AT ALF WITH SUSPICION. ALF SEES WILLIE WATCHING HIM AND SWITCHES GEARS IN THE MIDDLE, TRYING VERY HARD TO PAINT HIMSELF OUT OF THE CORNER)

ALF But, then, it's wrong to lie to people who trust you. Very wrong. Absolutely. I'd never do anything like that.

(BEFORE WILLIE CAN RETORT, BRIAN AND LYNN ENTER THROUGH THE FRONT DOOR. LYNN IS DRESSED IN A PETER PAN COSTUME. BRIAN RUNS OVER TO KATE)

BRIAN Is it ready, Mom?

KATE Just about, Brian.

BRIAN (ALMOST POUTING) It'll be time to go trick or treating in an hour. If I don't have it, I'll be the only kid in the neighborhood who doesn't have a costume.

WILLIE
I don't think not having a costume is so terrible.

(KATE LOOKS ANNOYED AT WILLIE'S REMARK)

KATE You're not going to try to get out of going to the Murdochs' Halloween party, are you? I've been working on our costumes for weeks now. I'm really looking forward to going... And there's no way you're going to go without a costume!

LYNN (TO ALF) I can't wait to see what she's come up with this year. Dad looked hysterical in the Bugs Bunny outfit Mom made him last Halloween.

WILLIE (OVERHEARING) Hysterical, ah! Everybody came over to ask "What's up, Doc." Then, Buzz Murdoch kept stalking me, saying, "Be vewy, vewy quiet, I'm hunting wabbits!" I had a terrible time!

KATE (POUTING) Well, I had a lot of fun!

WILLIE Sure you did! You went as Cinderella. They all wanted to dance with you. They weren't trying to feed you carrots!

KATE (TRYING TO APPEAL TO WILLIE'S GOOD NATURE) We really have to go, Willie. We can't just cancel out at the last minute...

ALF (INTERRUPTING) Can we have a little quiet around here? Bob and Jerry are just about to give in on the raise. It's a very moving moment.

WILLIE (SARCASTICALLY) Sorry for interrupting such an important event.

ALF Hey, no sweat. I've seen this episode before... You know what? Why don't I help you guys sort this whole thing out?

WILLIE (DEFINITELY WANTING ANYTHING BUT ALF'S HELP) No, please, don't help. We can manage. We don't need your help.

ALF Sure, you say that now, but you'll be grateful later!

WILLIE (SIGHING) I doubt that. Besides, we don't want to interfere with your watching television, do we?

ALF (MAGNANIMOUS) No, really, it's no problem, Willie. I'm happy to do it. Show's over anyway.
(HE GETS OFF THE COUCH)

133

What's all this Halloween stuff, anyway? I thought Halloween was about a raving, murderous maniac who escapes from an asylum and starts killing everybody in his family...

(SUDDENLY STRUCK BY AN IDEA, HE GETS WORRIED)

ALF (CONT'D) Hey, you guys don't have another son somewhere that I don't know about, do you? Because, if you do, I'm moving out!

LYNN (LAUGHING) No, no, Alf, that's only a movie! Halloween's an old custom about warding off evil spirits. It goes back to the times of the harvest festivals and...

BRIAN (INTERRUPTING) And it's really neat, 'cause we get to put on funny costumes and go trick or treating!

ALF What's this trick or treat stuff?

WILLIE (WARMING TO THE SUBJECT) It's a wonderful American tradition, Alf. The kids put on costumes and go door-to-door, asking people for candy, or else they'll do a trick -well, they don't really do that anymore, but they say they will...

ALF I get it. It's like institutionalized blackmail?

WILLIE (SOUNDING TIRED) No, no, it's not like that... I guess it's kind of complicated... Why am I trying to explain this to you...

ALF No, really, I understand. We've got something just like it back on Melmac...

WILLIE (SURPRISED) You do?

ALF Yeah. We call it "Krunchenkat." Everybody dresses up like French chefs with phony French accents, then they go door-to-door asking for cats. If they don't get one, they spread garlic paste all over the house. It's a gas.

(WILLIE, KATE, BRIAN AND LYNN LOOK AT EACH OTHER IN DISBELIEF AND DISGUST)

WILLIE That's not only one of the most disgusting things I've ever heard, I can't even imagine how a tradition like that could get started.

ALF What tradition? We just started it a couple of years ago after they ran a Jerry Lewis Film Festival on the Melmac Public Television Network. (TO BRIAN) So, Bri. What kind of costume are you going to wear for that Halloween of yours? I might have a chef's hat around somewhere if you want it.

KATE That's okay, Alf. Brian's costume is all ready.

(SHE GETS UP FROM THE SEWING MACHINE, CARRYING A PILE OF ORANGE-LOOKING FUR, WHICH SHE UNFURLS WITH A FLOURISH IN FRONT OF BRIAN -- IT IS AN AMATEUR, BUT QUITE RECOGNIZABLE ALF SUIT)

KATE (PROUDLY) Ta-da! Well, what do you think, honey?

(BRIAN RUNS OVER TO GRAB THE COSTUME)

BRIAN Oh, boy! Oh, boy! It's neat! I'll look just like Alf! What do you think, Alf?

(ALF IS LOOKING AT THE COSTUME, WITHOUT SAYING A WORD)

KATE Well, Alf, what do you think?

ALF (COMING OUT OF IT) Amazing! It looks just like my cousin Spike, back on Melmac. Especially the nose. Spike had an enormous honker. You sure he didn't model for you? (TO BRIAN) You'll be the coolest dude in the neighborhood, Brian. Now that I think of it, Spike was pretty cool too. He used to go out picking up babes, then he'd take them back to his place and get out the rubber chicken, then...

(WILLIE INTERRUPTS, BEFORE ALF'S STORY CAN GET REALLY OBJECTIONABLE)

WILLIE I think we all get the picture, Alf.

ALF You do? I didn't know you were into that kind of perversion, Willie. Besides, you don't have the nose for it, no offense!

(MEANWHILE, BRIAN STARTS TO GET INTO HIS COSTUME)

KATE Lynn, are you sure you don't mind taking Brian around the neighborhood while your father and I go to the Murdochs?

WILLIE But if you mind, it's okay, honey, we can cancel...

(KATE GIVES WILLIE A LOOK THAT TELLS HIM NOT TO CONTINUE THE DISCUSSION IN THAT VEIN)

WILLIE (FORCED LAUGH) But then, why should we... We had so much fun last year -- ah, ah!

LYNN Of course, I don't mind, Dad. It'll be fun. Like when I was Brian's age.

KATE Thanks, honey. I'll feel safer if I know you're with your brother.

ALF You don't have to worry, Kate. Besides, I'll be there making sure both of the kids are safe.

WILLIE (UPSET) What? Oh no, you won't! I absolutely forbid you to set foot outside of this house. That's just what we need, another alien sighting in the neighborhood. I can see the headlines now.
(SPREADING HIS HANDS)
"Alien on Rampage!" "War of the Worlds: Part Two!"

ALF Gee, I didn't know you guys were advanced enough to get involved in intergalactic warfare. It must have been pretty messy.

WILLIE No, we weren't, it was... Oh, just forget it. You're just trying to change the subject again. I want you to promise that you won't go out of the house tonight.

ALF (POUTING) Yeah, yeah. Just lock the alien up in the garage while everybody else gets to go out and have a good time.

WILLIE (FIRM) You heard me, do I have your word?

ALF Oh, okay, don't look at me like I'm Eddie Haskell or something...
(BEFORE WILLIE CAN COMMENT ON THIS, HE RUSHES TO ADD)
I promise. Sacred word. Most unbreakable Melmacian oath. Cross my tonsils, hope to granulate!

(BRIAN, IN HIS ALF SUIT, WALKS OVER TO SIT NEXT TO ALF ON THE COUCH, AND PUTS HIS ARM AROUND HIM)

BRIAN Don't feel bad, Alf. Halloween's not really that much fun. Mom doesn't let me eat any candy until I get home, and a lot of people give out stuff that's not very good, like granola bars. Besides, I'll share my candy with you.

ALF (PERKING UP) Fifty-fifty?

BRIAN Sure, fifty-fifty! Anyway, now that there's this really scary lady that moved into the old house at the top of the hill, Halloween's not as much fun. She looks mean, she talks weird, and all the kids are really scared of her...

ALF Hey, don't tell me you're afraid of an old woman, Bri?

(BRIAN NODS SEVERAL TIMES)

BRIAN Some of the kids said that she's a witch.

ALF Really?

(LYNN COMES TO SIT ON THE OTHER SIDE OF ALF)

LYNN I don't know, Alf, she's really spooky. Sometimes, late at night, there are strange lights and weird noises coming out of her house. And it always smells funny.

ALF (ACCUSINGLY TO KATE AND WILLIE) I don't believe it! How can you let your own flesh and blood go out alone with people like that in the neighborhood? Haven't you heard of Hansel and Gretel, or is that just another of Willie's intergalactic fantasies? (BEAT) At the very least, I should go too, so I can protect them!

WILLIE We don't need your advice on child rearing, Alf, thank you.

KATE (TO LYNN AND BRIAN) I'm surprised at you, kids. Especially You, Lynn. Just because a person looks a little different, it doesn't mean she's bad. This woman's probably a very nice person.

(THE KIDS LOOK UNCONVINCED)

BRIAN But, Mom...

WILLIE (SARCASTIC) Your mother is right. Look at Alf. In the middle ages, they would have thought he was an evil imp, and they'd have burned him at the stake. In fact...

(A BEAT -- HE CHUCKLES SILENTLY, OBVIOUSLY PICTURING ALF AT THE STAKE.)

ALF Thanks a lot, Willie. When I need a character witness, I'll make sure you're in Tasmania!

WILLIE (IGNORING ALF) Anyway, everybody knows there's no such thing as witches.

ALF (SEEING A CHANCE TO GET EVEN) Izzat so, Willie? Then, how come you always say Kate's mother is a real witch?

(KATE THROWS A SURPRISED AND HURT LOOK AT WILLIE, WHO SMILES MEEKLY AND TRIES TO PAINT HIMSELF OUT OF THE CORNER. ALF EXPECTANTLY LOOKS AT HIM FOR AN ANSWER)

WILLIE (EXTREMELY EMBARRASSED) I didn't say it that way. Besides, that's not what I meant, and it's not the same thing...

ALF (TWISTING THE KNIFE) You mean, she doesn't have a broom?

WILLIE Oh, stuff it, Alf!
(TO BRIAN AND LYNN)
Anyway. I'm sure you two get the point, and aren't going to say things like that about our neighbor anymore.

LYNN Sure, dad.

BRIAN Okay, dad.

KATE I feel kind of bad that I haven't gone over to welcome her to the neighborhood. I'll give you kids a plate of cookies to take over there when you go out.
(TO ALF)
And I'd appreciate if you didn't eat them before they have a chance to get out the door.

ALF (THE VERY IMAGE OF INNOCENCE FRAMED) How can you say that, Kate? I'm really shocked. Me, betray a sacred trust? For a few measly cookies... (BEAT) What kind of cookies, anyway. Do they have raisins?

KATE Well, I won't say it again, you've been warned.
(TO WILLIE)
I think we'd better start to get ready now, dear.

(SHE LEAVES THE ROOM TO GO INTO THE KITCHEN)

ALF Picky, picky, picky.

WILLIE I wouldn't ignore that warning if I were you, Alf. She means it. I've seen her with that look before.

ALF (GLUMLY) Yeah. After you proposed to her, I bet.

(WILLIE STANDS UP AND STARTS TO LEAVE THE ROOM. HE LOOKS AT ALF, AND BRIAN WEARING HIS ALF SUIT)

WILLIE (SIGHING) I feel that my life is complete. We're now a two alien family.

(HE EXITS)

DISSOLVE TO:

INT. TANNER LIVING ROOM - NIGHT (Alf, Willie, Kate, Lynn, Brian)
(IT IS NOW LATER ON. ALF IS ALONE IN THE LIVING ROOM, STILL WATCHING TELEVISION,STILL SUR-ROUNDED BY BAGS OF JUNK FOOD, AND STILL EAT-ING NOISILY. OCCASIONALLY A LOUD HOWL EMA-NATES FROM THE SET, CAUSING ALF TO JUMP IN HIS SEAT)

SFX: WILD GROWLS AND SNARLS

ALF (HE PAWS AT THE EMPTY BAGS ON THE COUCH AND THROWS THEM OVER HIS SHOULDER) Wow! That movie always makes me hungry... I need more food.

TELEVISION (V.O.) (AN ELVIRA-LIKE VOICE) Stay tuned, Fright Fans. Blood Curdle Theater will be right back with more spine-tingling horror from tonight's feature, "The Cat People..."

(LYNN, STILL DRESSED AS PETER PAN, AND BRIAN, STILL IN HIS ALF SUIT, WALK INTO THE ROOM)

BRIAN Hi, Alf!

ALF (STILL UNDER THE SPELL OF TELEVISION WATCHING) Hey, Spike, my man. They're showing "Cat People." Grab a bag of kitty claws and pull up chair.

BRIAN (CONFUSED) Alf, it's me, Brian!

ALF (REGAINING HIS COMPOSURE) Oh, right, Brian. Sorry, I always get a little carried away when I watch this film. (BEAT) So, what's going on?

LYNN (REALLY ENJOYING HERSELF) Mom and Dad are ready for their party. Wait till you see this!
(CALLING OUT OF THE ROOM)
Okay, Mom, we're ready.

(KATE MAKES AN ENTRANCE FROM THE BACK OF THE HOUSE. SHE'S DRESSED LIKE JUDY GARLAND'S DOROTHY IN "THE WIZARD OF OZ," COMPLETE WITH RUBY SLIPPERS, AND STUFFED "TOTO." SHE BOWS TO AN IMAGINARY AUDIENCE)

KATE Ta-da! (BEAT) So, what do you think?

LYNN (VERY IMPRESSED) You look great!

ALF Yeah. Great stuffed dog! You don't look bad either.

KATE (SHE GIVES ALF A DIRTY LOOK THEN CALLS OUT OF THE ROOM) Willie! It's your turn, now. Don't be difficult.

WILLIE (O.C.) I'm not coming out.

KATE Don't be silly. You look fine.

WILLIE (O.C.) Everybody's going to make fun of me!

ALF So what? Everybody always makes fun of you, Willie. Besides, how bad can it be?

(WILLY FINALLY ENTERS THE ROOM. HE'S DRESSED AS A REALLY TACKY OZ SCARECROW, WITH A SIL-LY CARROT-LIKE NOSE AND A RIDICULOUS LOOK-ING STUFFED CROW SEWN ON HIS SHOULDER)

ALF I was wrong. It's pretty bad. Especially the bird.

(KATE GIVES HIM A DIRTY LOOK)

ALF No, I swear. It looks just like a Schtumple. On Melmac, it's supposed to be the epitome of bad taste to carry one on your shoulder... (BEAT) And you should see the dry cleaner's bills, because the bird will...

KATE (INTERRUPTING) That's enough. I think you look terrific, Willie. We're going to have the best costumes at Buzz Murdoch's party.

WILLIE (RESIGNED) Somebody will probably come over and set me on fire. That's just the kind of stuff Buzz finds funny.

KATE (TO THE KIDS) Brian, you remember you're not sup-posed to eat anything until I have a chance to look at it, don't you?

ALF Don't worry about it, Kate. I'll make sure there isn't any-thing bad for him left.

KATE (IGNORING HIM) Don't come home too late, Lynn. And before you leave, I'm going get you that plate of cookies for our new neighbor.

BRIAN (WIDGETING) Do we have to, Mom?

KATE (FIRM) You most certainly do, young man. I want to the two of you to be very nice to that old woman. And I don't want to hear anymore of this nonsense about witches.

(SHE WALKS INTO THE KITCHEN. MEANWHILE, ALF WALKS TO WILLIE, LOOKING FALSELY CONTRITE)

ALF Hey, Willie, ol pal, forget what I said about you looking ridiculous. It was a crock. You look great. Even the schtumple looks great. You'll be the toast of the party. (BEAT) Now, knowing that you're going to have lots and lots of fun, you're not the kind of guy that wants his best buddy to be the only one who stays home and has no fun at all, are you?

WILLIE (STARTING TO CRACK) Yes, I am, Alf. Every time you've gone out, something terrible has happened. It will not happen tonight because...
(MARKING EACH WORD) You-are-not-going-to-go-out, get it?

(JUST THEN, LUCKY WALKS INTO THE ROOM. ALF TURNS TO LOOK AT HIM AND TRIES A LAST PLOY)

ALF Well, if I'm grounded here, perhaps I can find something else to keep me occupied.

WILLIE (NOT FALLING FOR IT) You are staying here, Alf. Lucky, however, is going out.

(WILLIE CHASES LUCKY OUT THE FRONT DOOR)

WILLIE (CONT'D) We've lived in this house a long time, and I'd like us to be able to stay a lot longer, which wouldn't be possible once you ate everybody's cats!

ALF (DESPERATE) Would groveling at your feet and otherwise totally humiliating myself cause you to change your mind?

WILLIE (FIRM) No.

ALF Well, it was worth a try. (BEAT) I'm disappointed in you Willie, you just don't have any faith in your fellow man -- or alien.

(KATE ENTERS THE ROOM FROM THE KITCHEN, HOLDING A PLATE OF COOKIES. SHE HANDS IT TO LYNN.)

KATE Here's what's left of the cookies. Somehow, someone appears to have gotten to the rest of them while we were getting dressed. I will have words with that someone later.

(SHE LOOKS MEANINGFULLY AT ALF, WHO CHOOSES TO RETURN AN INGENUOUS "WHO ME?" LOOK.)

KATE (CONT'D) (TO LYNN) Anyway, I want you to stop by the new neighbor's house on your way out, okay? She must be very lonely if all the kids on the block think she's a witch. (TO BRIAN) And you're not going to say bad things about people anymore, just because they look different, are you?

BRIAN No, Mom. But I still think she's scary.

(KATE LOOKS AT HIM AND SIGHS. WILLIE COMES OVER AND PATS HIM ON THE BACK, THEN WALKS TO THE FRONT DOOR WITH BRIAN AND LYNN)

WILLIE Just remember. There's no such thing as a witch.

(HE LOOKS OUTSIDE THE DOOR FOR A SECOND, THEN CLOSES IT AND TURNS BACK INTO THE LIVING ROOM)

WILLIE (LOOKING AT ALF) Who ate all the candy we left out for the trick or treaters?

ALF Hey, what can I say? Watching "The Cat People" always makes me extra hungry.

(WILLIE WALKS OVER TO THE PASS-THROUGH FROM THE KITCHEN AND PULLS OUT ANOTHER BAG OF CANDY. THEN HE GOES BACK TO THE FRONT DOOR AND EMPTIES IT O.S.)

WILLIE Don't eat this, okay? Please?

(KATE WALKS OVER TO JOIN HIM AT THE DOOR)

KATE And, Alf, don't answer the doorbell!

(THEY LEAVE. ALF SETTLES DOWN TO WATCH MORE TELEVISION)

ALF (GRUMBLING) Not only do I miss the chance to go out and eat as much free food as I want, but: now I've missed all the best parts of "The Cat People." It's just not my night.

(HE GRABS THE REMOTE CONTROL AND TURNS OFF THE SOUND)

TELEVISION (V.O.) (STILL THE ELVIRA-TYPE VOICE) Okay, Jitter-junkies, now that the cat's out of the bag, it's time for our next fear-filled flick, "Rosemary's Baby." Wow, talk about looking at little old ladies in a new light.

(ALF SITS UP AND TAKES NOTICE AT THIS SPEECH)

TELEVISION (V.O. CONT'D) If this picture doesn't make you afraid of the granny brigade, nothing will. Witches in our midst, for sure! And you all know what happens when a witch gets hold of you... especially children...

(THIS MAKES ALF SIT BOLT UPRIGHT)

ALF (HORRIFIED) Oh, no! Brian and Lynn!

(HE BEGINS PACING ACROSS THE ROOM)

TELEVISION (V.O.) ... It's dinner time! Yum, yum!

ALF What if that neighbor really is a witch! Willie and Kate are too tolerant. The kids should have never listened. A man who's willing to go out wearing a schtumple bird can't possibly know what he's talking about! I've got to do something!

(WITH THAT, ALF RUSHES OUT OF THE DOOR. A LOUD HOWL FILLS THE NIGHT AS WE FADE OUT.)

ACT TWO

FADE IN:

EXT. THE NEIGHBORHOOD – NIGHT (Alf, Melvin)
(ALF IS OUTSIDE WHERE IT IS DARK, AND VERY, VERY SPOOKY. HE'S TRYING TO STAY HIDDEN IN THE BUSHES, BUT HIS FUR KEEPS GETTING CAUGHT ON TWIGS, AND THE ATMOSPHERE IS STARTING TO GET TO HIM)

ALF Brian! Lynn! Where can they be? It's dark, spooky and creepy out here... (BEAT) Boy, those kids sure know how to have fun...

SFX: RUSTLING NOISES

ALF (CONT'D) (NERVOUSLY) What's that? Izzat you, Brian? Don't play with my nerves, buddy. Say something!

SFX: BLOOD-CURDLING HOWL

ALF (CONT'D) (SCREAMING) Yiiikes! Help!

A CAT RUNS OUT OF THE BUSHES)

ALF (CONT'D) (ANNOYED AT HIMSELF) Darn! It was a cat -- and I missed it! I've got to stop watching that Blood Curdle Theater, it dulls my instincts... Or maybe, it's the pepperoni-marshmallow pizza...

(HE STEPS OUT OF THE BUSHES, ONTO THE SIDEWALK)

ALF (CONT'D) Forget the bushes. Nobody's going to notice me out here anyway.

(SUDDENLY, MELVIN APPEARS. HE IS AN EXCEEDINGLY OBNOXIOUS KID WEARING A CHEAP "E.T." MASK, AND CARRYING A FAKE RAYGUN)

MELVIN (TO ALF, IN A BULLYING TONE) Hey, where do you think you're going, hose-nose!

(HE FIRES THE RAYGUN)

SFX: FLASHING LIGHTS AND ONE OF THE MOST ANNOYING SOUNDS EVER CREATED

ALF You know, kid, on some planets you'd get turned into plantfood for using that thing.

MELVIN Nobody talks to me that way, bug face. Who are you anyway? Do you live around here?

ALF (ANNOYED) Who are you calling bug-face, rodent breath?
(POINTING AT THE "E.T." MASK)
I don't take kindly to people impersonating my buddies, kiddo, so you'd better phone home fast.

(MELVIN KEEPS POKING AT ALF WITH THE RAYGUN)
SFX: MORE LIGHTS AND IRRITATING NOISE)

MELVIN That's it, you're dead meat, jerk. I'm gonna make you eat your stupid suit. It's the dumbest costume I've ever seen. Where'd you find it, the city dump? Lemme take a look at you. I bet you're even uglier under your crummy mask...
(HE STARTS PULLING AT ALPS NOSE, TRYING TO TEAR OFF HIS "MASK")
What'd you put this on with, Krazy Glue?

(ALF HAS HAD IT. HE PUSHES MELVIN'S HAND AWAY AND GRABS THE RAYGUN, WHICH HE TURNS ON THE LITTLE BRAT)

ALF (TALKING LIKE JIMMY CAGNEY) All right. I'm through messing around, see. It's time we evened the score... I'm really an alien from outer space, see... And I've come to Earth looking for food... Guess what, you little creep, you've been elected as tonight's main course!

(ALF PUTS HIS HANDS UP LIKE FRANKENSTEIN'S MONSTER AND SLOWLY STARTS ADVANCING ON MELVIN)

MELVIN (WORRIED) Whadda ya mean, main course... You can't mean... You can't be...

SFX: ALF MAKES THAT STRANGE, MELMACIAN "CHITTERING" SOUND OF HIS

MELVIN (CONT'D) (NOW SCARED) Hey! You're not kidding! You're really an alien! A slimy, disgusting alien! Eeeek!

(MELVIN TURNS AND TAKES OFF AT HIGH SPEED)

MELVIN (CONT'D) (SCREAMING) Heeeeelp! Heeeelp! Mommmmmy!

ALF (PLEASED WITH HIMSELF) I wouldn't have put it quite that way, but I guess it's the feeling that counts. (BEAT) And Willie said watching TV isn't good for anything. Ha!

(ALF TURNS AND CONTINUES ON HIS MISSION)

ALF (CONT'D) I hope that little brat hasn't made me too late to save Brian and Lynn.

DISSOLVE TO:

EXT. VERONIKA'S HOUSE - NIGHT (Alf)
(ALF ARRIVES AT THE DOOR OF VERONIKA'S HOUSE. THE PLACE REALLY IS CREEPY. THERE IS AN OLD, ROTTEN LOOKING PORCH, AND LOTS OF OVERGROWN, WEEDY PLANTS)

ALF I wonder when the Munsters moved out...

(HE RAISES HIS HAND TO KNOCK ON THE DOOR, BUT BEFORE HE HAS THE CHANCE, IT SLOWLY CREAKS OPEN ALL BY ITSELF)

ALF (CONT'D) (SURPRISED) Hey, this place is more modern than it looks... (BEAT) At least, I hope that's what it is.

(ALF GINGERLY STICKS HIS HEAD THROUGH THE DOORWAY)

ALF (CONT'D) Brian! Lynn! Are you guys in here?

(NO ANSWER. HE ENTERS CAUTIOUSLY.)

ALF (CONT'D) I wish Willie hadn't confiscated my Vampire-Slayer kit.. What the heck, they probably weren't real silver bullets anyway...

CUT TO:

INT. VERONIKA'S LIVING ROOM - NIGHT (Alf, Veronika)
(ALF IS ALONE INSIDE A HEAVILY GOTHIC-DECORATED ROOM. THERE ARE PRESERVED ANIMALS EVERYWHERE, INCLUDING A STUFFED BLACK CAT)

ALF (LOOKING AT THE CAT DISAPPROVINGLY) What a waste of a perfectly good cat. And I bet it's full of all kinds of unappetizing preservatives.

(HE COMES TO A PODIUM, WHERE A LARGE BOOK IS PROMINENTLY DISPLAYED)

ALF (CONT'D) What's this? Oh, oh! "Everything You Wanted to Know About Stuffing Little Furry Animals, But Were Afraid to Ask"... (BEAT) This is worse than I thought. I've got to find the kids and get out of here!

VERONIKA (O.C.) (WITH A STRANGE FOREIGN ACCENT) Ah, you're just in time, dear...

(ALF TURNS AND SEES VERONIKA. SHE LOOKS LIKE A CARTOON VERSION OF A WITCH. SHE HAS JUST

ENTERED THE ROOM, CARRYING A BUBBLY COOK-
ING POT AND A LARGE KNIFE)

VERONIKA (CONT'D) I've been eager to meet you...

(SHE MOVES TOWARDS ALF)

ALF (SCREAMING) Eeeek! Brian! Lynn! Run for your lives!

CUT TO:

EXT. VERONIKA'S HOUSE - NIGHT (Brian, Lynn, Alf)
(BRIAN AND LYNN ARRIVE AT VERONIKA'S DOOR.
LYNN IS STILL HOLDING THE PLATE OF COOKIES.
BRIAN IS SCARED, AND SO IS LYNN, BUT HER SENSE
OF DUTY IS STRONGER)

BRIAN (CAJOLING) Come on, Lynn. We'll give Alf the
cookies to eat before Mom and Dad get home. They'll never
know the difference.

LYNN Brian! I'm surprised at you. You've been spending too
much time with Alf.

BRIAN I don't want to do this. I'm scared.

LYNN I know you are. But we can't just go home. Mom and
Dad wouldn't like it. Besides, I'm sure she's just a lonely old
lady. There really isn't any such thing as a witch.

(SHE RINGS THE DOORBELL)

SFX: DOORBELL RING, FOLLOWED BY A CACKLING,
MANIACAL LAUGH

(THE TWO CHILDREN TURN TO EACH OTHER, TERRI-
FIED)

BRIAN What was that?

LYNN I don't think I want to know... (BEAT) You know, I like your idea better. Let's go home and give these cookies to Alf!

(SUDDENLY, ALPS HAND COMES O.C. AND GRABS THE COOKIES)

ALF (O.C.) Thank you. I knew you'd see it my way, eventual- ly!

(THE DOOR IS WIDE OPEN, AND THERE IS ALF, HAP- PILY STANDING INSIDE THE HOUSE)

ALF (CONT'D) Hey, Brian, my man, Lynn, what took you so long? Come on in.

DISSOLVE TO:

INT. VERONIKA'S LIVING ROOM - NIGHT (Alf, Brian, Lynn, Veronika)
(BRIAN AND LYNN ARE SITTING NEXT TO ALF ON A SOFA)

LYNN (TO ALF) What are you doing here? And how did you get here in the first place?

ALF I walked. How did you get here?

LYNN But you were supposed to stay home... Why did you come over here?

ALF I thought you and Brian might need a little protection. But it turns out I was wrong. Veronika's really okay. Although, I'll admit that when she came at me with the knife, I thought for a moment that it was curtains for the old Alfer.

BRIAN (HORRIFIED) She came at you with a knife!

ALF Yep. And I didn't bat an eye either. But it turned out she just wanted me to carve her pumpkin.
(POINTING TO AN EXTREMELY UGLY JACK O'LANTERN SITTING ON A TABLE IN A CORNER) What do you think?

LYNN (TRYING NOT TO LAUGH) Oh, it's just great, Alf. Really.

(VERONIKA ENTERS THE ROOM WITH THE COCOA AND A PLATE OF COOKIES)

VERONIKA So, you two are Gordon's friends?

(THE KIDS LOOK NERVOUSLY AT ALF, WHO ACTS COOL)

LYNN Gordon? Er, yes...

VERONIKA Good. I'm glad you got here in time for us to all have some cocoa together. (BEAT) You do like cocoa, dears, don't you?

BRIAN & LYNN (TOGETHER) Yes, Ma'am. Thank you, Ma'am.

(VERONIKA STARTS POURING CUPS OF COCOA)

VERONIKA (TO ALF) Your friends are very polite. You'd almost think they were afraid of me.

ALF (SLURPING HIS COCOA DOWN LOUDLY) Oh, that's because they think you're a witch.

(HE GRABS A HANDFUL OF COOKIES AND SLOPPILY SHOVES THEM INTO HIS MOUTH, WHILE BRIAN AND LYNN STARE AT HIM, HORRIBLY EMBARRASSED. VERONIKA, HOWEVER, SEEMS UNPHASED)

VERONIKA Is that all? I thought it was something serious.
(TO BRIAN AND LYNN)
Whatever gave you children such a fanciful idea?

(LYNN LOOKS AT BRIAN AS IF TO SAY, "YOU GOT US INTO THIS, NOW YOU GET US OUT")

BRIAN (EMBARRASSED) There's always strange noises and lights coming from your house. And it smells funny too.

(VERONIKA STARTS TO LAUGH)

VERONIKA Oh my, oh my! So that's why none of the other children have come by for Halloween! I guess I'd better explain.

(SHE GETS UP AND GOES OVER TO THE PODIUM WHERE THE BOOK IS)

VERONIKA (CONT'D) In the old country, I learned to be a taxidermist, you know, stuff and preserve animals. I am very good at it, in fact, you might say I'm the world's expert on preserving difficult species. So, I wrote this book, and my publishers very kindly asked me to come to America to lecture. I liked it here, so I stayed. What you have seen, heard, and, I'm afraid, smelled, coming from this house, has to do with my work. I'm terribly embarrassed that I frightened anyone.

(ALF PICKS UP THE COOKIE PLATE AND SHOVES THE
REST OF THE COOKIES IN HIS FACE, THEN WIPES HIS
MOUTH WITH HIS HAND)

ALF (SLIGHTLY DISAPPOINTED) So, old Willie was right.
There really isn't any such thing as witches. I guess sometimes
he does know what he's talking about. I'll have to remember
to tell him. It'll make him happy.

(VERONIKA LOOKS AT ALF AND BRIAN, WHO IS
STILL IN HIS ALF COSTUME)

VERONIKA Maybe you boys would be more comfortable if
you removed those lovely costumes...

ALF No problem. I'm fine this way.

LYNN (LOOKING FOR EXCUSES) He can't remove his
costume. You see, he's sewn into it... and he wouldn't be able
to get it back on again, so he'd have to go home without any
clothes on...

BRIAN Yeah, and then he'd catch cold. But I can take mine
off.

(BRIAN PUSHES THE HEAD OF HIS COSTUME BACK
LIKE A HOOD)

VERONIKA (UNCONVINCED) Whatever makes you comfortable, dear.

(BRIAN AND LYNN STAND UP TO LEAVE. LYNN
HOLDS OUT KATE'S PLATE OF COOKIES, NOW
COOKIELESS)

LYNN Thank you very much for your hospitality. Our Mom wanted you to have these, er, this plate.. to welcome you to the neighborhood.

(VERONIKA REACHES OUT AND TAKES THE PLATE)

VERONIKA Thank your mother for me, dear. I have been very lonely since I moved here. I hope you'll all come back and visit me.

LYNN We will, but we'd better get going now. I'm not supposed to bring Brian home too late. Come on, Brian, Alf.

VERONIKA (TO ALF) Alf? I thought your name was Gordon?

ALF It is. Sometimes the kid mixes me up with somebody else. It's a sad case.

(HE SHAKES HIS HEAD AS IF IN SORROW)

ALF (CONT'D) (TO LYNN AND BRIAN) I'm going to hang around a little longer. Veronika promised me some of her candied apples.

VERONIKA (REMEMBERING) You're absolutely right, dear. Where has my head been! I'll go and get them.

(SHE LEAVES THE ROOM BY THE KITCHEN DOOR)

LYNN (TO ALF) If Mom and Dad get home and find that you went out, we're all going to get in trouble. What if somebody sees you? And what about Veronika?

ALF (UNCONCERNED) Don't worry. I got her eating out of the palm of my hand! I'll make it back before Willie and Kate. There's absolutely no problem.

(BEFORE LYNN HAS THE CHANCE TO RESPOND, VERONIKA WALKS BACK INTO THE ROOM CARRYING A PLATE FULL OF APPLES AND A BAG, WHICH SHE HANDS TO BRIAN)

VERONIKA You might as well take some apples too. After what you have told me, I don't imagine that there will be many of the other children coming visiting tonight.

(BRIAN LOOKS VERY CONTRITE)

BRIAN I'm sorry about being scared of you just 'cause you were different. My Mom and Dad were right about not saying bad things about people you don't know. I bet all the kids'll want to come when I tell them how neat you are.

VERONIKA (MOVED) Well, that's very sweet of you, dear. You're all welcome back anytime you wish.

LYNN Well, thanks again for the cocoa. Bye!

BRIAN Yeah, bye!

(THEY WALK OUT THE DOOR)

VERONIKA Good-bye, my dears.

(SHE CLOSES THE DOOR AND TURNS TO ALF WHO IS MUNCHING ON SOME APPLES)

VERONIKA (CONT'D) Well, I suppose you'll need to be going soon as well, Gordon. But you must be very careful going home. Someone from so far away has to take some precautions...

(ALF IS TAKEN ABACK, BUT NOT QUITE SURE VERONIKA REALLY KNOWS)

ALF (PLAYING IT COY) I don't live that far away. Just down the street.

VERONIKA Come on, Gordon, we all have our little secrets, don't we?

(VERONIKA MAKES SOME MYSTICAL PASSES WITH HER HANDS, THEN POINTS AT THE STUFFED BLACK CAT, WHICH GOES "POOF" AND TURNS INTO A LIVE CAT)

ALF (IMPRESSED) Wow! Well, well... So Willie was wrong, after all. It figures.

VERONIKA I wanted to thank you for bringing in your young friends. People like myself have suffered from a lot of, er, bad publicity in the past. As you know, it can be very lonely without friends. But now, it will be much nicer, I'm sure...

(ALF WALKS OUT THE DOOR)

ALF No sweat. I understand. There's lot of rubbish written about people like me too. So, I'm glad I was around to help you out. (BEAT) Say, you don't think I could learn that cat trick of yours sometime...

DISSOLVE TO:

INT. TANNER LIVING ROOM - NIGHT (Alf, Willie, Kate, Lynn, Brian)
(ALF, LYNN AND BRIAN ARE WATCHING THE TV. WILLIE AND KATE WALK IN THROUGH THE FRONT DOOR. WILLIE DOES NOT LOOK HAPPY)

WILLIE (SUSPICIOUS) Alf, did you keep your word about staying in the house tonight? And, please, don't lie to me this time.

ALF Why do you ask?

WILLIE On the way home from the Murdochs, I heard a radio report of someone dressed like an alien terrorizing a child. You wouldn't be involved in that, would you?

ALF (PATRONIZING) Willie, Willie, is it my fault if your planet is full of neurotic people whose latent alien phobias are just waiting to bloom... (BEAT) As you often say, Willie, it's all the fault of television!

WILLIE (HE DOESN'T KNOW WHAT TO THINK ANY-MORE) Yes... I guess you're right.

ALF (EAGER TO CHANGE SUBJECTS) So, how was the bash?

(WILLIE GOES TO SIT NEXT TO ALF ON THE COUCH)

WILLIE (DEPRESSED) It was a disaster. It seems that Buzz neglected to tell us that this year he decided not to have a costume party. When he said we should dress fancy, he meant tuxedoes and long dresses. Kate and I were the only ones who wore costumes. It was very embarrassing.

KATE At least, we both looked silly together.

BRIAN But I thought you said it was okay to be different? We went to see the weird old lady, and she was really neat. Just like you said.

(KATE HUGS HIM)

KATE You're right, Brian. Being different is okay. And I think it would be hard to find a family that's more different than ours...

(SUDDENLY, VERONIKA'S GENTLE, CACKLING LAUGH ECHOES AROUND THE ROOM AND THEY ALL LOOK UP, AS WE

FADE OUT.)

The Bionic Six was an American-Japanese animated television series that aired from 1987 to 1989, by TMS Entertainment and distributed, through first-run syndication, by Universal television. It was very loosely based on The Six Million Dollar Man*, and featured a family of machine-enhanced human beings each possessing a unique power thanks to bionic technology. The series was story edited by Gordon Bressack.*

The Bionic Six: The Hive

ACT ONE

FADE IN:

EXT. ALIEN FORTRESS - NIGHT
This is the alien fortress to end all alien fortresses. Craggy, evil, utterly dreadful. Two huge blue moons light up the purple sky. In the foreground, the HERO (think Flash Gordon), holding the HEROINE (think Dale Arden), is facing a horde of winged monsters and assorted gargoyles, sword in hand.

HERO (corny) Courage, Dalia, we shall escape from the Queen's foul fortress...

As the Hero begins slicing away at the monsters, CAMERA TRUCKS BACK to reveal that we are really in

INT. BENNETT HOME - TV ROOM - DAY
where Eric, J.D. and Bunji are watching a somewhat futurist big-screen TV set, upon which the previous action is taking place. They are all munching popcorn, obviously enthralled by the film.

ERIC Wow! Look at that backswing!

BUNJI Pfft! I can do better any time. If you ask me...

J.D. Shh!

ANGLE ON TV SCREEN

The giant face of the QUEEN, a beautiful but evil-looking woman, has just appeared above the Hero. Her hair looks like that of Elsa Lanchester in "Bride of Frankenstein", except that it's got spikes around the ears, and it's almost fluorescent. Her eyes shoot off a ZAP BEAM that causes the Hero to fall to his knees.

QUEEN You won't escape my clutches so easily, Dash! Ah! Ah! Ah!

HEROINE (scream)

The picture on the set FADES TO BLACK and the HOSTESS of the program -- a girl dressed in a Vampirella-like costume – enters.

HOSTESS (syrupy) Don't go away, fright fans! Our screen gem of the week, "Blood Queen of Mars", will continue after these messages...

ANGLE ON THE THREE BOYS, FAVORING ERIC

They get up to stretch their legs.

ERIC Boy, what a movie! Amazing the stuff they can do today. Did'ja see that Queen!?

ANGLE ON BUNJI

He grabs his empty glass and walks towards the door.

BUNJI (slightly superior) It's all special effects... (beat) I'm gonna get a drink...

He opens the door. (NOTE: We do NOT see what's behind it as he does so.) Suddenly, he screams and drops his glass.

BUNJI Argh! It's the Blood Queen!

CAMERA TURNS 90 DEGREES - ANGLE WIDENS

to reveal MEG coming into the room. Her hair looks almost exactly like that of the Queen.

ANGLE ON MEG

MEG (peeved) Well, thanks for the show of support, guys! I'm definitely underwhelmed.

ANGLE ON ALL OF THEM, FAVORING ERIC

The guys can't believe their eyes.

ERIC What's... that!?

ANGLE ON MEG

She pulls on her "hair," revealing that it is actually a wig. Her real hair, flattened and messy, is underneath.

MEG (pouting) Well! I'll have you know that it's the latest fashion. All the kids are doing it. Just like the "Frankensleazies..."

ANGLE ON J.D.

J.D. (confused) The Franken-what?

ANGLE ON MEG

She raises her eyes heavenward and shakes her head in pity at the ignorance of her poor, unenlightened friend.

MEG The Frankensleazies, you megadrip! You mean you haven't heard their last holog -- "Singing in the brain?" It's all over the waves!

ANGLE WIDENS

Eric points at the wig that Meg is still holding in her hand.

ERIC Er, yeah, but have Mom and Dad seen you wearing that yet?

MEG (embarrassed) Um, no. I thought I'd spring it on them later.

BUNJI Oh, boy! I want to see their faces when you do! They're going to go into orbit!

CUT TO:

INT. BENNETT HOME - KITCHEN
JACK is wearing his cook outfit. The general state of messiness on, and around him, shows that he's been puttering in the kitchen. HELEN holds a half-closed book, indicating that she's probably been interrupted in the middle of some kind of study.

JACK (firm) I'm sorry but my answer's no!

ANGLE ON MEG

MEG (begging) But, Dad, it's a "Frankensleazies" wig. All the kids are wearing them. I don't want to be a gred!

ANGLE ON HELEN

HELEN Your father's right, Meg. I'm not sure what a, er, gred, is, but I don't want you wearing that thing!

ANGLE ON JACK

JACK Just because everyone else is wearing one doesn't mean you have to. What's wrong with being an individual for a change?

ANGLE ON MEG

MEG (pouting) It's not fair! Eric got to wear his "Devil Brood" shirt, and it was mega-gross!

ANGLE WIDENS, FAVORING ERIC

He is not pleased at being dragged into the argument.

ERIC Hey, waitaminnit! First, it was Halloween... (beat - revenge time) ... and anyway, "Devil Brood" is a real group, not chumps like the "Frankensleazies!"

MEG (furious) Oooh! I'll...

ANGLE ON JACK

He makes pacifying gestures at the kids.

JACK This argument's over. I want you to go back to your rooms now. And, Meg, sorry, but no wig, unless it's Halloween...

AS HE SPEAKS, CAMERA TRUCKS IN on a console behind him. A light on the console starts to FLASH, emitting an electronic BEEP.

JACK (CONT) Uh-oh! Professor Sharp's signal!

ANGLE WIDENS TO INCLUDE THE ENTIRE FAMILY

They gather to look at the console.

ANGLE ON CONSOLE

The console rises up, revealing a video screen. The picture on the screen flickers for a second or so, then PROF. SHARP appears.

PROF. SHARP Sharp to Bionic Six! Sharp to Bionic Six! Please report to the SPL A.S.A.P!

ANGLE ON JACK

He walks up to the console and flicks a switch (SFX).

JACK Bionic One here, Professor! Ten Four -- we're on our way!

ANGLE WIDENS TO INCLUDE THE ENTIRE FAMILY

They assume their STOCK FAMILY POSE, raising their fists, etc.

ALL Bionics on!!!

With a FLASH, they turn into the Bionic Six.

BIONIC WIPE TO:

EXT. SPECIAL PROJECTS LAB - DAY

ESTABLISHING SHOT.

PROF. SHARP (VO) Diamonds, Bionic Six, diamonds!

CUT TO:

INT. SPL - PROF. SHARP'S LAB
Sharp sits in a mechanized chair, with various buttons at his fingertips. The Bionic Six are gathered in front of a giant wall screen, divided into a number of smaller display "windows" which pop in and out of existence at Sharp's commands.

PROF. SHARP (CONT) Diamonds are pure carbon, as you know...

ANGLE ON SPORT ONE AND I.Q.

Sport One looks questioningly at I.Q., who nods silently.

ANGLE ON SCREEN

Several display windows appear, which first show the computer-generated image of a cut diamond, then rotate it, then just show a line drawing of its atomic structure, then zoom in for a C.U.

PROF. SHARP (VO - CONT) Because of their perfect atomic structure, we use them in micro-chip technology just as silicon was used a few decades ago...

ANGLE ON SHARP

PROF. SHARP (CONT) That is why any threat to diamond production is a most serious one indeed!

ANGLE ON BIONIC ONE

BIONIC ONE I understand, Professor. Dr. Scarab must be planning to steal the world's diamond stock and you want us to...

ANGLE ON SHARP

PROF. SHARP (interrupting) Not this time, Bionic One, not this time! Look!

He presses a button and points at the screen (OS).

ANGLE ON THE BIONIC SIX

Their heads turn accordingly.

ANGLE ON SCREEN

Suddenly, the computer-generated picture of an ANT in C.U. fills the entire screen, while we hear an electronic SCREECH (SFX).

ANGLE ON THE BIONIC SIX, FAVORING KARATE ONE

They all react in various displays of amazement.

KARATE ONE What.... What's that!?

ANGLE ON SHARP

PROF. SHARP (somewhat pretentious) Dorylus Formicidae, more commonly known as driver ants, and found in nomadic swarms in Africa... (beat) Meet your enemy, Bionic Six!

ANGLE ON MOTHER ONE

MOTHER ONE Ants?! But surely, Professor, there must be specialized organizations equipped to deal with pests. We...

ANGLE ON SHARP

PROF. SHARP (chuckling) Not this kind of pest, Mother One, trust me! Let me enlarge the picture for you...

He presses another button.

ANGLE ON SCREEN

The camera appears to zoom back, and the ant is shown to be standing next to the picture of a man. They are the same size!

ANGLE ON THE BIONIC SIX, FAVORING BIONIC ONE

BIONIC ONE Great Scott, giant ants!

ANGLE ON MOTHER ONE

She looks at the screen in amazement.

MOTHER ONE What could have caused such a mutation, Professor? Are there any chemical dump sites nearby?

ANGLE ON SHARP

PROF. SHARP We're not sure what the cause is, Mother One. All we know is, that anyone who goes into the diamond mine... disappears!

ANGLE ON I.Q.

I.Q. What made you suspect giant ants, Professor?

ANGLE ON SHARP

PROF. SHARP Formic acid was found all around the area...

ANGLE ON SCREEN

Various windows display a rapid cut of snapshots of insect-like shapes, strange footprints, chemical readings, etc.

PROF. SHARP (VO) This confirmed several mysterious sightings...

ANGLE ON SPORT ONE

SPORT ONE Wow! It's just like that movie they were running on the Horror Marathon Fest last week, "Them!"

ANGLE WIDENS, FAVORING BIONIC ONE

BIONIC ONE So, where do you want us to go, Professor?

PROF. SHARP The Kalahari Desert, in the southern tip of Africa...

ANGLE ON SCREEN

Now, the windows display a view of Africa, zooming in on the KALAHARI DESERT in South Africa. (We may still show the images of the ant and the diamond in a corner of the screen.) CAMERA then TRUCKS IN on a spot on the map marked "KALAHARI CITY" as we

WIPE TO:

EXT. KALAHARI CITY - AIRSTRIP - DAY
ESTABLISHING SHOT. This is the African equivalent of a mining town, and these look the same all over. The overall impression is that of a desert outpost: lots of dust, makeshift

habitations, rough living, etc. The high-tech Bionic Six aircraft looks out of place among the old DC-10s sitting on the airfield.

CAMERA TRUCKS IN to reveal the Bionic Six unloading a MULE. The vehicle is being driven out of the plane, down a ramp and onto the field. Bionic One is at the wheel, while Mother One gives him directions through the microphone on her shoulder pack.

MOTHER ONE (with appropriate hand signals) A little bit more to the right, Bionic One... That's it...

ANGLE ON THE KIDS

They're standing by nearby, looking around.

SPORT ONE So this is South Africa... (beat) I saw something about it in the history tapes. Didn't they use to have some kind of weird social system? Apart-something...

I.Q. (he knows) Apartheid.

ANGLE ON KARATE ONE

He is looking at a dust cloud getting closer.

KARATE ONE I think the welcome wagon is here!

ANGLE WIDENS

By now, Bionic One has parked the MULE next to the plane. As he gets out of the vehicle, a jeep arrives and stops, tires SCREECHING. A man (TULLEY) gets off. He is a big, burly black man, wearing safari-like clothes.

ANGLE ON TULLEY

TULLEY (smiling) Welcome to Kalahari, Bionic Six! I'm Edward Tulley, general manager of the mines. We're happy to have you here.

ANGLE ON BIONIC ONE

BIONIC ONE Thank you, Mr. Tulley. Have there been any further disappearances?

ANGLE ON TULLEY

He looks resigned and almost defeated.

TULLEY No, but we've all but closed the mines down since the last one. If you don't do something to help us, we're ruined!

ANGLE ON MOTHER ONE

MOTHER ONE (comforting) Don't worry, Mr. Tulley. I'm sure we can help you. The Bionic Six are experienced at this kind of thing.

ANGLE ON THE KIDS

SPORT ONE (whispering) We are? When's the last time we experienced giant insects?

ROCK ONE (sarcastic) The last time we cleaned your room!

ANGLE WIDENS, FAVORING BIONIC ONE

BIONIC ONE Come on, kids, no time to chat. Get on board the MULE!
(to Tulley) You lead, we'll follow.

They all climb into the vehicle. Sport One still smarts over his sister's remark.

SPORT ONE (under his breath) Clean my room! Ha! Wait till she needs to borrow my can of Raid!

He closes the MULE's door behind him.

CAMERA TRUCKS BACK to reveal Tulley's jeep leaving the airfield, followed by the MULE, and PANS ALONG to show them taking a trail leading right into the desert.

INT. MULE
Bionic One is driving. Mother One sits at his right, and the others sit behind.

KARATE ONE Where are we going exactly?

ANGLE ON BIONIC ONE

BIONIC ONE The mines are fifty miles inside the desert. We'll be there soon.

ANGLE ON MOTHER ONE

MOTHER ONE Make sure you kids use your sunscreens. Desert sun can cause severe burns. Do you hear me?

ANGLE ON THE KIDS

They all nod, except Rock One who's seemingly lost to the outside world, swinging in time to her "Walkman".

ANGLE WIDENS TO INCLUDE MOTHER ONE

She turns and unplugs her daughter.

MOTHER ONE Rock One, I want you to pay attention when I'm saying something! (beat) You've been spending way too much time with that thing. Give it to me.

ROCK ONE (slightly whining) Mother One!

MOTHER ONE (firm) Rock One, I won't say it again. Give it to me.

ANGLE ON ROCK ONE

Reluctantly, she hands her "Walkman" to her mother, whose arm comes INTO FRAME and takes it away.

ROCK ONE It's not fair!

ANGLE WIDENS TO INCLUDE ALL OF THEM

SPORT ONE (happy to have a revenge of sorts) Peuh, it's only the "Franken-sleazies"! Who wants to listen to that anyway!

ROCK ONE Oh, you! I'll...

ANGLE ON BIONIC ONE

BIONIC ONE (pointing ahead) Stop squabbling! We're almost there!

ANGLE WIDENS TO INCLUDE ALL OF THEM

The kids lean forward to look ahead.

I.Q. Look! There are the mines!

POV ALL - THE DIAMOND MINES

Vast, open-sky mines. Huge mountains of piled-up sand and rocks. Metal barracks, crouching under a merciless sun. Weird metallic structures (cranes, derricks?) silhouetted against the burning sky, like primeval skeletons. Not a hospitable sight.

EXT. DIAMOND MINES

The two vehicles enter the mining compound.

INT. MULE

They all look through the windows at the rather depressing view.

KARATE ONE Gee! What a downer! I wonder what the people who work here do for fun?

CUT TO:

INT. MESS BARRACK - EVENING

EXTREME C.U. of the cover of a "Frankensleazies" compact disk (portraying the group's definitely aberrant look, not forgetting the wigs, of course).

ROCK ONE (VO) So it's a deal. I'll let you copy all my "Frankensleazies" disks, in exchange for the sculpted sandstone necklace...

CAMERA TRUCKS OUT to reveal the Bionic Kids sitting around a table with a crowd of YOUNG MINERS.

YOUNG MINER #1 (excitedly) You bet! The "Frankensleazies"! Oh, boy!

YOUNG MINER #2 (equally excited) Yeah! I can't believe our luck!

ANGLE ON SPORT ONE

He raises his eyes and shakes his head, like he can't believe these guys are really interested in the "Frankensleazies".

SPORT ONE Why don't you just give them the disks. You can't play them anyway. Mother One confiscated your player.

ANGLE ON ROCK ONE

She displays something that looks like an earplug.

ROCK ONE (mischievous) That's what she thinks! But I brought a micro-player with me!

ANGLE WIDENS TO INCLUDE ALL THE KIDS

SPORT ONE Hey, way to go! You're smarter than I thought!

I.Q. (disapproving) Well, I don't approve. I don't think you should...

Bionic One ENTERS FRAME, and Rock One quickly hides her micro-player.

BIONIC ONE I think you kids should go to bed. Tomorrow, we'll start exploring the mines.

DISSOLVE TO:

EXT. DIAMOND MINES - DAWN
ESTABLISHING SHOT, followed by a TRUCK IN showing the Bionic Six being escorted towards a mine shaft by Tulley and a few men.

TULLEY Well, this is it. Shaft No.1 will take you to the main mining area. The tunnels spread over a 20-mile radius. Some of them are pretty old...

ANGLE ON THE BIONIC SIX, FAVORING BIONIC ONE

They step into an elevator cage.

BIONIC ONE The map you gave us will be very helpful, I'm sure.

ANGLE ON TULLEY AND BIONIC ONE

They shake hands.

TULLEY Good luck, then!

CAMERA ZOOMS IN for an EXTREME C.U. of Tulley's hands. He sticks an almost indetectible flat, transparent disk on B.O.'s sleeve.

BIONIC ONE Thanks, we may need it!

ANGLE WIDENS

With a loud, groaning NOISE (SFX), the cage begins its descent.

BIONIC WIPE TO:

INT. SHAFT NO. 1
A loud KLANG (SFX) tells us that the cage has hit bottom. We are in a wide corridor, dug within the rock, with rails on the ground, lots of cables and halogen lights on the walls. Bionic One steps out. A beat. The others follow right behind.

ANGLE ON BIONIC ONE

BIONIC ONE (using his X-ray vision) I don't detect anything dangerous, but be careful anyway.

178

ANGLE ON MOTHER ONE

MOTHER ONE (scanning) No, I sense something... but I can't be sure what... (beat) It's getting closer...

ANGLE WIDENS TO INCLUDE ALL OF THEM

They all gather together, looking very tense. Suddenly, a small, metallic FLYING DRONE zooms in at incredible speed from the other end of the shaft and releases billows of green gases.

ALL (coughing sounds)

As the Bionic Six sink into unconsciousness, CAMERA PANS TO THE RIGHT, where a huge, insect-shaped SHADOW has appeared on the wall. We TRUCK IN on the shadow and

FADE OUT.

ACT TWO

FADE IN:

EXT. DIAMOND MINES - DAY

ESTABLISHING SHOT.

DR. SCARAB (VO) This won't do at all, Mr. Tulley. It just won't do!

CAMERA TRUCKS IN

INT. MINES - TULLEY'S OFFICE

Lots of charts on the walls, including a large, "cut-out" map of the mines. There is a window, and a videoscreen on a wall shelf. In the room are Tulley, DR. SCARAB, GLOVE, MECHANIC, CHOPPER and several CYPHRONS. Scarab is pacing the room, quite unhappy.

DR. SCARAB (CONT) I spent an inordinate amount of time and my precious resources gaining control of these mines so I could monopolize the world's diamond market...

ANGLE ON TULLEY

Looking properly scared.

DR. SCARAB (VO - CONT) I even put you, Mr. Tulley, in my employ, and what is the result... failure!

ANGLE ON SCARAB

DR. SCARAB (CONT) Workers start disappearing. Production stops. The authorities are alerted. And now, this!

ANGLE WIDENS

Scarab walks to the videoscreen and turns a few knobs.

DR. SCARAB (CONT) The Bionic Six disappear too, and the vid-spy you planted on them appears to have failed!

ANGLE ON MECHANIC

MECHANIC But, uh, boss, why did'ya call dem Bionic Six. It ain't fair. I could've sorted out dat mess by mesself.

ANGLE ON SCARAB

CAMERA TRUCKS IN for a C.U. on Scarab's face.

DR. SCARAB Perhaps you could have, Mechanic, and then perhaps not... (beat) No, there is something wrong down there, and it's much better to let our old enemies make it right first! Ha! Ha! Ha!

DISSOLVE TO:

INT. HIVE - OUTER PERIMETER
In a POV shot, CAMERA GOES OUT OF FOCUS and SPINS, revealing silver metal lined corridors, halogen lamps and insect-looking humanoid shapes (DRONES).

BIONIC ONE (VO) (groggy) Ugh... Where am I?

GREEN DRONE #1 (emotionless) The humans are coming to. Alert Hive Leader.

Still in POV, CAMERA REFOCUSES to reveal the Drones in full detailed clarity. Their outward appearance is that of insects, but it is now obvious that they are in fact men wearing green armor, shaped like insect bodies. Their faces are completely covered by featureless helmets, with red goggles and antennae.

ANGLE ON THE BIONIC SIX, FAVORING BIONIC ONE

The Bionic Six are all regaining consciousness, in various states of awareness. Bionic One is already up and talking.

BIONIC ONE (to the Drones) Who are you and why did you attack us? We come in peace...

ANGLE ON DRONE

Prodding him back with a short, nasty-looking lance.

GREEN DRONE #1 (emotionless) The outsiders will wait. Leader will take them to Hive Core soon.

ANGLE ON THE BIONIC SIX, FAVORING THE KIDS

KARATE ONE Outsiders? Leader? Hive? What's all that stuff? Did we find the secret World Bug Lovers Convention or something?

SPORT ONE Why don't we just pile into these bozos and find out the answers ourselves!

ANGLE ON BIONIC ONE

BIONIC ONE Be patient, boys. We don't know what we're up against. It's obvious there's more here than Prof. Sharp suspected...

ANGLE ON DRONES

Their ranks open up to let HIVE LEADER through. Behind her armor, she is obviously a woman. Her armor itself is more elaborate and decorated than that of the Drones. Her faceless helmet also is more elaborate, with more complex antennae. Her voice is not as emotionless as that of the Drones.

HIVE LEADER The outsiders will follow me.

ANGLE ON THE BIONIC SIX, FAVORING BIONIC ONE

BIONIC ONE (whispering) We'll do what she says... for now.

ANGLE WIDENS

and CAMERA PANS to follow the Bionic Six, led by Hive Leader and escorted by the Drones, as they exit the corridor and enter

INT. HIVE

OVERVIEW SHOT. We are in a HUGE cavern, filled with multilevel abstract buildings (think Fritz Lang's "Metropolis" redesigned by Jack Kirby), linked by small silver bridges. At the center is a massive tower, covered in insect-like motifs and sporting huge antennae on top (HIVE CORE). The place is, ahem, buzzing with people, all dressed in insect armor of various colors.

The Bionic Six et al. have entered at about mid-level, from a tunnel emanating from the rock, joining onto one of the silver bridges, leading towards Hive Core. CAMERA TRUCKS IN.

I.Q. Incredible!

KARATE ONE You bet! It's like... Metropolis. Fritz Lang's, not Clark Kent's...

MOTHER ONE I wonder where they're taking us.

ANGLE ON BIONIC ONE

He points at something O.S.

BIONIC ONE There. What they called the Hive Core, I think. I bet we find all the answers there...

ANGLE ON HIVE CORE

as described above, in a POV shot. An ominous HUM (SFX) emanates from the giant antennae on top of the structure.

MATCH CUT TO:

the same picture, this time framed on a videoscreen. CAMERA TRUCKS OUT, revealing that we are now back in

INT. TULLEY'S OFFICE
Tulley is sitting at a keyboard in front of the videoscreen. Dr. Scarab and the other villains stand behind him.

TULLEY (apologetic) The reception's fine now, Dr. Scarab. Something inside the tunnels must have been blocking the signal...

INT. HIVE
QUICK CUT to a C.U. of Bionic One's sleeve, where the transparent disk affixed by Tulley at the end of Act 1 PULSES faintly.

INT. TULLEY'S OFFICE - ANGLE ON SCARAB

DR. SCARAB Lucky for you, Tulley. (beat) A human Hive. Hmmm. I must learn more. This is prodigiously interesting...

CUT TO:

INT. HIVE
Hive Leader and the Bionic Six enter Hive Core. The Drones remain behind.

INT. HIVE CORE - THRONE ROOM
We are in a vast hall, all gleaming and shining. The walls are decorated with insect motifs. At the opposite end there is a throne, with a huge screen above it, and doors leading into other chambers on each side. Hive Leader goes to sit on her throne, leaving the Bionic Six standing in the middle of the room, looking in awe at their surroundings.

HIVE LEADER (pondering) You are different from the others. I knew that sooner or later, my Hive would attract the attention of people such as you. Who are you?

ANGLE ON THE BIONIC SIX, FAVORING BIONIC ONE

BIONIC ONE I'm afraid we must be the ones asking the questions...

SPORT ONE Yeah. And now that your goons aren't around anymore, you better answer them!

ANGLE ON HIVE LEADER

She acts almost as if she hadn't heard them.

HIVE LEADER I was prepared, of course. The gas you breathed contains chemical secretions that prevent you from attacking me...

ANGLE ON THE BIONIC SIX, FAVORING SPORT ONE AND KARATE ONE

They both spring into action, as if to test the truth of Hive Leader's statement. They take a couple of steps forward, then stop as if caught in an invisible grip. Beads of sweat appear on their faces as they struggle (in vain) to move forward.

SPORT ONE She's right! I can't - move!

KARATE ONE I want to -- but I just can't!

ANGLE ON HIVE LEADER

HIVE LEADER So, you outsiders haven't changed. Always ready to use force...

ANGLE ON THE BIONIC SIX, FAVORING MOTHER ONE

MOTHER ONE We didn't get here entirely under our own steam either!

ANGLE ON HIVE LEADER

HIVE LEADER Silence! I shall brook no argument from you! You are soldiers, worse, mercenaries!

ANGLE ON THE BIONIC SIX, FAVORING BIONIC ONE AND MOTHER ONE

They look at each other in surprise.

BIONIC ONE If that's what you think, you're mistaken. We're not...

ANGLE ON HIVE LEADER

She points an accusatory finger at them.

HIVE LEADER Do not lie to me! I know warriors when I see them. I have founded my Hive to protect the Human Race from ones such as you!

ANGLE ON THE BIONIC SIX, FAVORING KARATE ONE

KARATE ONE The human race is doing fine without your help, thank you!

ANGLE ON HIVE LEADER

HIVE LEADER Young fool! Can't you see the signs all around you? Mankind is doomed to self-destruct. War, pollution, scientific disasters!

ANGLE WIDENS TO INCLUDE THE SCREEN ABOVE THE THRONE

Images of life inside an anthill fill the screen.

HIVE LEADER Unlike the world of insects, where all is peace and order, the society of men is filled with anarchy and chaos...

ANGLE ON THE BIONIC SIX, FAVORING ROCK ONE

ROCK ONE (chuckling) Yeah, but it sure is fun!

ANGLE ON HIVE LEADER

Ignoring the interruption.

HIVE LEADER When Man destroys himself, my followers will be ready to build a new world, a perfect world.

ANGLE ON THE BIONIC SIX, FAVORING SPORT ONE

SPORT ONE Living like insects sure doesn't seem like perfection to me!

ANGLE ON HIVE LEADER

She gets up, stung by Sport One's remark.

HIVE LEADER What do you know of perfection! Come, I will you show the beauties of my Hive...

ANGLE WIDENS AND CAMERA PANS TO FOLLOW HIVE LEADER, EXITING THE THRONE ROOM, THE BIONIC SIX IN TOW, AS IT WERE.

INT. HIVE CORE - REPRODUCTION CHAMBERS
From the viewpoint of a platform overlooking the entire scene, Hive Leader shows the Bionic Six the Hive's Reproduction

Chambers: a vast cave, filled with numerous vats in which one can guess at humanoid shapes, bathed in a bubbly green liquid. There are white-armored Drones running all over the place.

HIVE LEADER In these reproduction chambers, I use insect-derived cell regeneration processes to breed our new race.

C.U. ON HIVE LEADER

HIVE LEADER (CONT) No longer are the sexes forced to do battle. Our emotions are under total control. We live in complete harmony.

ANGLE ON MOTHER ONE

MOTHER ONE But what about love?

ANGLE ON HIVE LEADER

HIVE LEADER We have no need for love, outsider. Soon, you will be part of the Hive Mind and you will understand.

ANGLE ON BIONIC ONE

BIONIC ONE The Hive Mind?

ANGLE WIDENS TO INCLUDE ALL OF THEM

Hive Leader walks to a side compartment and presses a hidden switch. The platform on which they stand slides down rapidly, like an elevator, into

INT. HIVE CORE - MASTER COMPUTER
Yet another cave, this one occupied almost entirely by a huge computer. Blue-armored Drones are manning the machine.

HIVE LEADER This is the computer that controls the thoughts of every member of the Hive...

ANGLE ON BLUE DRONES

Two blue-armored Drones, each carrying a silver tray with three "insect" Hive helmets on them, enter.

HIVE LEADER (VO - CONT) Once you wear these helmets, you will all become part of the Hive, as have all the other outsiders who have come here.

ANGLE WIDENS TO INCLUDE HIVE LEADER

She grabs a helmet and walks towards the Bionic Six.

HIVE LEADER (CONT) You will see that our society is the perfect one...

ANGLE ON THE BIONIC SIX

They all attempt to resist -- but can't seem to shake free.

ANGLE WIDENS TO INCLUDE HIVE LEADER AND THE DRONES

Hive Leader puts the helmets over the heads of the Bionic Six.

HIVE LEADER (CONT) ...And you will stay of your own, "free" will!

MATCH CUT TO:

INT. TULLEY'S OFFICE
CAMERA TRUCKS OUT from the videoscreen (showing the above scene) to reveal Dr. Scarab and his minions.

189

DR. SCARAB Ah! Ah! Ah! Poor Bionic Six! Turned into Drones! Ah! Ah!

ANGLE ON MECHANIC AND GLOVE

MECHANIC Uh, what's a drone?

GLOVE You are, you brainless imbecile!

MECHANIC (perplexed) Uh?

ANGLE ON SCARAB

DR. SCARAB (thinking aloud) This changes everything. The stakes are more than diamonds. With these reproduction chambers, I could create invincible armies...

C.U. ON SCARAB

DR. SCARAB (CONT) (increasingly excited) An endless number of warriors to help me take over this miserable globe!

TULLEY (VO) Er, Dr. Scarab...

ANGLE WIDENS TO INCLUDE TULLEY

TULLEY (CONT) (embarrassed) I agreed to help you steal the diamonds, but I didn't agree to this kind of scheme. It's... too dangerous, too risky...

DR. SCARAB (the soul of kindness) Of course, Mr. Tulley, we must make sure that you are not involved in this...
(to Glove, OS)
Glove, would you make sure that Mr. Tulley is not involved in our present business...

ANGLE ON GLOVE AND TULLEY

Glove puts his hand on Tulley's shoulder.

GLOVE (chuckling) Of course, Doctor. My pleasure.
(to Tulley)
Come with me.

TULLEY You're... you're sending me away?

CAMERA FOLLOWS them as they walk to the door, and exit the room, and then STAYS on the door.

GLOVE (VO) Yeah. You might say that!

TULLEY (loud scream, cut short)

Glove re-enters the room.

GLOVE All taken care of, Doctor.

ANGLE ON SCARAB

DR. SCARAB Very well. Now, we can concentrate on our primary objective: invade and take control of the Hive, and destroy anyone or anything in our path!

ANGLE WIDENS TO INCLUDE ALL THE MINIONS

who laugh in anticipation of the coming massacre.

CHOPPER Piece o'cake. They're all chicken – even if they are bugs! Ha! Ha!

ALL Ha! Ha! Ha! Ha!

BIONIC WIPE TO:

INT. HIVE - FOOD FACTORY

Another huge cave, this one occupied by an assembly line producing yellow, cubic wax-like blocks (obviously food!) and manned by Drones in yellow-armor. The Bionic Six, all wearing faceless helmets (but identifiable because they still wear their uniforms) enter, led by a green-armored Drone.

CAMERA TRUCKS IN to show the Drone talking to Mother One, Rock One and I.Q.

GREEN DRONE #2 You will work on food preparation.

ANGLE ON THE THREE

They all sound as emotionless as the Drone, except Rock One who delivers her lines with a slightly delayed beat, almost as if she needed to hear what the others are saying first (hint, hint).

ALL THREE We will work on food preparation.

ANGLE ON THE DRONE AND THE OTHER THREE

GREEN DRONE #2 You three will be trained to become Protectors, like myself. Follow me.

ALL THREE We will become Protectors. We follow.

They leave. CAMERA PANS BACK to show Mother One and I.Q. walk to an empty spot on the line and diligently do whatever complex manipulations are required there. Once more, Rock One shows signs of not being "with it" by acting with a slight delay.

ANGLE ON ROCK ONE

ROCK ONE (whispering to the others) Hey, guys, you can stop pretending now. He's gone!

ANGLE ON MOTHER ONE AND I.Q.

They don't answer and keep working.

ANGLE ON ROCK ONE

She removes her helmet and shakes her hair.

ROCK ONE (realization sinking in) Giga Bytes! It's not an act. They did get plugged into that Hive Computer. But how cum I'm okay?

A beat. Then, an idea strikes her. She removes something from her ear. CAMERA TRUCKS IN to reveal the microplayer.

ROCK ONE I got it! My microplayer! The "Frankensleazies" music must block out the Hive's signals!

She places it back in her ear, and then puts back her helmet.

ROCK ONE I always knew they were high-voltage! I'll just keep this in, and no one'll guess I'm not, er, one of them. Now, I need to get out of here...

ANGLE WIDENS TO INCLUDE MOTHER ONE AND I.Q.

Rock One turns to talk to them in a not too convincing emotionless Hive speech pattern.

ROCK ONE I just received, er, new orders. Gotta, er, I must go.

The other two nod silently. Rock One leaves in a hurry. CAMERA then FOLLOWS Rock One as she exits the food factory.

INT. HIVE - VARIOUS LOCATIONS (GOING TOWARDS HIVE CORE)

Outside, Rock One takes a few seconds to decide on a plan.

ROCK ONE If I could disable that Computer, their whole system will freak out.

POV ROCK ONE - HIVE CORE

ROCK ONE (VO - CONT) If I'm going to do it, I've got to get back inside Hive Core! Hmm, not easy, but I have to try!

CAMERA FOLLOWS Rock One as she acrobatically jumps from bridge to bridge, dances along domed tops, races at super-speed along passageways, etc. until she reaches

INT. HIVE CORE - THRONE ROOM

We see Rock One's face appear through the door, and look right and left. There's no one in sight. She tiptoes in and crosses the Throne Room, retracing their previous itinerary.

INT. HIVE CORE - REPRODUCTION CHAMBERS

Rock One steps onto the platform where Hive Leader stood earlier with the Bionic Six, and is about to access the side panel that contains the elevator controls.

WHITE DRONE #1 (VO) Who are you? What are you doing here?

ANGLE WIDENS

to reveal two white-armored Drones, standing guard.

WHITE DRONE #2 You are one of the Food Workers. You should not be here.

ROCK ONE (nervously) Er, I've been reassigned. Yes, I've received new instructions...

ANGLE ON THE WHITE DRONES

They remain silent and inscrutable.

ANGLE ON ROCK ONE

ROCK ONE (improvising fast) ... From Hive Leader. Must report to Hive Core. Immediately.

ANGLE ON THE WHITE DRONES

WHITE DRONE #1 You may pass.

ANGLE ON ROCK ONE

She breathes with relief as she activates the elevator. The platform begins its descent.

<u>INT. HIVE CORE - MASTER COMPUTER</u>
Rock One sets foot inside the Master Computer chamber. There are two blue-armored Drones working on the machine. She walks towards them as automaton-like as she possibly can.

ANGLE ON BLUE DRONES

They react in confusion at the sight of her.

BLUE DRONE #1 Alert! Unauthorized Visitor! Alert!

ANGLE ON ROCK ONE

Using her super-speed, she swiftly disables the two Drones with two well-placed karate chops. She then turns her attention to the Computer.

C.U. of her hands reaching for the controls

ANGLE WIDENS

At the very instant she touches the Machine, she is struck by a violent ELECTRO-BLAST (blue flash surrounding her body, "ZZTAK" SFX, etc.) and slumps to the floor, barely conscious.

HIVE LEADER (VO) Foolish child!

ANGLE WIDENS FURTHER

to reveal Hive Leader and two Green Drones (armed with lances) walking into the room from a secret wall panel. Hive Leader goes to Rock One, pulls off her helmet and examines her head.

HIVE LEADER We were quite aware of your resistance, girl, but we had to discover the cause...

In a few seconds, she has found and removed the microplayer.

HIVE LEADER (CONT) Ah, one of these toys that you outsiders like so much...

CAMERA TRUCKS IN as Hive Leader drops the microplayer, grabs the helmet and slowly puts it back on Rock One's semi conscious head.

POV ROCK ONE

The helmet obscures the top half of her vision, as it descends lower and we

FADE OUT.

ACT THREE

FADE IN:

INT. HIVE - OUTER PERIMETER
The same, large silver-lined corridors seen at the opening of Act Two. A trio of green Drones, armed with electro-lances, stand watch. Suddenly, an indicator light on a box affixed to the wall starts BLINKING.

GREEN DRONE #3 Intruders in Shaft B.

GREEN DRONE #4 Release the Flying Drone.

ANGLE WIDENS

to show the same flying device shown at the end of Act 1 ZOOM In from the right end of the screen, past the Drones, towards the left. CAMERA FOLLOWS the Flying Drone and TRACKS IN.

ANGLE ON DRONE

A miniature rocket enters from O.S. left and destroys the Flying Drone in an explosion (SFX)

ANGLE ON VILLAINS

Glove, Chopper and Mechanic, followed by the Cyphrons, rush into the corridor.

ANGLE ON THE GREEN DRONES

Two of them point their lances and begin firing electro-blasts (SFX) at their attackers, while the third one cries out an alert. His antennae glow a very bright green to show he is communicating with Hive Core.

GREEN DRONE #3 Alert! Alert! Outsiders have invaded our perimeters! Alert!

WIDE ANGLE, FAVORING CHOPPER

While Glove and Mechanic go after Green Drone #3 and #4 in their own, inimitable styles, Chopper sends one of his bionic chains whirring into the air, and neatly lassoes Drone #5.

CHOPPER (revving loudly) Bugs ain't fer talkin' -- they're fer squashin'!

ANGLE ON GLOVE

Glove, standing next to an unconscious Drone, pulls out a small, communicator. The screen lights up and we SEE Dr. Scarab's face.

GLOVE (triumphantly) No problems down here. I think we'll be able to "exterminate" the opposition without any trouble! Ha! Ha! Ha!

ANGLE ON COMMUNICATOR SCREEN

DR. SCARAB Excellent! Excellent! Proceed as planned!

BIONIC WIPE TO:

INT. HIVE CORE - MASTER COMPUTER
We reprise the last seconds of Act Two from Rock One's POV.

The top half of the screen is dark because of the helmet coming down. Before the whole screen goes dark, however, a PIERCING SIREN (SFX) is heard, and a FLASHING RED LIGHT illuminates the room.

ANGLE WIDENS, FAVORING HIVE LEADER

Hive Leader pulls the helmet off Rock One and rushes to the computer. She punches a few keys, and several screens light up.

ANGLE ON SCREENS

These show Scarab's minions making mincemeat of the Hive's green-armored security drones.

HIVE LEADER (VO) (alarmed) We're being invaded!

WIDE ANGLE. FAVORING HIVE LEADER AND ROCK ONE

Hive Leader turns and points an accusatory finger at the girl, still laying on the floor, but now fully conscious.

HIVE LEADER (angry) Are these men your friends? Have they come to rescue you?

ANGLE ON ROCK ONE

She gets up an goes to look at the screens.

ROCK ONE No! They're our enemies! Evil men... completely ruthless!

ANGLE WIDENS TO INCLUDE HIVE LEADER

ROCK ONE (CONT) We've had a lot of experience fighting those guys. Believe me, your people are never going to be able to beat them...

ANGLE ON SCREENS

depicting more scenes of carnage. The Hive People are running away from Dr. Scarab's forces, like headless chickens, SCREAMING (SFX), stumbling over each other, etc.

ANGLE ON HIVE LEADER

HIVE LEADER (to herself) They're coming this way... What can I do?

ANGLE WIDENS TO INCLUDE ROCK ONE

ROCK ONE Listen, I'll make you a deal. Like I said, we know all about fighting those bozos. Let my, er, friends go and we'll help you beat them.

C.U. ON HIVE LEADER

She is thinking hard about this one, then:

HIVE LEADER You win, outsider...

ANGLE WIDENS

to show Hive Leader typing a few commands into the Computer.

HIVE LEADER It is done. Your friends are now free...

CAMERA PANS UPWARD TO THE SCREENS AND TRUCKS IN.

ANGLE ON SCREEN

Bionic One is part of a little squad of Green-armored Drones clumsily fighting Mechanic and two Cyphrons. In the segment of Hive where they are located, are several out-croppings of rock, or small ledges.

Mechanic is shooting from two guns at once, one of which is firing big, metal rivets, the other, small sawblades. When hit, the Drones fall like dummies. CAMERA PULLS IN FURTHER on the scene.

MATCH CUT TO:

INT. HIVE
The same scene. Suddenly, Bionic One, whose movements were slow and sluggish, stands erect and pulls off his helmet.

BIONIC ONE (immensely happy) Free! I'm free!

ANGLE ON BIONIC ONE

He looks around and notices the bad position they're in.

BIONIC ONE Mechanic! We're under attack by Dr. Scarab!

ANGLE WIDENS TO INCLUDE THE THREE DRONES

Bionic One, automatically assuming command, pushes the Drones down to the floor, and behind one of the ledges.

BIONIC ONE Get down, he'll make mincemeat of you!

ANGLE ON MECHANIC

He becomes suddenly aware that his opponent is Bionic One, and relishes the situation.

MECHANIC Bionic One! Wit dem bugs! Come outta here where I kin crush ya!

He redoubles his firing.

ANGLE ON BIONIC ONE

Still hiding behind the ledge, he uses his "Zoom Vision" to focus upward and far away.

POV BIONIC ONE

Two Flying Drones are floating, aimlessly, near a shaft entrance.

ANGLE ON BIONIC ONE

He uses his bionic beams to "take over" the two machines.

ANGLE ON THE FLYING DRONES

They zoom towards the scene of the fight.

WIDE ANGLE

Bionic One comes from behind the ledge and runs to the right, waving at Mechanic, in an effort to distract him.

BIONIC ONE Hey, Mechanic, my dog is a better shot than you!

MECHANIC (furious) Argh! I'll show you! Crush you! Kill you!

ANGLE ON MECHANIC AND THE CYPHRONS

The two Flying Drones zoom in from O.S. right and BONK (SFX) the two Cyphrons. Mechanic, surprised, turns right and left.

MECHANIC Uh? Whazzat?

Bionic One's fist ENTERS FRAME (left) and CONKS (SFX) him.

BIONIC ONE (VO) Nothing that you can't take!

ANGLE WIDENS

to reveal Bionic One standing over the unconscious Mechanic, the two demolished Cyphrons, and inviting the Green Drones to come out from behind the ledge.

BIONIC ONE Come on! We've got to get rid of these guys!

He turns to take a good look at the situation.

POV BIONIC ONE

of the Hive being overrun by Cyphrons, etc.

ANGLE ON BIONIC ONE

He starts running towards Hive Core.

BIONIC ONE We can't stop them alone. We need help...

CAMERA TRUCKS OUT AND INTO...

<u>INT. HIVE CORE - MASTER COMPUTER CHAMBER</u>
... where Hive Leader and Rock One have just watched the previous scene on one of the Master Computer screens.

HIVE LEADER You are good fighters...

ROCK ONE Yeah, but he's right. We're probably not going to be enough...

CUT TO:

INT. HIVE - FOOD FACTORY
Mother One and I.Q., now free of their helmets, are running towards the exit. Suddenly, Chopper and a squad of Cyphrons appear in their way.

CHOPPER (nasty) Where ya goin', beautiful?

ANGLE ON CHOPPER

He fires one of his chains.

CHOPPER (CONT) How could ya forget our date, ha, ha, ha!

ANGLE ON THE TWO HEROES, FAVORING I.Q.

With his super-strong bionic arm, he grabs the chain right out of the air, before it hits, and breaks it in two.

I.Q. Sorry, Chopper, but we don't have time to continue this delightful conversation right now!

ANGLE WIDENS

to show Mother One and I.Q. running off, while Chopper, furious, urges the Cyphrons after them.

CHOPPER Little Runt! Hurry up! Don't let 'em get away!

<u>INT. HIVE</u>
Mother One and I.Q. are now running on one of the silver bridges, towards Hive Core.

ANGLE ON MOTHER ONE

She speaks into her shoulder microphones.

MOTHER ONE Mother One to all, come in!

BIONIC ONE (VO) Bionic One here! Let's regroup at Hive Core. Over.

ANGLE WIDENS

to show them still running. Suddenly, there is a loud KRASH (SFX). CAMERA TILTS as the characters stagger and the bridge upon which they stand collapses.

They fall toward a lower level platform, upon which stands Glove, accompanied by a group of Cyphrons, who have just caused a metal support beam to collapse.

ANGLE ON GLOVE

He begins firing various beams and other weapons at them (SFX).

GLOVE (sadistic) Mother One! I.Q.! I couldn't hope for better shooting practice! Ha! Ha! Ha!

ANGLE ON MOTHER ONE AND I.Q.

falling, while Glove's rays ZIP (SFX) past them. Suddenly, a large cable swings past them.

KARATE ONE (VO) Catch!

They both grab the cable.

ANGLE WIDENS

to show Sport One and Karate One on a side bridge. They've just swung the cable, which now swings back, bringing Mother One and I.Q. safely to the bridge. Glove is still shooting at them from below.

CLOSER ANGLE ON THE FOUR OF THEM

MOTHER ONE Thanks, Karate One!

KARATE ONE Hey, what are friends for!

SPORT ONE Er, I hate to interrupt, but we've got to reach Hive Core before it's too late.

CAMERA PANS TO THE RIGHT to show a squad of Cyphrons rushing towards the Bionic Four. They are met by Karate One, who launches a vigorous kick, causing them to fall like dominoes.

KARATE ONE Ki-aiiii!

WIDE ANGLE, FAVORING GLOVE

He stands in the f.g. Up, in a corner of the screen, we can see the Cyphrons tumbling and the Bionic Four running off.

GLOVE (furious) Get 'em! Fry 'em!

CLOSER ANGLE ON GLOVE

He takes his communicator.

GLOVE (to himself) Bah, they can't escape, and they know it. We got this place sown up...
(switching on the communicator)
We're almost there, Dr. Scarab. The bugs are running scared, and so are the Bionic Six! It won't be long now! Ha! Ha!

CUT TO:

INT. HIVE CORE - MASTER COMPUTER CHAMBER
All the Bionic Six have made it to the Master Computer chamber. Hive Leader is pacing furiously.

BIONIC ONE (firmly) It's the only solution.

ANGLE ON HIVE LEADER

HIVE LEADER I can't! Turning off the computer would mean the destruction of everything I've built.

ANGLE ON THE BIONIC SIX, FAVORING BIONIC ONE

BIONIC ONE The six of us can't protect the entire Hive. We need the help of all your people. You have to free them!

ROCK ONE We told you what it would mean to let the Hive fall into the hands of Dr. Scarab...

ANGLE ON HIVE LEADER

HIVE LEADER (uncertain) Yes, I can see that you are honorable people. Perhaps, I was wrong. I don't know anymore...

She removes her helmet and reveals her true face: that of a white-haired, yet still young-looking woman.

ANGLE ON THE BIONIC SIX, FAVORING MOTHER ONE

All their faces register amazement.

MOTHER ONE Dr. O'Connor? It isn't possible! You're supposed to have...

ANGLE ON HIVE LEADER (O'CONNOR)

HIVE LEADER ...died? Yes, that's what I wanted the world to believe. And perhaps I did die in a way...

ANGLE ON THE BIONIC SIX, FAVORING I.Q.

I.Q. But you were the most respected entomologist in the world! You received all the awards, and the honors...

C.U. ON HIVE LEADER'S FACE

HIVE LEADER Yes, but what I really wanted was to escape to a safe, orderly place. Because I couldn't find it outside, I created one...

ANGLE WIDENS

Hive Leader walks to the Master Computer and starts programming.

HIVE LEADER (CONT) ... but you have made me realize that my beautiful Hive was not the answer. The world needs individuality to fight evil...

She grabs a microphone and speaks into it.

HIVE LEADER (CONT) Total erasure... I repeat, total erasure...

ANGLE WIDENS TO INCLUDE THE MASTER COM-PUTER

Lights start BLINKING, tapes begin WHIRRING (SFX), etc.

CUT TO:

INT. HIVE

A QUICK SERIES OF CUTS THROUGH THE HIVE

shows people pulling off their helmets and throwing them away. They then start grabbing things around them, or tearing them out of the decor, turning them into makeshift weapons and using them to fight the Cyphrons.

Glove is trying to keep the Hive people at bay by shooting various rays at them, but by using make-shift shields, and pipes, the mob manages to make him back off.

Mechanic shoots bolts at the crowd, but suddenly, a net of wire mesh is dropped from above, and he disappears under a mass of angry Hive denizens.

Chopper is keeping the Hivers away by whirling his chains like ninchakus, but several metal cables lasso him around the legs and torso, and he is dragged to the floor.

CUT TO:

INT. TULLEY'S OFFICE
Dr. Scarab is looking at a clock on the wall of the office. He looks as if he is having trouble controlling his impatience.

DR. SCARAB Why hasn't Glove called me? He should have taken over the Hive Core by now...

He flicks a switch on the video console, but the screen remains obstinately dark.

DR. SCARAB (CONT) Come in, Glove! Come in, you hare-brained incompetent! (to himself) What is going on down there?

GLOVE (VO) Ahem...

Dr. Scarab turns around, looking amazed.

POV SCARAB

Glove, Mechanic and Chopper have just walked into the room. They're in a sorry state (like the Coyote after an encounter with the Roadrunner!) bleeding from wounds, uniforms shredded, etc.

GLOVE (apologetic) Well, er, there were a few, er, bugs in the plan. We, er...

MECHANIC Yeah, them bugs jumped us from behind and...

ANGLE ON SCARAB

His face becomes red with fury.

DR. SCARAB You brainless nincompoops! You miserable worms! You...

Suddenly, we hear loud HELICOPTER noises (SFX). Dr. Scarab rushes to the window.

ANGLE ON MECHANIC AND CHOPPER

MECHANIC (to Chopper) Gee, I wuz scared he'd be mad at us!

ANGLE ON SCARAB

He is looking through the window.

DR. SCARAB The army!

POV SCARAB

Several huge military troop transport helicopters are landing outside. SOLDIERS are jumping out of them and begin securing various positions in the mining complex.

SOLDIERS (ad lib) Hup-two! Git! Move! (etc.)

ANGLE ON SCARAB

DR. SCARAB Quick! To the pneumatic tubes! I'll deal with you three later!

ANGLE WIDENS TO INCLUDE ALL OF THEM

as they rush out.

ANGLE ON CHOPPER AND MECHANIC

CHOPPER You see, dummy! He *is* mad at us!

CUT TO:

EXT. DIAMOND MINES
CAMERA PANS OVER the helicopters and the soldiers, then TRUCKS IN on a rocky hill behind them, upon which stand the Bionic Six and Dr. O'Connor.

SPORT ONE Well, I guess we showed those guys a thing or two!

CAMERA ROTATES 180 DEGREES: the seven of them are now in the foreground while down below, the Army is taking charge.

BIONIC ONE Thanks for not trying to stop us from calling the Authorities, Dr. O'Connor...

ANGLE ON DR. O'CONNOR

DR. O'CONNOR Please, Bionic One! I have much to account for, I suppose...

ANGLE ON THE BIONIC SIX, FAVORING MOTHER ONE

MOTHER ONE Your intentions came from the heart, Dr. O'Connor, but robbing people of their individuality won't ever accomplish what you desired...

CAMERA TRUCKS DOWN to reveal all the Hive People (without helmets, looking dazed) coming out of tunnels, shafts, etc.

MOTHER ONE (VO - CONT)
... Perhaps now, the people of your community can use their free will to make the world a better place.

ANGLE ON DR. O'CONNOR

DR. O'CONNOR I suppose we'll all need a little time to get reacquainted with the real world...

ANGLE ON THE BIONIC SIX, FAVORING THE KIDS

SPORT ONE We'll help. How about teaching them all a real team sport, like baseball?

ROCK ONE Or introducing them to the latest hit by the "Frankensleazies"?

As they run downhill, CAMERA TRUCKS OUT to show them joining with the still confused-looking Hive members.

DISSOLVE TO:

EXT. BENNETT HOME - DAY

ESTABLISHING SHOT.

MEG (VO) I really thought about what you said before...

CUT TO:

INT. BENNETT HOME - KITCHEN
All the family is sitting around the table, which is covered in empty dishes, etc., except for Meg, who has quite obviously just entered the room.

JACK That's terrific, Meg. (beat) What are you talking about?

ANGLE ON MEG

MEG You know, your speech about how we should all try to just be ourselves, just be individuals...

ANGLE ON HELEN

HELEN I'm glad you remembered, honey.

ANGLE ON MEG

MEG I've decided not to wear that ugly wig anymore. Besides, the "Frankensleazies" are out.

ANGLE WIDENS TO INCLUDE ALL

There is a general sigh of satisfaction from everyone around the table.

ALL BUT MEG (Loud sigh of joy)

ERIC (smug) I knew those weezies wouldn't last!

ANGLE ON MEG

MEG (unfazed) So, I've decided to start my own trend...

She reaches her hand to her head and pulls off what had at first appeared to be her own hair. It is, in reality, just a wig.

Her real hair has been styled into porcupine-like spikes. At the end of the spikes are multi-colored globes, which blink on and off like Christmas tree ornaments.

MEG (CONT) (proudly) I call it the "Glitterbug!"

ANGLE WIDENS TO INCLUDE ALL

The rest of the family looks at each other in silent dismay as we

FADE OUT.

The Real Ghostbusters *was an American animated television series, a spinoff of the 1984 movie. The series ran from September 1986 to October 1991, and was produced by Columbia Pictures Television, DiC Enterprises, and Coca-Cola Telecommunications. J. Michael Straczynski was story editor. This is the second of the two scripts we wrote for it.*

The Real Ghostbusters: The Headless Motorcyclist

ACT ONE

FADE IN:

<u>EXT MANHATTAN - NIGHT - ESTABLISHING SHOT</u>
CAMERA PANS over the Manhattan skyline. The lights of the buildings shine prettily against the dark blue sky, conveying a festive and relaxed atmosphere.

CAMERA TRUCKS IN SLOWLY towards Central Park, on to an elegant penthouse terrace.

<u>EXT PENTHOUSE</u>
A chic party is in progress. We HEAR a STEREO BLARING in the b.g. Elegantly dressed PEOPLE walk in and out with drinks, mingling on the terrace and savoring the night.

<u>INT PENTHOUSE</u>
CAMERA MOVES into the penthouse and PANS OVER the party. It is a scene very similar to the one outside. We HEAR mindless PARTY CHATTER over the music.

CAMERA TRUCKS IN on a large buffet table, amply covered with drinks and hors d'oeuvres, near which we discover

MEDIUM ANGLE ON PETER AND BANKER

PETER VENKMAN, looking very smooth and dapper in a fancy evening suit, a (fruit juice) cocktail in hand.

Peter is leaning forward with a canny look on his face and is talking to a silver-haired, conservative-looking gentleman who looks very much like a Wall Street BANKER. Which he is.

PETER (smoothly) I'm telling you, what you really need is our new, Year-Round Ghost Protection Policy. Keeps you safe from spooks, or your money back!

ANGLE ON BANKER

He looks slightly befuddled, as if events are moving too quickly for him.

BANKER (with a slight stutter) Gh-ghost Protection Policy... Er, I'm not sure we have a need for... .pn2 .h1# .h2 .h3 .fl
MEDIUM ANGLE

The Banker tries to slide away from Peter, who puts a hand on the man's arm to prevent any possibility of escape.

PETER (earnestly) Need! Of course you have a need! We're living in troubled times...

ANGLE ON PETER

PETER (CONT) (lyrically) Think of all the dead accountants who must haunt your vaults at night, the embezzlers that shot themselves, rather than face the shame of a long trial, the...

ANGLE ON BANKER

Now he looks somewhat worried and defensive.

BANKER Embezzlers? We've never had any embezzlers!

CAMERA PANS to the right to reveal RAY STANTZ walking by. He is stuffing a sandwich into his mouth and looks bored. Although he is wearing formal attire, he still manages to look less well groomed than anyone else in the room.

ANGLE ON RAY

FROM OUT OF FRAME, Peter's arm grabs hold of Ray, just as he is about to take another large bite of his sandwich. He is put off balance by the gesture. The food misses his mouth, flies past his ear and over his shoulder.

ANGLE ON SANDWICH

which finishes its trajectory, landing in the glass of KATE, a very attractive young woman, who is presently talking to another male PARTYGOER.

ANGLE ON KATE AND PARTYGOER

Kate looks somewhat taken aback, but not angry. She shrugs and smiles the incident away.

KATE Well, I guess that blows my diet!

PARTYGOER Let me get you a new glass...

KATE No, that's all right, I'll get it.

She turns and heads for the buffet table.

ANGLE ON PETER, RAY, AND THE BANKER

Peter introduces Ray, who automatically beams at the befuddled Banker.

PETER This is one of my associates, Dr. Ray Stantz. He can tell you about all the deadly ghosts that haunt the banking world.

Ray enthusiastically shakes hands with the Banker, who looks as if he can't believe Ray is expert at anything.

RAY (excitedly) Banking! Yes, the world of banking is full of ghosts! There was the Axe Murderer of First National Trust, and the Spectre That Ate Tax-Exempt Bonds...

BANKER (genuinely worried) *Ate* tax-exempt bonds?

CAMERA PULLS OUT to show Kate coming towards the group to get to the buffet.

ANGLE ON KATE

She extends her arm past them to take a glass.

KATE Excuse me.

ANGLE ON PETER

Peter turns his head to look at her, and obviously is taken with her great beauty.

PETER (muttering to himself) Wow!

MEDIUM ANGLE ON THE GROUP

While Ray and the Banker are involved in deep conversation, Peter walks away to follow Kate.

RAY ... and the strangest thing is that it only ate bonds that were issued by defense contractors...

PETER'S POV

We follow Kate elbowing her way through the party crowd to

EXT PENTHOUSE
Kate walks over to an attractive young man, whom she kisses lightly on the cheek. It is obvious that they are together. His name is BUD, and he has the look of a Madison Avenue yuppie executive.

CAMERA PULLS OUT to reveal a grimacing Peter. Suddenly, a hand comes from OUT OF FRAME to land on his shoulder. It is WINSTON ZEDDMORE'S.

WINSTON (VO) Looks like you struck out, buddy.

ANGLE ON PETER AND WINSTON

Peter shrugs.

WINSTON (CONT) Don't worry about it! The night's still young, and there's plenty more fish in the sea!

The two men are turning to walk back inside when we HEAR very LOUD voices.

ANGLE ON KATE AND BUD

The two are involved in a sudden, heated argument, and are behaving in an agitated fashion -- especially Bud.

BUD (angrily) We're supposed to be at this party together! I didn't come over here to watch you hanging around with some other guy!

KATE (defensively) You're being ridiculous! I already told you that he was an old friend I haven't seen for years!

ANGLE ON PETER

He was about to leave the terrace with Winston, but stops to see more of what is going on.

ANGLE ON KATE AND BUD

Bud is getting more agitated. He grabs Kate by the shoulders, as if to shake her.

BUD He didn't look very "old" to me!

KATE Let me go, you're hurting me!

ANGLE ON PETER

He fumes over the treatment, and goes over to the couple to see if he can help Kate.

ANGLE ON THE THREE OF THEM

PETER (threatening) That's no way to treat such a pretty lady!

ANGLE ON BUD

Bud stops yelling at Kate and turns his attention to Peter.

BUD (very irritated) Buzz off, Buddy! We don't need you butting into our business!

MEDIUM ANGLE

Peter puts his hand on Bud's shoulder.

PETER You may not need me, but I'm sure this beautiful lady does.

Peter's remarks are the last straw. Bud forcefully removes Peter's hand from his shoulder and then shoves him, hard.

CAMERA PULLS BACK to include other PARTYGOERS, and Winston, watching the action.

It looks like the argument is going to escalate. Both Bud and Peter put themselves in "macho" fighting stances, ready to come to blows. PETER (really furious) Okay! You've had your chance! Now I'm going to take you down a peg or two!

BUD (smirking angrily) Yeah, you little wimp? When I'm through with you, you're going to look like day old Brie!

Several Partygoers then hold Bud back, while Winston attempts to calm Peter.

ANGLE ON WINSTON AND PETER

WINSTON Come on, Pete. Let's leave these folks alone to settle their own problems...

ANGLE ON KATE AND BUD

Kate tries to placate Bud, putting her hand on his arm.

KATE I'm sorry Bud. Why don't we go and talk...

Bud shrugs her hand away angrily.

BUD I'm going, but not with you!

CAMERA FOLLOWS HIM as he pushes his way into the

INT PENTHOUSE
and, through the crowd inside, to the apartment door which he jerks open and SLAMS behind him.

CUT TO:

EXT PENTHOUSE
Peter and Kate both stand looking in the direction of Bud's exit. Kate has a worried expression on her face.

PETER Good riddance!

KATE (extremely worried) Oh, my! Now he's really in for trouble! Peter does a double take and looks at Kate, trying to understand what she means. CAMERA TRUCKS IN on Kate's worried expression.

DISSOLVE TO:

EXT FIFTH AVENUE - NIGHT
CAMERA PANS OVER the almost deserted street and TRUCKS IN onto a fancy, red SPORTS CAR, ZOOMING along at a fast clip.

INT SPORTS CAR
Bud is driving. He is still grumbling about his night.

BUD Who does she think she is! I bet that guy was another "old friend"...

As he crosses Broadway, he glances at his rearview mirror.

CLOSE UP ON REARVIEW MIRROR

A small dot of light rapidly grows larger and larger, and blindingly bright. We HEAR the ROAR of a powerful motorcycle motor.

ANGLE ON BUD

He squints his eyes, and tries to shield himself from the glare of the painfully bright light.

BUD (annoyed) Geez! I hate that! The guy's blinding me! Why doesn't he pass or something!

EXT SPORTS CAR
Bud puts his hand out of the window, gesturing impatiently at his follower to pass him.

For a second, nothing happens, except the SUPERCHARGED ROAR of the motorcycle engine REVVING angrily.

ANGLE ON BUD

Puzzled that he has not yet been passed, Bud turns his head to see who is following him.

BUD'S POV

At last, we SEE the shape of the HEADLESS MOTORCY-CLIST, carrying a FLAMING HELMET in one of his bony hands. With a LOUD SCREECH of tires, and a super ROAR of the engine, the Motorcyclist rears his bike on its back wheel, where it is silhouetted against the lights of Manhattan.

WIDER ANGLE

The unnerving sight of the horrifying motorcyclist almost causes Bud to lose control of the sports car as it makes a skidding right turn into Washington Square Park.

INT SPORTS CAR

Bud's knuckles turn white as he angrily grips the wheel.

BUD (fury in his voice) If this is someone's idea of a joke, I'll give them their money's worth!

EXT SPORTS CAR - A SERIES OF SHOTS

takes the two vehicles through a spine-tingling chase through the narrow streets of GREENWICH VILLAGE. The car ZOOMS, making hairpin turns and burning rubber. But the Motorcyclist is not shaken.

INT SPORTS CAR

Bud's expression changes from anger to worry.

BUD (nervously) That guy's good, but I know how to get rid of him!

EXT SPORTS CAR

Bud drives the car into a basement parking lot. Assuredly, he spirals through it and comes to another exit, barred by a metal curtain.

INT SPORTS CAR

Bud points a radio-control device at the shutter.

BUD (maniacally happy) Ah, ah, I got him! Obviously the jerk doesn't work here!

EXT SPORTS CAR

The metal gate opens with a CLANGING WHIR to let Bud's car through, and then closes behind him, equally LOUDLY.

Bud zips the car into an alley, and stops in the shadows.

INT SPORTS CAR

Bud wipes the sweat from his brow.

BUD Well, let him find his way outta there!

Suddenly, we HEAR a RESOUNDING LAUGH. The effect is very chilling and scary. Bud's eyes open wide.

BUD'S POV

We see the Headless Motorcyclist zooming RIGHT OUT OF THE SOLID METAL GATES!

ANGLE ON BUD

Bud swears and starts the car again.

BUD I'm getting outta here! I don't know who that guy is, but I'm not gonna wait around to find out!

EXT SPORTS CAR
The car REVS UP at incredible speed, and leaving a cloud of dust behind it, heads down Broadway.

Instead of driving with his earlier assurance and skill, Bud now zigzags his car nervously all over the road. We keep HEARING the frightening and unnerving sound of the Motor-cyclist's ghostly LAUGH.

INT SPORTS CAR
Jerkily, Bud keeps looking over his shoulder, in a state of rap-idly increasing panic.

BUD I've got to shake him! I've got to get out of here! This baby can do 120 once I get her on a straight road!

EXT SPORTS CAR

He makes a left turn from Broadway onto Canal Street, almost causing the other cars there to have an accident. Then, he ZOOMS towards the MANHATTAN BRIDGE, pursued by a CACOPHONY of HONKING HORNS and SHOUTED IN-SULTS.

The Motorcyclist is still hot on his tail, but he is no longer laughing.

EXT MANHATTAN BRIDGE - ANGLE DOWN CANAL STREET
Bud's car grows very quickly from a small dot on the horizon as it ROARS onto the bridge with a WHOOSH!

The Motorcyclist is in hot pursuit, also growing from a mere speck to full size. But, instead of getting onto the bridge he SCREECHES to a total and complete halt!

ANGLE ON MOTORCYCLIST

He ROARS and shakes his fist in anger.

INT SPORTS CAR
Bud, seeing in the rearview mirror that the Motorcyclist has stopped, brings his car to a SCREECHING, twisting halt.

EXT MANHATTAN BRIDGE
The two opponents stare at each other for a micro-second.

ANGLE ON MOTORCYCLIST

In a superhuman display of strength and accuracy, the Motor-cyclist throws his flaming helmet at Bud's car.

ANGLE ON SPORTS CAR

The helmet CRASHES through the passenger side of the windshield, and the entire car goes up in SOARING FLAMES.

Bud scrambles out of the burning car. Standing there, he sees

BUD'S POV

The Motorcyclist once more raising his fist in the air, but this time in an unmistakable display of triumph. Then, the Ghost REVS his engine and ROARS away into the night, LAUGHING maniacally. In the distance, we HEAR the approach of POLICE SIRENS.

DISSOLVE TO:

EXT GHOSTBUSTERS CENTRAL - DAY
ESTABLISHING SHOT of the Ghostbusters' firehouse.

CAMERA PANS OVER to a fire hydrant. A DOG walks INTO FRAME and examines the hydrant with a "Will I or wont'I?" look.

Before he can make up his mind, we HEAR a SIREN. SCREECHING INTO FRAME, a POLICE CAR ROARS up to the curb and parks in front of the hydrant, causing the dog to run away.

ANGLE ON POLICE CAR

With a bit of Wagnerian-like b.g. MUSIC, the feet of LIEUTENANT FRUMP appear on the sidewalk. Then, he slowly, and almost painfully, extracts himself from the car.

ANGLE ON FRUMP

Frump is a gigantically fat man (somewhat like JACKIE GLEASON before he lost all that weight), but there is nothing kindly about his face. He's dressed in a blue suit, a tan raincoat, a slouch hat, and the ugliest tie this side of a Moose convention!

MEDIUM ANGLE

A YOUNGER COP gets out of the driver's side of the car, then walks around to join Frump on the sidewalk. FRUMP (scratching his face) Come on, kid. Let's get down to business.

CUT TO:

INT JANINE'S DESK
JANINE is reading a woman's magazine at her desk. A sheet of paper is rolled into the typewriter. Suddenly a HUGE SHADOW falls across the desk. Startled, she looks up.

JANINE'S POV

CAMERA TILTS SLOWLY UP from around the area of Frump's belt to his very mean-looking face.

ANGLE ON FRUMP

FRUMP (commandingly) I want the Ghostbusters!

ANGLE ON JANINE

She is surprised but not daunted. JANINE Which one? Doctor Spengler is quite busy in his lab at the moment. Doctor Stanz is occupied in the motor pool...

MEDIUM ANGLE

Frump bends his bulk slightly over Janine and interrupts.

FRUMP (roaring) All of them! Now!

CUT TO:

INT CONFERENCE ROOM
CLOSE UP on a series of photos of Bud's destroyed car.

FRUMP (VO) ... and the guy was lucky not to end up the blue plate special at Bob's Barbecue Hut...

CAMERA TRUCKS OUT to reveal Frump, the younger Detective and the four Ghostbusters, all sitting around a long table.

Egon grabs the pictures, looks at them very closely (about an inch from his face) and goes "Hmm, hmmm..." several times. He will remain absorbed in them for most of the scene.

ANGLE ON PETER

Peter obviously believes Frump has come for their help. Smelling a client, he beams.

PETER Okay, so of course, you want us to investigate this motorcycle spook?

ANGLE ON FRUMP

FRUMP (very coolly) No.

ANGLE ON PETER

PETER (quite surprised) No?

MEDIUM ANGLE ON PETER AND FRUMP

Frump pulls out a photo of Bud and pushes it towards Peter.

FRUMP Know this guy?

PETE (he hasn't got it yet) Yeah, sure. I met him last night. He had an argum...

FRUMP (interrupting) That's the guy who was almost barbe-cued.

CLOSE UP ANGLE ON PETER

He gets it -- at once -- and clams up.

PETER Oh.

MEDIUM ANGLE ON PETER, FRUMP AND RAY

Ray, who has followed the exchange with interest, has not gotten it and, despite Peter's angry glances, carries on.

RAY You mean, the guy that Peter had a fight with last night almost got killed by a ghost...

There is a pregnant pause.

RAY (CONT) (genuinely amazed) What a coincidence!

FRUMP (very meaningfully) Yep! Quite a coincidence.

WIDER ANGLE, NOW INCLUDING EGON

He grabs the photos. Those that Egon is still looking at, he has to pull from his hands inch by inch.

FRUMP (CONT) (to Peter) Why don't you make both of our lives easier and tell me how you did it.

RAY (turning to Peter) Did what? What did you do?

ANGLE ON PETER

PETER (angry) Nothing! I didn't do anything! I'm innocent!

ANGLE ON RAY AND FRUMP

He sounds completely convinced of Peter's innocence.

RAY (to Frump, righteously) You heard him. He didn't do anything. He's innocent.

FRUMP Yep. And he's the only guy in New York with a motive and easy access to ghosts...

ANGLE ON PETER

PETER Hey, wait a minute! I barely knew the guy. Besides, a ghost isn't a hit man. You can't get them to do whatever you want...

WIDER ANGLE

At that very moment, SLIMER ZOOMS into the room, and goes "coo, coo" very affectionately all over Peter, who then tries desperately, but unsuccessfully, to "shoo" him away.

ANGLE ON FRUMP

Frump looks at the scene and nods knowingly.

FRUMP Yep, I can see ghosts don't like you...

ANGLE ON PETER AND SLIMER

He is still trying to get rid of Slimer.

PETER (exceedingly annoyed) No, you can't! Slimer isn't... Well, he is, but...

He realizes that his explanation is going to sound too complicated, even to himself, so he just shuts up.

ANGLE ON RAY

RAY (carrying on) You can't say things like this to my buddy. Besides, we were all together all the time last night.

WIDER ANGLE

All the Ghostbusters turn immediately to look accusingly at Ray, who goes "Oops" silently.

ANGLE ON FRUMP

Frump nods, a large smile on his face.

FRUMP Hmm, hmm.

WIDER ANGLE

Frump gets up, walks towards the door, followed by the younger detective, and turns before he leaves.

FRUMP I can see we're getting nowhere fast. But I want you weirdos to know I never let a guy go free. Never. I'll be back.

ANGLE ON RAY AND PETER

RAY (to Peter) You didn't do it, did you?

Peter gets up and starts pacing the room angrily.

PETER Of course, I didn't do it! How could have I done it, anyway?

EGON (VO) (matter of factly) By reversing the polarity of the neutron flow.

WIDER ANGLE

Peter turns angrily towards Egon.

PETER I didn't reverse any polarity. I don't even know what you're talking about. I tell you I didn't do it. WINSTON (the voice of common sense) Then, there's a killer ghost on the loose, and we better catch it.

ANGLE ON RAY

RAY (meaning it) Yes, besides it'd be bad for business if Peter goes to jail...

ANGLE ON PETER

He throws a furious glance at Ray.

DISSOLVE TO:

INT GARAGE - NIGHT
CAMERA PANS OVER the Ghostbusters' Garage. The door is open. Out there, it is NIGHT. Next to ECTO-1 is an exact copy of Bud's SPORTS CAR.

The four Ghostbusters are standing by, dressed in full ghost-busting gear -- except for Peter who does not wear his PROTON PACK. They look like they're arguing.

ANGLE ON PETER AND RAY

PETER I don't like this plan. I think it's a stupid plan.

RAY (patiently) But we need somebody to drive the car and retrace that guy's itinerary. Besides, we'll be following you. He smiles a smile that spells doom.

RAY (CONT) Nothing can go wrong!

PETER (not at all convinced) Yeah, sure... But why do I have to be the bait?

MEDIUM ANGLE, TO INCLUDE WINSTON

WINSTON (with a large, wicked grin) Well, for one, you're the one who stands to go to jail! Besides, we drew for it, re-member?

WIDER ANGLE

Grumbling, Peter gets into the sports car, SLAMS the door, starts the car and ZOOMS into the night.

CUT TO:

EXT FIFTH AVENUE - A SERIES OF SHOTS
enable us to follow Peter as he drives through nocturnal Man-hattan, followed by Ecto-1.

INT ECTO-1
Ray is at the wheel, with Winston in the passenger seat. Egon is in the back, looking at the usual array of super- scientific instruments.

RAY Anything yet?

EGON Nope.

INT SPORTS CAR

PETER (grumbling) Go to jail, go to jail...

EXT SPORTS CAR
The Headless Motorcyclist ZOOMS IN from a cross street, between Peter's car and Ecto-1. He REARS UP his bike as he negotiates the sharp turn and rushes after Peter.

He then proceeds to throw a flaming helmet at Peter, while LAUGHING maniacally.

INT SPORTS CAR

PETER (gasping) Holy smokes!

EXT SPORTS CAR
The surprise causes Peter to swerve, and the flaming helmet to miss. It CRASHES harmlessly a few yards away.

INT ECTO-1
Egon raises his eyes from the equipment and points.

EGON (impressed) I think we have something here. It seems to have quite a strong concentration of PK energy.

ANGLE ON RAY AND EGON

Ray hasn't waited for Egon to tell him that the Ghost has arrived. He turns to answer Egon, thereby completely taking his attention away from the road.

RAY I kind of noticed! The question is, what do we do with it now that we've got its attention?

WINSTON (VO) Hey!

EXT ECTO-1

Ray has almost shot past a right turn, where Peter and the Ghost have gone. He gives the wheel a sharp twist, almost sending Ecto-1 into a tailspin, but the car recovers.

RAY Good girl! Atta boy!

ANGLE ON WINSTON

Leaning out the window, he SHOOTS several ion beams at the Ghost, but misses.

EXT MANHATTAN STREETS

The beams HIT the traffic light overhead. The energy flows across the wires, from light to light, causing them to change in haphazard fashion, creating chaos.

A SERIES OF SHOTS shows the pursuit intensifying. The choreography of the chase bears some resemblance to that of "The Keystone Kops."

For example, Peter's car goes down one street, followed closely by the Ghost, while Ecto-1 is going in the opposite direction on the next street. They all skid, swerve, go through lights, leaving chaos in their wake.

ANOTHER QUICK SERIES OF SHOTS shows Peter dodging the Motorcyclist's fireballs; Ray doing his best not to lose sight of Peter's car; Egon hunching over his instruments; Winston shooting ion beams.

EXT SPORTS CAR

The chase has now taken Peter near the Civic Center, and he ZOOMS towards the Brooklyn Bridge.

WIDER ANGLE

CAMERA PULLS OUT to show the car speeding onto the bridge, while the Motorcyclist SCREECHES to a halt at its foot.

Ecto-1 SQUEALS to a stop just beyond. The Motorcyclist throws a last flaming helmet (which misses), shakes his fist, and ROARS off into the night.

EXT BROOKLYN BRIDGE
Ray, Winston and Egon get out of Ecto-1, while Peter makes a U-turn on the bridge and drives back to join his friends.

Peter gets out of the car, and goes over to the last spot where the ghost stopped. Egon is there, holding a PKE meter, while Ray looks very excited.

ANGLE ON EGON AND RAY

EGON There's something funny about these readings, but I can't seem to put my finger on what...

RAY (excitedly) I know! I know! It's the water! Water is a natural ionizing agent and...

MEDIUM ANGLE TO INCLUDE PETER

PETER (barging in) I said it was a stupid plan before. Well, I was right and I won't do it again!

EGON (not noticing Peter) Yes, that would explain the sudden drop in power readings as we got closer to the river. But I still don't understand...

PETER Why me?

Egon and Ray turn toward Peter and simultaneously answer his rhetoric question.

EGON AND RAY Yes, that too...

WINSTON (snapping his fingers) I think I've got it!

The other three turn toward him.

WINSTON (CONT) Doesn't it all ring a bell? The chase, the bridge, the headless spook? It's that old Washington Irving tale... (a pause) "The Legend of Sleepy Hollow!"

A look of realization dawns on the Ghostbusters' faces. They all look at each other as we

FADE OUT:

ACT TWO

FADE IN:

EXT MANHATTAN - DAY
CAMERA PANS from the U.N. Building, up Franklin D. Roosevelt Drive along the East river, STOPS at the QUEENSBORO BRIDGE, and then TRUCKS IN on a posh, riverside, condo building.

CLOSE UP on Ecto-1, parked under a no-parking sign in front of the place.

CUT TO:

INT BUILDING
All four Ghostbusters are standing on the landing in front of a set of heavy doors. Peter's hand is still on the doorbell.

The door opens. Kate appears in the opening. She looks more embarrassed than surprised.

KATE Oh, it's you.

PETER (not making things easier) Yeah, it's us.

ANGLE ON KATE

There is silence. Then, she moves back from the door.

KATE (somewhat reluctantly) Why don't you come in?

INT KATE'S APARTMENT
They all walk in. Egon pulls out a PKE meter and starts "sniffing" around the apartment, while Ray looks at the elegant decor. Peter confronts Kate.

ANGLE ON PETER AND KATE

Peter is in a hurry to get to the point.

PETER We think there are certain things you can tell us about a certain ghost...

Kate attempts to interrupt him.

KATE (embarrassed) A ghost? Why should I...

Peter raises a finger in the air to silence her.

PETER (a bit obnoxiously) You were kinda worried the other night, when there was no particular reason for you to be... (a pause) Except, of course, if you knew in advance what would happen... He points his finger at her.

PETER (CONT) ... which you did, didn't you?

Kate puts her head down to hide her embarrassment, but remains silent. Pete continues, lecturing.

PETER (CONT) Then I remembered the Washington Irving folk tale...

ANGLE ON WINSTON

frowning at Peter's attempt to hog all the credit.

ANGLE ON PETER

He notices and tries to worm out of it.

PETER (CONT) (embarrassed) Well, er, we remembered the story of the Headless Horseman!

ANGLE ON KATE

She GASPS, collapses onto a chair, her face in her hands.

MEDIUM ANGLE TO INCLUDE PETER

Peter, who can't resist a pretty face, goes to her and gently pats her on the shoulder. He looks embarrassedly at the others, as if to say, "Well, it's not my fault if she's emotional!"

PETER Hum, er, is this ghost a friend of yours?

ANGLE ON KATE

She raises her face, stained with tears.

KATE Friend! He's my family's curse!

WIDER ANGLE TO INCLUDE EVERYONE

At the word "curse," Ray visibly perks up. Even Egon gets closer to the group, to listen to Kate's story.

ANGLE ON KATE

KATE My ancestor was the man Washington Irving called Ichabod Crane...

SHIMMER DISSOLVE TO:

EXT WOODED TRAIL - NIGHT - ESTABLISHING SHOT
A lone horseman is riding through the moonlit woods. In the b.g. we HEAR the approaching THUNDER of HOOFBEATS.

KATE (VO - CONT) One night, in the Catskills, Irving heard the tale of poor Uncle Ichabod, and how he brought upon himself the wrath of the Headless Horseman...

ANGLE ON ICHABOD

as he turns his head to see who is following him. A look of pure TERROR crosses his face.

ICHABOD'S POV

Rapidly approaching is the nightmarish sight of the HEAD-LESS HORSEMAN, a flaming pumpkin held high in his hand.

WIDER ANGLE

Ichabod is urging his horse to go faster, but in vain. The Horseman is getting closer and closer.

KATE (VO - CONT) As Uncle Ichabod felt the Horseman's hot breath approaching the back of his neck...

A bridge comes in sight and with barely a second to spare, Ichabod urges his horse across.

KATE (VO - CONT) ...he ran, faster and faster, to the far side of the bridge, knowing full well the next moment could very well be his last... ANGLE ON HORSEMAN

He stops dead at the foot of the bridge, and is quite obviously furious. He rears his horse on its hind legs, then throws the pumpkin at the retreating Ichabod.

ANGLE ON PUMPKIN

It EXPLODES in front of the CAMERA, causing a FADE TO WHITE, followed by a

SHIMMER DISSOLVE TO:

INT KATE'S APARTMENT

The Ghostbusters listen in rapture to Kate's story.

KATE (CONT) The next morning, Ichabod was nowhere to be found. Out by the bridge, the townspeople found the broken-down old nag he'd been riding...

SHIMMER DISSOLVE TO:

EXT BRIDGE - DAY
A group of TOWNSPEOPLE stands at the foot of the bridge, where Ichabod's horse is munching on some grass.

CAMERA TRUCKS IN to highlight broken pieces of pump-kin, and Ichabod's hat, scattered on the bridge.

KATE (VO - CONT) ... And some pieces of a shattered pumpkin, scattered around on the bridge floor... WIPE TO:
EXT RIVER - DAY

Ichabod is pulling himself out of the river, wet but alive.

KATE (VO - CONT) But what Washington Irving didn't know, or chose not to tell, was that Uncle Ichabod had escaped the fury of the Horseman...

CUT TO:

EXT COUNTRY ROAD - DAY
Ichabod is walking away on a lonely country road, never looking back.

KATE (VO - CONT) However, he chose to move and never return to his little Catskills village...

CUT TO:

INT EARLY AMERICAN HOUSE - DAY
An older Ichabod, and his wife proudly look at a baby.

KATE (VO - CONT) Eventually, he married and had a son, and they lived happily ever after. But...

SHIMMER DISSOLVE TO:

INT KATE'S APARTMENT
CLOSE UP on the Ghostbusters' eager faces.

ALL OF THEM But? Yes? Yes?...

ANGLE ON KATE

KATE Twenty years later, on the anniversary of the date Uncle Ichabod had first met the Horseman, the Ghost returned...

SHIMMER DISSOLVE TO:

EXT EARLY AMERICAN TOWN - NIGHT
The Headless Horseman, dressed in the period's clothes, pursues a man who looks like he could be Ichabod's SON.

EXT BRIDGE
Ichabod's son rides over a bridge, which causes the Ghost to stop, SCREAM SILENTLY in anger and gallop away.

KATE (VO - CONT) Like his father, Ichabod's son found that the Ghost could not pursue him over running water...

SHIMMER DISSOLVE TO:

INT KATE'S APARTMENT

RAY (to Egon) Ha! You see, it's the ionization factor. I told you so.

Peter shoots him a dark glance.

PETER Shhsh!

SHIMMER DISSOLVE TO:

EXT EARLY AMERICAN TOWN - DAY

KATE (VO) When the Ghost began to pursue his friends, Ichabod's son decided to move, since this seemed to be the only cure...

A QUICK SERIES OF SHOTS

now depict the Headless Ghost chasing various descendents (male or female) of Ichabod Crane, in different cities and different times -- but always at night.

As we are going forward in time to the present, the Ghost's and the victim's costumes change to represent the respective periods during which the action takes place.

Somewhere around 1920, as car transportation becomes more common, the Ghost now appears on a motorcycle.

KATE (VO - CONT) Ever since, the Headless Horseman has pursued my family and our friends, forcing us to move again, and again...

SHIMMER DISSOLVE TO:

INT KATE'S APARTMENT
The Ghostbusters shake their heads in sympathy.

ANGLE ON KATE

KATE (CONT) ... And now it's after me!

She gets up and goes to the bay window. Through it, we definitely see the shape of the QUEENSBORO BRIDGE.

KATE (CONT) Living next to a bridge isn't good enough. It's going after my friends. First, Bud, then yourselves...

She walks back to the center of the room and faces them bravely.

KATE (CONT) I guess I'll just have to move...

ANGLE ON PETER

He jumps to his feet, and rushes to her.

PETER Of course, you won't! Remember, we're the Ghost-busters. Busting ghosts is what we do for a living. There's no reason why this ghost should prove more difficult than any of the thousands of other ghosts we've busted!

ANGLE ON EGON

looking at his PKE meter.

EGON Actually, there is. This ghost packs more energy than...

WIDER ANGLE TO INCLUDE PETER AND EGON

Peter rushes to Egon's side and covers his partner's mouth, in spite of Egon's vehement denegations.

PETER I mean, no serious reason.

EGON Mumble, frumble, grumble.

Peter then walks back to the center of the room.

PETER Okay, gang, it's settled. We're going to take care of the young lady's pesky paraphysical pest. Besides, it's for a good cause!

ANGLE ON RAY

RAY (moved) Yeah, she deserves a break.

ANGLE ON PETER

PETER (genuinely surprised) What?

WIDER ANGLE ON EVERYONE

246

RAY (pointing at Kate) I said, she deserves a break.

PETER (annoyed by what he perceives to be Ray's lack of sympathy) Oh yeah, that too. But I meant me! Clearing my good name. That should count for something too!

ANGLE ON RAY

His face bears a puzzled look, as if the idea had never crossed his mind.

DISSOLVE TO:

INT GHOSTBUSTERS LAB - DAY
CLOSE UP on a newspaper cutting showing a picture of Frump being interviewed. Above the photo is a large headline saying "FRUMP PROMISES ARRESTS SOON."

SUDDENLY a large, dart ZIPS into frame, and plants itself smack dab on Frump's forehead.

CAMERA TRUCKS OUT to reveal that Peter has thrown the dart, and is preparing to throw another. In the b.g., Egon and Ray are busy tinkering with various bits of scientific equipment. Winston is trying to help.

ANGLE ON WINSTON

He is carrying a tray containing microchips, while Slimer is rubbing up against him and trying to get him to play.

WINSTON Come on now, be a good boy and let Daddy work.

JANINE (VO) (shrieking) You can't just barge in there like that!

FRUMP (VO) (assuredly) You wanna bet?

ANGLE ON SLIMER

At the sound of Frump's VOICE, he takes off for parts unknown.

WIDER ANGLE

The Ghostbusters stop what they're doing to watch the door, which opens wide to admit Frump. Behind him, Janine is partly visible, looking slightly red in the face.

FRUMP (CONT) Listen up, you Bozos! I wanted to be the one to tell you that you've got the honor of having my full, personal attention...

During the rest of the scene, through A SERIES OF CUTS, we see Peter casually sidling towards the dart board, in an effort to retrieve Frump's photo before it can be noticed.

Meanwhile, Frump is walking around, touring the work tables. His first stop is Egon's station. He peers at the various bits of electronics machinery spread on it.

FRUMP (fake friendly) What have we here? Preparing to let some ghosts loose, are we?

ANGLE ON EGON

Egon raises his nose in disdain, but says nothing.

ANGLE ON FRUMP

Frump now meanders over to Ray, who looks like he is working on an old fashioned crystal radio set.

FRUMP (CONT) Maybe to clean up a few loose ends at the...
Police Department?! ANGLE ON RAY

Ray attempts to quell Frump's suspicions.

RAY (superior) Really, Lieutenant. If we wanted to get rid of
you, we wouldn't put this blue plug into the red socket, we
would put the green plug into the red socket...

MEDIUM ANGLE TO INCLUDE EGON

EGON (interrupting) But that's what you're supposed to do,
Ray. The green plug always goes into the red socket.

RAY (surprised) Are you sure?

He tries it, we here a loud PFZITT!

RAY (CONT) Oops!

ANGLE ON PETER

He is now standing next to the dart board, and his hand is at
the photo, ready to take it down. Suddenly, Frump's hand
reaches INTO FRAME and grabs it down first.

TWO SHOT ON PETER AND FRUMP

Peter looks like a school boy who has been caught drawing
unflattering pictures of his teacher. Frump pulls a police wanted poster up in the photo's place.

FRUMP How d'ya like that for target practice?

ANGLE ON FRUMP

He then turns and walks out of the room.

CAMERA TRUCKS IN on the poster, revealing that it features the Ghostbusters' faces.

DISSOLVE TO:

EXT KATE'S APARTMENT - DUSK
ESTABLISHING SHOT of the sun setting on Kate's apartment building. In the b.g., we clearly see the QUEENSBORO BRIDGE. CAMERA TRUCKS IN to the bay window of

INT KATE'S APARTMENT
Winston, in full Ghostbuster's equipment, is briefing Bud and Kate.

WINSTON Okay. We're going to go over everything again. We can't afford to have any mistakes.

He points towards two chairs. Attached to the top of each one is something that looks like a hair-dryer helmet sporting parabolic antennae.

ANGLE ON WINSTON

In his hands are sheets of a script. He holds them out to Bud and Kate (OS).

WINSTON Remember. You sit in the chairs, hold hands, and then you read from the script.

ANGLE ON BUD AND KATE

They take the scripts, go over to sit in the chairs, and place the helmets over their heads.

MEDIUM ANGLE

WINSTON (CONT) The way Egon explained it to me, those helmets are going to broadcast your psychograms to the ghost, and draw him here like a fly to honey.

Winston grabs his walkie-talkie to begin checking with the rest of the team.

A QUICK SERIES OF CUTS

EXT STREET - NIGHT
Ray is cruising down the street, at the wheel of Ecto-1.

RAY Check!

EXT QUEENSBORO BRIDGE - NIGHT
Egon is standing next to a ton of fancy equipment at the base of the Bridge.

EGON Check!

INT BASEMENT GARAGE
Peter is wearing a helmet in CLOSE-UP, in someplace that looks like an underground garage.

PETER Yeah, yeah... Check!

INT KATE'S APARTMENT
WINSTON Check!

He switches off his walkie-talkie, lowers the antenna, and puts it back on his belt. Then, he turns to Kate and Bud.

WINSTON (CONT) Okay! It's a go!

ANGLE ON KATE AND BUD

Bud starts reading from his script.

BUD (very stilted) Oh, Kate, my darling. I am so happy to be in the same room with you.

KATE (also stilted) Yes, Bud. My heart throbs passionately as we sit here holding hands.

Bud raises his eyes from the paper.

BUD (condescending) This stuff sucks eggs! Who wrote this drivel?

ANGLE ON WINSTON

He shrugs his shoulders and looks kind of matter of fact.

WINSTON Peter.

ANGLE ON BUD

BUD Nobody talks this way!

ANGLE ON WINSTON

He agrees with Bud, but what can he say.

WINSTON Peter does.

ANGLE ON BUD

He rolls his eyes skyward, then resumes reading the script.

BUD (still stilted) Our two hearts beat...

CUT TO:

EXT STREET - NIGHT
CAMERA TRUCKS IN on Ecto-1 as it patrols around the block.

INT ECTO-1
Ray is driving while looking at a radar-like green screen, which sits on the passenger seat.

CLOSE UP ON SCREEN

where a green blip appears, accompanied by a BEEPING SOUND.

RAY (excited) That's it! That's him!

EXT ECTO-1
In the middle of traffic, Ray makes an almost impossible U-turn, with causes the tires to SQUEAL and WHINE. Then, he peals off in the direction from which he just came.

RAY'S POV

Through the windshield of Ecto-1, we SEE the silhouette of the Headless Motorcyclist in the distance. As Ray gains speed, it gets closer.

EXT STREET
Ray is gaining on the Ghost.

RAY Good girl! We're gaining on him. With a bit of luck, we'll get him before he even gets to the building.

WIDER ANGLE

In front of us is Kate's building. The Ghost makes a hairpin turn into an alley behind the building.

Ray almost misses the turn, but makes it, although he's slower about it because of Ecto-1's greater inertia.

RAY That's it, he's sewn up. This is a dead end!

ANGLE ON MOTORCYCLIST

He reaches the wall of the building, and makes a ninety degree turn -- STRAIGHT UP! He LAUGHS demonically as he drives STRAIGHT UP THE WALLS OF THE BUILDING!.

CAMERA PANS to follow the Ghost up for a few seconds then

UPSHOT to a SHARP ANGLE from the ground, showing the Motorcyclist as he gets smaller and smaller.

ANGLE ON RAY

His head is tilted straight back, as he watches the Ghost's progress.

RAY (amazed) Gee! That ghost is some driver!

CUT TO:

INT KATE'S APARTMENT
Winston is fully armed, proton gun aimed at the bay window.

We HEAR the sound of the engine GROWING LOUDER then, the Ghost comes across the balcony. He reaches the CLOSED windows and drives right THROUGH them.

Winston tries to keep the Motorcyclist at bay with his ion beams, but without success. The Ghost throws a flaming helmet at him, which causes him to duck behind a chair.

WINSTON (yelling) Go on, you two! Part two! Part two!

ANGLE ON BUD AND KATE

They rush out of the apartment into

INT LANDING
They run into the open elevator. The doors close behind them.
Numbers above the door show it is descending.

INT KATE'S APARTMENT
Winston is doing his best to delay the Ghost by shooting a
barrage of ion beams at it.

But the Ghost is able to drive him back with his flaming helmets, until he gets a clear run at the door.

Then, with a ROARING LAUGH, the Headless Motorcyclist
rushes past Winston and THROUGH the door onto

INT LANDING
The Ghost drives straight THROUGH the elevator doors.

CUT TO:

INT BASEMENT GARAGE
The elevators door open. Kate and Bud come rushing out.

CAMERA TRUCKS OUT to reveal a large underground parking lot. Ray stands next to the idling Ecto-1. Peter stands next
to an idling motorcycle.

ANGLE ON PETER

He does not look happy. He is dressed EXACTLY like Bud.
On the motorcycle is a human-size inflatable doll, looking

vaguely like Kate. Various bits of electronic equipment are attached to the doll.

ANGLE ON RAY

He motions to Kate and Bud to hurry.

RAY Quick! Quick!

WIDER ANGLE

Ray ushers them into Ecto-1.

RAY I've turned on the psycho-dampers. As long as you stay in the car, the Ghost won't be able to detect your presence.

ANGLE ON BUD

He crawls into the car.

BUD But how are you going to?...

WIDER ANGLE

Ray points at Peter, who is climbing onto the motorcycle and REVVING UP the engine.

RAY The recorder attached to the dummy is now transmitting the same signals you broadcast earlier...

ANGLE ON PETER

The motorcycle ZOOMS UP the ramp.

RAY (VO - CONT) As far as the Ghost will be able to tell, that's your psycho-imprints leaving.

INT ECTO-1

Ray gets into the car. Kate and Bud are visible in the back seat. KATE Isn't that dangerous? I mean, if the ghost catches up with him...

ANGLE ON RAY

RAY (smiling) Yes, but we drew lots for it and he lost!

EXT STREET - NIGHT

Peter ZOOMS out of the garage, and into the street.

PETER (annoyed) It's another stupid plan!

CUT TO: INT BASEMENT GARAGE

Ray drives Ecto-1 into the shadows. In the b.g., we hear the now-familiar ROARING sound of the Headless Motorcyclist.

RAY Not a minute too soon, I see!

WIDER ANGLE

The Motorcyclist comes out and THROUGH the elevator doors.

CAMERA PANS and follows him as he speeds across the garage, and out the entrance.

INT ECTO-1

Ray grabs a walkie-talkie.

RAY The Eagle is landing!

CUT TO:

EXT QUEENSBORO BRIDGE - NIGHT
Egon is sitting next to his equipment at the foot of the bridge.
He is holding his walkie-talkie.

RAY (VO) The Eagle is landing!

EGON (slightly annoyed) I wish you wouldn't be so melo-
dramatic, Ray. This is just a simple ectoplasmic manifestation
of 12.5 on the Flammarion scale, not some kind of "Aquila
Vulgus."

CUT TO:

INT ECTO-1
Ray folds down the antenna of his walkie-talkie, and looks
slightly wounded.

RAY Well, excuuse me!

INT BASEMENT GARAGE
The elevator doors open, and Winston runs out of them, out of
breath. Ray HONKS at him, and he rushes towards the car and
gets into the passenger seat.

The car BURNS RUBBER as it drives away, up the exit ramp.

EXT STREET
Ecto-1 exits onto the street. CUT TO:

EXT STREET (CLOSER TO THE BRIDGE)
Things are getting hot for Peter. He's ZOOMING along on his
motorcycle. The Ghost is gaining on him, and there are flaming helmets ZIPPING past his handlebars.

PETER This plan is even stupider than I thought. He leans his
head down to a microphone on his collar.

PETER (CONT) Okay, Egon, here we come. I hope that stuff of yours works, or I'm barbecue!

CUT TO:

EXT QUEENSBORO BRIDGE
Egon is standing next to a large circuit-breaker type of switch. One hand is on the switch, and the other is holding a stopwatch. He's wearing a headset.

Suddenly, we HEAR the sounds of the rapidly approaching motorcycles. So does Egon, and he flips down the giant switch.

ANGLE ON EQUIPMENT

Electricity CRACKLES and DANCES over the equipment. CAMERA TRUCKS OUT to encompass the entire bridge. We see the same electricity coursing up wires that hang in front of the entrance to the bridge.

The entire entrance to the bridge SHIMMERS like a mirage, and RECONGEALS to resemble an ordinary avenue.

CUT TO:

INT ECTO-1
Ray is driving with one hand, gesturing with the other.

RAY (lecturing) You can only fight fire with fire, and a curse with a curse. First we trapped the Ghost with the recording of your psychic emissions, then we get him onto the bridge. The laws of Physics take care of the rest.

ANGLE ON KATE

KATE (curious) But, how are you going to get him onto the bridge?

ANGLE ON WINSTON

WINSTON Egon created a hologram that makes the bridge look just like any other street.

CUT TO:

EXT QUEENSBORO BRIDGE
Peter's motorcycle ZOOMS past Egon, and into the fake "street."

Hot in pursuit, the Headless Motorcyclist follows. Suddenly, as he hits the middle of the "street," the Ghost literally FREEZES in his tracks. He SCREAMS in rage.

ANGLE ON EGON

He switches off the hologram.

WIDER ANGLE

The "street" becomes a bridge again.

ANGLE ON MOTORCYCLIST

He's trapped at the very center of the bridge, his form wavering, right next to a GHOST TRAP.

WIDER ANGLE

Ecto-1 arrives at the entrance of the bridge, and stops.

Ray and Winston get out. They are joined by Bud and Kate. They all walk over to join Egon.

ANGLE ON EGON AND KATE

Egon holds the foot pedal.

EGON (very much the gentleman) I think the honor of the final capture should be all yours.

WIDER ANGLE TO INCLUDE EVERYONE

Kate smiles as Egon puts the foot pedal in front of her foot. The others surround her, smiling.

CLOSE UP ON KATE'S FOOT ABOVE THE FOOT PEDAL

She steps on it.

ANGLE ON MOTORCYCLIST

He is SUCKED DOWN into the trap, and the lid SLAMS closed.

WIDER ANGLE

Now that the Ghost is gone, Peter ROARS back across the bridge to join the group. He stops the motorcycle and gets off.

PETER I still think it was a stupid plan!

RIPPLE DISSOLVE TO:

EXT ANOTHER MANHATTAN PENTHOUSE - NIGHT
This is another party, reminiscent of the one at the opening of the show. However, we HEAR the WEDDING MARCH being played.

CAMERA TRUCKS IN to

<u>INT PENTHOUSE</u>
and PANS OVER what is obviously Bud and Kate's wedding party.

CAMERA then TRUCKS IN TO Peter, Ray and the same Banker, all standing next to a buffet table.

RAY Well, I'm glad you decided to sign up with us.

Suddenly, a WOMAN's hand reaches in between them from OUT OF FRAME to take an hors d'oeuvre.

CAMERA PULLS OUT to reveal that it belongs to another very beautiful woman.

Peter turns to follow her as she leaves, but Ray grabs the back of his coat and shoves a plate of food in his hand.

RAY Why can't you just eat at these things like everybody else. It's safer.

Peter shrugs, and bites into a large sandwich as we

FADE OUT:

Following the success of Hellraiser *and* Hellbound: Hellraiser II, *Marvel's Epic Comics imprint began publishing a series of comic book spinoffs for the franchise, under the editorship of Dan Chichester. The series ran from 1989 to 1993, each issue containing a set of short stories, with Clive Barker acting as a consultant on all of them. This is the first of two scripts we did for them; this one appeared in #4, wonderfully illustrated by British artist John Ridgway.*

COMICS

Hellraiser: Blood of a Poet

What I most remember are the smells, the sweet smells of Paris in September, in the year of our Lord 1925.

Now, they call them the "Crazy Years", but they were so much more. They reshaped the Old Order, swept away what little the Great War had left. Paris was the capital of the *Avant-Garde*.

Jazz and the Surrealists reigned on the Rive Gauche. Picasso, whose paintings scandalized the Bourgeois, proudly proclaimed: "I'm not looking, I've found it!"

And I, a naive Midwestern boy who decided to live in the eye of this tornado, sought a bed... Or rather someone willing to take a chance on a struggling , young poet, with no means of support.

I still remember the intoxicating smell of freedom in the air, of futures unbound... of rebirth!

I never think of that smell without seeing the tall, gaunt figure of Jean Cocteau sitting at La Coupole.

His plain-chant had stripped my blood, more than anyone else, he was responsible for my becoming a poet.

Later he wrote about himself and poetry: "...*by pouring my blue ink in them, I made the ghosts turn visible. To say that the task is simple or without danger would be insane, to dare disturb the angels.*"

And that he told me my poems did not do! But what could I know of disturbing the angels when the only thing I had experienced were the pure skies .and golden fields of native Kansas?

I remember casting my eyes around, looking for a sign, any sign. Then I saw it. *The Eye of Pan.*

It was one of the many bookstores in Paris, dabbling in a mixture of poetry and the occult. It was exactly my kind of bookstore.

So, how perfect that it should also advertise rooms to rent, I entered, and there, I saw her....Melanie.

She loved Cocteau, Rimbaud and even Lautreamont, whose *Songs of Maldoror* had been passed around my college in secrecy.

I can still smell her subtle perfume, as it cut through the store's musty air, like a beam of sunlight piercing the clouds.

None of the rooms she suggested were within my meager budget. I asked if she knew of anything else and caught her hesitation.

Whatever she might have said remained unvoiced, silenced by the arrival of her employer. She introduced him as Monsieur Daniel.

He reprimanded her for not telling me of the Pension Veneur, although I cannot now recall if he actually uttered that accursed name. There was no thunderclap, no bolts of lightning in the sky, merely the soft-spoken voice of a young woman; one I did not heed.

Daniel explained that it housed a community of artists who lived there, free under the provisions of a trust arranged by a deceased patron of the arts. He gave me the address and indicated that there had been a recent vacancy.

I clearly remember that he said I would be welcomed with open arms. And so I was.

But I am getting ahead of myself. Those who speak of poets' intuition could not have seen me that day, foe I felt nothing but elation at having found a place to stay. But all that changed as soon as I arrived at the Pension Veneur.

It was located in a tranquil *cul-de-sac* and, at first, I thought it looked like my austere, imposing French bourgeois house, but then I felt an odd sense of finality about it. In the declining light of the day, its facade exuded an air of quiet obdurate hatred towards its surroundings, the kind of hatred that ugliness often feels towards beauty. I thought of the snout of an obstinate, evil beast, just standing there, refusing to heed his master's voice, meeting him instead with waves of silent loathing. "I am the ultimate challenge," it seemed to proclaim. "dreadful shall be the harm to your soul if you dare come nigh".

Still, the hour was late, and passing another damp night beneath a bridge held no charm. The concierge was a gnome-like creature, whose name, I later learned, was Sebaud. At first he looked at me with suspicion, but when I mentioned M. Daniel, his eyes cleared, and he confirmed that indeed, there had been an unexpected vacancy.

He offered to take me to Monsieur Barsac, the director, who would decide whether I could stay.

I recall as if it were yesterday his unhealthy wheezing as we climbed the great marble stair-way lined with old-fashioned oil paintings. He caught my questioning glance, and volunteered that they were portraits of the Veneur family.

Now, of course, I well know the reason for the strange scratches on the paintings, but then.... Then I was but a naive Midwestern boy...

Sebaud told me that Barsac, like myself, was an author, as I had never heard of him, I asked what he had written.

"Monsieur Barsac does not so much write as record," chuckled Sebaud, leaving me to puzzle his meaning.

I confess to forming an immediate antipathy for Barsac, although his invitation to enter was perfectly congenial. Sebaud, he curtly dismissed.

Our conversation remained on a formal level. He spouted several banalities about having himself once been a young starving writer. There was a faint, fetid smell to his apartment, which reminded me of the office of Mr. Christian, our town's undertaker, yet, everything appeared well polished and clean.

I no longer recall what I said, but my credentials must have satisfied him for he offered me a small studio on the top floor.

He led me up to the top floor, towards one of those narrow service stairway the French call "*l'escalier de la bonne*" – the maid's stairs. I couldn't get that smell out of my nostrils.

And then, in that confined space, I realized from where it came. Him!

Barsac explained the pension's rules, which were few: dinner at eight, no overnight guests. And, due to the nature of the trust, there was an obligation to produce art while living on the premises.

I began to reassure him that I had every intention of becoming a famous poet, but he told me not to concern myself with that, apparently, no one else did.

After the dark corridor, the cozy little studio felt like heaven, besides, it was free, what else would you have done? I took it.

The tradition of the Pension Veneur required formal attire to be worn a dinner, which was held in the great *salle à manger* – the dining room. There, Barsac introduced me to the other artists of the residence.

I thought I detected a note of contempt in his voice as he made the presentation.

Legrand, a stout vital painter, heartily chewing on meat that looked disgustingly rare.

Mademoiselle Curval, a blonde waif-like sculptress, who seemed cold and remote, as she ate without passion.

Mathieu, an old musician, whose eyes were glazed and who muttered to himself...

And finally, Restif, an engineer whose passion was automata and clock-work toys.

It was he who first broke the strained silence, offering to show me his wondrous singing birds.

"Whose birds? Yours – or Lemarchand's?" interrupted Legrand sarcastically.

I did not understand the reference, but it obviously infuriated Restif, for the two men began to argue, until Barsac stopped it with a few , curt, unchallenged words.

That was when Mlle Curval complained to Sebaud about her meat. So he was not only concierge and butler, but cook as well. I thought it interesting.

"We still whip dogs in this house," said Barsac to no one in particular. But somehow, we all knew whom he meant.

Never before had I seen such pure hatred radiate from a man as I saw from Sebaud that night.

When we reached the *consommé*, I asked Mlle Curval about her sculptures, but elicited very little response. No one appeared interested in discussing their work, except for Legrand, who made another of his cryptically sarcastic remarks:

"Oh, but we're all quite famous in certain quarters," he said with an annoying chuckle.

That's when Barsac told him he had enough wine.

Suddenly, something seemed to grip Mathieu. He began shaking violently, spewing soup everywhere.

Petit mal, I thought, an epileptic fit.

He babbled incoherently about a plate of doves' heads.

Barsac remarked that Mathieu had been working too hard lately and apologized on his behalf. I caught Legrand shaking his head in bemused tolerance, the way a teacher would at a student's prank.

Sebaud entered and dragged the poor wretch from the room. Perhaps they are playing tricks with my memory, and none of this happened, but that is how I recall my first dinner at the Pension Veneur.

That first night, as I worked on a new poem, I dozed off and beheld monstrous visions such as I had never seen before.

Could these have been the angels Cocteau had advised me to disturb?

I woke up and immediately began committing these images to paper, engaging in what the surrealists called Automatic Writing. My nerves still tingled, and such action proved excruciatingly painful, yet I persevered.

Slowly, blood began to seep from beneath my fingernails.

Finally, I could stand it no longer, I screamed...

...and woke up. It was yet another dream, my fingers were unharmed.

...but fresh blood stained my notebook.

Then, I heard another scream. Was I still dreaming?

As I reached the door, I stopped, for in the pallid light, something had suddenly caught my eye.

A name was scratched into the frame...

PAQUET.

The Tao says "*a man dreams that he is a butterfly, when he awakes, he is not sure if he is a man who dreamed he was a butterfly, or a butterfly who dreams he is a man.*"

And that best describes how I felt that first night, as slowly, I sank, body and soul, into the stygian depths of the Pension Veneur.

Dawn brought small succor.

I had decided I would try to learn more about the mysterious Paquet. My first step was to stop by Sebaud's loge.

He did not welcome my inquiries, and indeed, appeared to rebuff them.

Only my insistence caused him to relent, and reveal that Paquet was the previous owner of the studio.

Still, no matter how hard I tried, I could not extract more information that that from him. Mulling this, I decided to ask Barsac.

However, my knock yielded no answer. Did he ignore me, or did he just sleep soundly, I never learned.

Then, I noticed that the next door over was ajar, it was Restif's apartment. Already, unconscious fears burrowed through my subconscious, causing me to become suspicious... Otherwise, what could have possessed my to enter it uninvited?

Was it oil, grease, or some kind of monstrous ichor that oozed from the spilled guts if Restif's mechanical creations? The whirr of the cogs droned on, in an endless mockery of life. And there in the center of it all...

How does a young bird react to its first snake? Can our souls recognize things our eyes have never beheld? I approached the thing, and never saw Restif come in behind me.

Wordlessly, he threw a sheet over it. There was an odd respect to his gesture. I muttered some words of apology, though these fell on deaf ears.

But I had not forgotten my original purpose; I asked about Paquet.

"He went. They all went", he replied, dismissively.

"They all went?"

The friendly eccentric of the previous night had turned into a wall of solid indifference.

I was about to press for more, when the sound of Barsac's voice coming from just over my shoulder caused me to jump.

With his usual curt tone, he sent a grumbling Restif scurrying. It all seemed so banal on the surface.

As trivial as Barsac's eventual explanations about Paquet, given later that morning, as he led me past Sebaud's watchful eyes. After all this time, I have forgotten what they were, but I do recall they were rendered utterly unbelievable by the oppressive atmosphere of the Pension Veneur.

In the street, the suffocating environment of the Pension seemed unreal. I breathed long and deep, cleaning my lungs of the miasmic atmosphere that held sway within. I felt a pressure upon my breast, the gentle nudge of a close friend... my notebook...

Looking in the cold unmerciful light of the day upon the poem I had written the night before, I found it beautiful, powerful and at the same time, frightful and terrible!

Could it truly have been me, the innocent American boy, who had written such monstrous verse? Had my night's feverish visions (for what else could they be?) inspired me to such heights?

My almost somnambulic meandering somehow led me back to *The Eye of Pan...* To Melanie and to her ever-so-helpful employer, Monsieur Daniel. He recognized me as I entered, and probably felt bound by convention to ask if I liked my new home.

My sour face must have told him much about my feelings. I quite clearly recall mentioning how unsatisfied I was with Barsac's explanation of Paquet's disappearance.

Daniel rose to the defense, making preposterous claims about Barsac's respectability...

He had started spinning a yarn when another client forced him to abandon me to my own designs, which suited me just fine.

The one I had really come to see stepped from behind a shelf, and told me that Daniel was lying, which, even then, I remember, came as no great surprise to me.

What I did not know, however, and what I learned that day from Melanie's whisper in my ear, was that Daniel was Sebaud's brother!

It was then that I understood how he had come to send me to the pension, but not yet why.

Melanie told me of other young, struggling artists sent there before me, but none had ever been seen, or heard from again! That was to come later.

Melanie's curiosity, had made her distrustful of the mysterious Pension Veneur, hence her earlier reluctance to send me there.

As Restif had said, "they all went."

We agreed to meet the following day—her day off—at the Luxembourg Gardens.

That night, dinner was, if anything, more bizarre and repulsive than before. Restif was furious at not being able to assemble or disassemble something... a machine perhaps? There was much I must have missed.

"Lemarchand could do it, why can't I?" he shouted.

But one thing I could never forget: that name.

Barsac tried to get him to shut up, but Restif would not be silenced. Legrand called him a "*bricoleur*"—a tinkerer.

Mathieu had another fit, but no one seemed to care, or notice. Dear Lord, no one even lifted a finger to help him.

He rolled on the floor, frothing, foaming. I turned for help, but Legrand and Curval were fighting, shouting the foulest obscenities, emitting animal-like grunts. And yet, it looked like a ritual? At last Mathieu lay still.

I didn't dare approach him. I was afraid to know. Instead, like the lamb who detects the tiger's arrival from its rank breath.

I ran away.

That second night, the fragile bound'ries 'tween my soul and the horrors which suffused the Pension Veneur just crumbled away, As my brain burned, I tried to shut out the visions, but in vain. I cursed the white hot flow of words that tried to escape through my bleeding fingers.

I sought only to reach the cool refuge of the darkness outside. As I ran from my room, the name on the door mockingly reminded me of the as yet unguessed fate which lay ahead.

On the second floor, I noticed that a door was ajar, light spilled out into the darkness, It was Legrand's room.

I hesitated but a moment.

The room was filled with weird, obscene paintings and sculptures, none of them were as sickening as its two human occupants.

Barely bothering to stop their loathsome behavior, they invited me in. Curval even dared suggest that I join them. I shrank back in terror.

Legrand called me a fool and a coward. He bragged that all the Pension's residents purveyed works of a nature so filthy and perverse, I could barely comprehend it. Their creations commanded high prices from secret collectors whose depraved tastes thrived on such abominations.

He taunted me, calling me a hypocrite, turning up my nose at them, yet drinking from the same source.

I ran to my room, their foul, mocking laughter still ringing in my ears. Had I truly accepted the meaning of his words, I could still have escaped the Pension's insidious trap.

But as I looked at my night's work, I saw that, as morbid and decadent as it was, my poetry had gained a life and strength it had never had before.

I felt an elation which horrified me more than the poetry itself. The Pension was nurturing my creativity into some gnarled and twisted shapes. What was the cost for this new-found excellence? Was I becoming a monster, like the others? Was that what had happened to Paquet?

The next morning, I saw a hearse and two undertakers outside. I was not the least bit surprised. Death seemed a natural visitor to the Pension Veneur.

I asked Sebaud, who revealed that Mathieu had killed himself during the night. He feigned the unctuous compassion which he quite obviously did not feel.

The two undertakers were *croque-morts*—crunchers of the dead--the colorful name the French give to those traffickers in death.

I overheard one remark that he'd never seen anyone do themselves in such a horrible way. The other replied about a case he'd once seen. They ghoulishly began to compare notes.

Barsac and Legrand stood nearby, watching the proceedings. As I walked past them, I caught a shred of their conversation:

"I thought he'd never go!" Barsac said.

I met Melanie in the Luxembourg Gardens. The bright sunny afternoon made the horrors of the Pension look even more unreal. Melanie told me the Pension Veneur used to belong to a man named Lemarchand. A strange maker of puzzle boxes and other weird mechanical wonders, someone with a decidedly unsavory reputation. One day, he disappeared. No one knew how, why or where.

For all she knew, Lemarchand might have been the founder of the trust that kept the Pension going. The house itself was built upon the catacombs: bone powder was mixed into its very mortar, blood used in its cement. A house of death, a house of pain.

She urged me not to return, I felt compelled to go.

I knew then, that if I remained at the Pension, I could become the best poet who had ever lived.

That was my calling, I suppose it could be said that it was in my blood. I never saw her again, but I like to think that she cried as I ran back to the Pension in the rapidly falling dusk.

Later, I confronted Barsac in his apartment. He was expecting the encounter. In his eyes, I was a resourceful young man, but a fool, nonetheless.

He freely admitted that each of the Pension's residents was beholden to something or someone he called the *Cenobites*.

They wished us all to produce work of so horrifying a nature that few but those hellish creatures could even manage to stand its sight. In exchange, they allowed the artists to sell some of the lesser pieces on that abominable black market, where it still fetched incredible prices.

And speaking of prices, there was a price to pay.

"A small one," Barsac said.

The Cenobites periodically required the delivery of new victims, hence the disappearances of Paquet and the other young artists who had preceded me.

The time had come to honor the age-old bargain; summon the Cenobites to take possession of their new offerings.

I tried to leap at Barsac, but Legrand and Restif suddenly seized me. I felt that same wretched helplessness which must be felt by the man on the guillotine, as he waits for the blade to fall.

Locked up in my studio, I scratched my name on the door, as a futile warning to those who would follow me. Suddenly, I heard a voice, Sebaud's. He said I did not have to share in the fate of the others.

I was different. Somehow, he had found my notebook and read my poems. I had become the troubadour of blood and pain. Barsac had erred by allowing me to join the Pension.

"In your heart you know what you must do," he said.

Then, he left, but he had been right.

In my heart, I knew what I must do.

So help me God, I knew.

Acting on Barsac's request, Restif activated the mysterious device in the cellars of the Pension.

I was tied on chair, watching impotently. Tied—but not muzzled

Lemarchand's cursed machine accomplished its wondrous, devilish work.

The Cenobites arrived. They brought a fitful phosphorescence, like a glow of deep-sea life, and a smell if vanilla, which barely hid the stench beneath.

I welcomed them with an impassioned speech.

I no longer damned the flow of mad poetry which welled within me. Oh, Cocteau , if you could have heard me then. Not only did I disturb your precious angels, but I shredded their silken wings and drank their heavenly ichor. I became the Cenobites' perfect instrument, glorifying the only feelings which they could still experience. I proved I could serve them better than Barsac, a dried-out husk; like Mathieu, an empty vessel, fit only to be discarded.

The Cenobites stopped.

Barsac began to rant, He shouted at them to take me.

But I showed them how to transmute pain into beauty...

...and to this, even the mighty Cenobites paused to listen.

I knew then that I had won. They moved towards Barsac. Terrified, he uttered a small animal whine, then turned and fled.

Legrand and Curval might as well have been made of stone, for they moved not an inch to aid him.

Not so Sebaud, who remembered old accounts yet to be settled, and tripped him as he tried to escape.

My last memory of that fateful night was of the Cenobites dragging Barsac away to whatever fate I had undoubtedly invoked for him in my demented verses.

Then mercifully, I lost consciousness.

The morning sun woke me, and found me in my bed. Fleetingly I prayed it had all been a nightmare, yet knew perfectly well the horrible truth.

Sebaud welcomed me, and told me Barsac's apartment would be ready for me to move into by early that evening.

I tried to explain I had only followed his mad advice to save my life, I did not want to become like Barsac. But he said I had no choice. It was to become my destiny.

I fled to the streets to escape his monstrous honesty. He yelled after me—"dinner at eight, young master!"

I ran towards the one and only person whom I thought could still save me from that abyss... Melanie!

Daniel was alone. I asked about her.

He threw his arms up in the air, in a typical gallic shrug.

"It is a big *malheur*, Monsieur!" he said, an unfortunate event.

She had died that morning, stabbed by a mugger, an innocent victim of the city's madness.

The rest of his sanctimonious clichés were drowned out by the sound of the brass gates of hell closing upon my cold heart.

They called them the "Crazy Years."

But the year before, in Munich, an obscure German political party had held its first congress—the Nazi party...

In the Soviet Union, Josef Stalin had become general secretary of the Communist party...

A quiet, German scientist named Albert Einstein was presently mulling thoughts that would someday explode the light of a thousand suns over Japan...

And I, no longer naive and innocent, I...

I moved into the Pension Veneur.

This is the original, far more ambitious, plot that was written for Alfredo Castelli, which eventually morphed into L'Ombra di Fantômas *in Martin Mystere's* Almanaco del Misterio 2012.

Martin Mystere: The Treasure of the Black Coats

THE VATICAN. 1769.

It is night. We are in the Vaults of the Vatican, where all the most precious and secret treasures of the Church are kept.

Two figures enter. One is a handsome, dark-haired, evil-faced man in his thirties: IL COLONNNELLO MICHELE BOZZO, a.k.a. "Bel Demonio," the current leader of the Bastia crime family and future leader of the Camorra.

The other man is a SWISS GUARD (his name is unimportant), who has secretly let Colonel Bozzo in.

They walk amongst the accumulated treasures of centuries.

The Guard says to the Colonel: "Now my little girl will be safe, eh?" making it clear that Bozzo used some kind of odious blackmail to force his way in.

They reach a glass case, which is inside an iron cage.

Bozzo smiles an evil smile.

"She is at peace," he replies, as the Guard unlocks the cage.

The Guard, worried by what the Colonel has said, turns – and Bozzo plunges a long dagger inside the man's chest, adding, "...and you shall now join her!"

The Guard dies, moaning:

"I was a fool to trust you, you whom they call Bel Demonio... Fra Diavolo..."

Then he dies.

The Colonel carefully opens the case. Inside is the SCAPULAR: basically a pendant, decorated with some ornate, cabalistic markings. Clearly, it is meant to contain something inside, but we don't see that.

The Colonel grabs the Scapular: "From the hands of Gerbert d'Aurillac to mine... Life without end..." he whispers.

We end the sequence on a CLOSE-UP of the Scapular.

SARTENE, THE CONVENT OF LA MERCI. NOVEMBER 1890.

We open the sequence on the same, identical CLOSE-UP of the Scapular.

It is now hanging on the chest of an ancient-looking Colonel Bozzo. In fact, he is over 150-years old! He looks very old but his eyes and his face radiate intelligence, cunning and power.

The Colonel closes his shirt. "As per the Law of our Brotherhood," he says, "I wear the Scapular of La Merci and therefore, I am Master here. None may deny me. So say I."

He sits at the head of a long table. Behind him is the MARCHEF, a tall, hulkish man wearing an executioner's hood, his henchman. On the wall behind is a classic painting, the portrait of a youngish man, who looks a bit like Martin Mystere. It is entitled: "PORTRAIT OF REMY D'ARX" by Ingres.

Around the table are eight members of the High Council of the Black Coats. To the right of the Colonel is COUNT CORONA, an older but still energetic man, looking evil and depraved. The other seven characters are: (i) COLONEL MORAN, a sturdy English businessman with a mustache, (ii) LECOQ a.k.a. TOULONNAIS L'AMITIÉ, a dandy Frenchman (iii) a fat bishop, (iv) the COUNTESS DE CLARE, a very beautiful blonde aristocratic woman, (v) VISCOUNT GIOJA, an older Corsican nobleman looking like old Casanova in the Fellini film, (vi) SALADIN, a Clark Gable-type rogue, and (vii) a Germanic "Herr Doktor"-type.

Somewhere during this sequence, we shall cut to an outside/exterior view of the Convent of the Brotherhood of Mercy, which is located on a cliff overlooking the sea, near Sartene in Corsica.

"None may deny him. So say we all," the assembly replies, respectfully and dutifully.

"You seem in good health, godfather," says Gioja.

The Colonel smiles benevolently. "Thank you, thank you, my dove." He looks and talks like an old avuncular grandfather. "It is very kind of you to say so... I'm sure I won't be in this world much longer, my children... This will be my last affair, I think..."

L'Amitié whispers to the Countess: "The old rascal. He's old as Methuselah and still he pulls this same trick every time."

The Colonel heard him. The man of steel suddenly emerges from behind the mask of the kindly old man. "You should respect your elders, L'Amitié. I can still teach you a thing or two," he says. "As I taught your father and your grandfather before you."

The Colonel turns towards Count Corona to his right. "My memory isn't what it used to be, Corona, my boy. Please refresh it by recapping the matter at hand today."

Corona says: "The business will take place on December 26. The Archeologist Schliemann will be staying at the Grand Hotel in Naples. He will have the Golden Apple with him. Our man is already in place, ready to strike."

"Very good, very good," says the Colonel, patting Corona's hand. "Daring. Bold. Just like me when I was your age. I was right to entrust you with this. You're my favorite son."

"How do we *pay the law*?" asks Moran.

The Colonel replies: "Colonel Moran is right, Corona. I should have thought of asking you first. *Sangodemi!* I grow forgetful. Tell us how we *pay the law.*"

Corona coldly pulls a photo of two characters: one is a 20ish-year-old, the other a 10-year-old boy. They look like they are brothers. They are respectively CIGALE and CIGALE'S OLDER BROTHER (who looks like Martin Mystere).

Corona explains: "This is a photograph of two orphaned boys who were forced to leave France after having stolen a few francs from their employer, a heartless miser and swindler who was abusing the youngest child. They will make perfect scapegoats."

Saladin says: "What is the Police ask too many questions? The Neapolitans are no fools. They will soon realize the boy is innocent."

"They will not have a chance to question them," replies Corona. "They will be discovered to have fled after having stabbed the officer sent to arrest them."

The Bishop: "You mean?..."

Corona: "Yes. To everyone's eyes, it will look like a daring escape, but their bodies will feed the fishes in the bay of Naples that very night."

The Countess: "Their bodies—plural?"

Corona: "The younger boy too. We can't leave any witnesses behind."

Herr Doktor: "What if someone comes looking for the boys later?"

Corona turns towards the Colonel, angry at being interrogated by the others. "Godfather, I thought I was to be solely in charge of this matter..."

But the Colonel is distracted. All this time, he has been lost in the contemplation of the photograph.

We show that the boys bear a resemblance to the portrait of Remy d'Arx hanging on the wall behind.

Corona: "Godfather? Godfather?"

We end the sequence on a CLOSE-UP of the portrait.

NEW YORK. THE GUGGENHEIM MUSEUM. TODAY.

We open the sequence on a CLOSE-UP of the same Portrait of Remy d'Arx by Ingres (1836).

It is part of an exhibition of French Masters at the Guggenheim Museum. We now are at the opening cocktail reception.

Amongst the crowds milling about are the current COUNTESS DE CLARE, a stunning British blonde, and the descendent of L'AMITIÉ, a dashing but sinister, dark-haired Frenchman.

MARTIN MYSTERE and DIANA are looking at the painting. Martin is dressed in a tuxedo and Diana wears a stunning haute-couture dress.

Diana: "He looks a bit like you, don't you think?"

Martin: "Oh, I don't think so..." He looks more closely. "Maybe the eyes," he concedes. He still appears unconvinced.

A white-tuxedoed waiter appears with champagne glasses on a tray and offers them to Martin and Diane, who each take a glass and continue talking.

Martin sees JAVA, dressed in a tuxedo one size too small, eating all the food off a buffet table under the horrified eyes of another waiter.

Martin looks at his watch and observes it's time to go home as he has lots of work to do the next day.

The trio walks out of the Museum and onto the sidewalk. It is night. Across the street is Central Park.

A tall valet whistles to summon cabs one at a time when the guests come out. L'Amitié and the Countess are behind Martin and Diana, but our heroes do not notice them.

A cab arrives. There's no room in it for Java obviously, so he'll have to take the next one.

Diana gets in first, then Martin sits in the cab and tells the driver their home address (Washington Mews). He looks at the cab driver when the man turns his head slightly to check traffic. It is the waiter from the Museum—the current MARCHEF, a big, burly Frenchman, the Foreign Legion-type.

Martin's frown shows first puzzlement, then concern – then we end this sequence with an ALL-BLACK panel as they both lose consciousness.

NEW YORK. BLACKSPEAR HOLDINGS TOWER

Martin comes to. He is sitting in a comfy period arm-chair. He is in what appears to be a salon in a French late-18th or early-19th century castle.

On the wall to his right is a giant fireplace, with a roaring fire. Above the mantelpiece is a period Venetian mirror. The walls are wood paneled with antique paintings hanging on them. Behind Martin is a wall-to-wall bookcase and leather armchairs. To his left is a French billiard table, and the double-doors leading into the room. In front of him is a massive, sculpted oak desk. Behind the desk is the COLONEL, looking exactly the same as he was in 1890. Behind the Colonel is another wood paneled wall with built-in shelves to the right and left with previous artifacts inside.

The painting on the wall is that of the Convent of the Brotherhood of Mercy in Sartene by the famous Corsican painter Lucien Péri (1880-1948).

In the room with Martin and the Colonel are LECOQ/TOULONNAIS L'AMITIÉ, who is practicing shots on the billiard table, and the COUNTESS DE CLARE, standing by the fireplace, looking very elegant and sexy. Behind the Colonel is the MARCHEF (waiter/taxi driver).

The Colonel: "I must apologize for having brought you here in such a cavalier fashion, Dr. Mystere..."

Martin: "Diana? What have you done to her?"

The Colonel makes an appeasing gesture. "Please, do not worry. Right now, she is at home, waking up, just like you. She will find a note telling her that you will be returned to her in just an hour. You have my word on it."

Martin has now fully recovered his senses. He looks around, notices L'Amitié and the Countess.

Martin: "I saw you at the exhibit. Who are you?"

The Colonel answers instead. "These are my, er, associates. The beautiful lady is Frances, Countess of Clare..."she nods "And the gentleman to your left is Monsieur Julien Lecoq a.k.a. L'Amitié. I am Colonel Bozzo-Corona."

Martin: "What do you want from me?"

The Colonel: "Before we get into that, you must first lean who we truly are... Let me ask you a question. Have you heard of the Black Coats?"

Martin frowns. "It was some kind of criminal society that operated throughout Europe in the early part of the 19th century, no? The French *feuilletoniste* Paul Féval wrote several novels about them, before he lost all his savings and became a born-again Christian and denounced his earlier works which, he thought, glorified evil..."

The Colonel smiles. "Not bad, not bad at all... Your knowledge is impressive. Yes, Monsieur Féval wrote about us. We had to bankrupt him, utterly destroy him, because he knew too much, he was getting too close..."

Martin (surprised): "About you? You mean, you are...?"

The Colonel: "We have gone by many names. In my youth, in Corsica, we were known as the Brotherhood of La Merci... In Napoli, we were the Camorra, in France the Habits Noirs, in London, the Gentlemen of the Night, in Germany, the Vehmgerichte... We were always drawn to the sites of power and wealth... From Napoli we moved to Paris, then to London, and then after the Great War, to this modern Babylon... New York... where we are now... (to L'Amitié) What do we call ourselves these days, my boy?"

Lecoq: "A holding company, godfather."

The Colonel: "Yes, a holding company. That's what we are now. Blackspear Holdings. I'm getting too old for this. This will be my last affair, you know..."

Martin: "If you really are the Black Coats, or their successors, surely you should know that I would never willingly assist any criminal organization."

The Colonel: "Yes, yes... Of course... But we are quite legitimate now, or so my Law Professor tells me... Dr. Mystere... What do you know of Gerbert d'Aurillac?"

Martin: "The man who became Pope Sylvester II in the year 999 AD.... A sorcerer... He built a bronze head which contained something that he had acquired from the Nine Unknown, and which would answer his questions with yes or no. They say it was the same gift that enabled Rabbi Loew to animate the Golem... The head told Gerbert that if he should ever read a mass in Jerusalem, the Devil would come for him. He then cancelled a pilgrimage to Jerusalem, but when he read a mass in the church of Saint Mary of Jerusalem in Rome, he became sick soon afterwards and, dying, he asked his cardinals to cut up his body and scatter it across the city... As for the head, it was never found..."

The Colonel: "That was a lie. His successor took the Head apart and the gift of the Nine was locked inside a Scapular, which was kept deep inside the vaults of the Vatican. More than 200 years ago, that Scapular came into my possession..."

Martin: "Into your possession..."

The Colonel: "Come on, Dr. Mystère, a man with your, er, colorful background has come in contact with a great many wonders... Cagliostro... The Elixir of Life... The Philosopher's Stone are no mysteries for you... What is inside the Scapular is the essence of life itself... Yes, it was I who wrested it away from the Church, I who built the Black Coats, and rules them still... We now call it the Scapular of La Merci... It is our most sacred possession... Whosoever wears it is Master of the Black Cots and, directly or indirectly, controls all the criminal empires of the world..."

The enormity of the matter is beginning to sink in.

Martin: "I think I'm beginning to understand..."

The Colonel continues: "What if the Scapular were to fall into the hands of someone like OHISVER MULLER?"

Martin: "Ohisver Muller disappeared in the failure of the Osaka Experiment on December 31, 1999. No one has seen him since."

The Colonel: "Ohisver Muller is alive and is trying to steal the Scapular."

Martin (thoughtful): "That would not be a good thing."

The Colonel: "I see that we understand each other."

Martin: "But why do you need me? An... organization... like yours has vast resources, I'm sure. Surely you must have the necessary... manpower... to stop even a man like Ohisver Muller?"

The Colonel: "Normally, you would be correct, Dr. Mystere. The Scapular is kept in a most safe place, the place where we keep our Treasure. It is well guarded. No ordinary man would have the power to breach it – but Ohisver Muller is not an ordinary man. He uses extraordinary weapons... against which my men are powerless... You know of what I speak..."

Martin: "Yes."

The Colonel: "Twenty-four hours ago, our vault was breached. Some kind of... magical barrier... now surrounds the place... L'Amitié, show him..."

L'Amitié hands Martin a folder that contains various scientific-looking charts, graphs, spectroscopic analyses, etc.

Martin studies them and whistles. "An Easter Island Egg," he says.

L'Amitié: "I don't understand. Our scientists can't make heads or tails of this."

Martin puts the folder down on the desk.

Martin: "Your 'barrier' is caused by a device that controls the rate of molecular vibrations. In my world, we call this an 'Easter Island Egg,' because it was used by the builders of Rapa-Nui to move the Statues of Easter Island. They are normally very rare and well-hidden."

The Colonel: "Can you... breach it?"

Martin: "Yes. In fact, if left unchecked, this could cause the entire structure around it to come crashing down..."

The Colonel and L'Amitié exchange a meaningful look.

Martin: "How do you know Ohisver Muller is behind this? It could be the Men in Black..."

L'Amitié hands Martin another photo: that of a man who looks a little like Oddjob from *Goldfinger*, leading a tight-suited commando in a tunnel.

L'Amitié: "We do have a CCTV. Well, we did anyway. That is the last picture it took."

Martin: "Machefer."

The Colonel: "Ohisver Muller's right-hand man."

There is a moment of silence. Then:

Martin: "I concede that I do not fancy the notion of someone like Ohisver Muller getting his hands on your Scapular, but what makes you think that I would want to help you, Colonel?"

The Colonel laughs, then coughs, then spits into his handkerchief.

The Colonel. "Ah, yes... I must have some fresh air... Will you walk with me outside, Dr. Mystère..."

He presses an invisible button and the wall behind him slides out, revealing a tree-lined terrace and a view over the night skyline of New York. The salon was located at the top of a mighty glass and steel skyscraper!

The Colonel grabs Martin's arm as an old man grabs his son's. In the garden outside, there is an old Italian stone fountain spouting water into a basin.

The Colonel: "Let me tell you a story, Dr. Mystere...."

CLOSE-UP on the Fountain.

FLASHBACK TO NAPLES. HOUSE CORONA. DECEMBER 1890.

CLOSE-UP on the same Fountain in a garden of a rich Mansion overlooking the Bay of Napes with Capri in the distance. It's a beautiful, sun-drenched winter morning.

In the CLOSE-UP we now see the water become tainted with blood.

Wider Angle: Count Corona and three henchmen of the Black Coats. Henchman No. 1 holds a bloody knife. At his feet is the corpse of the 20-year-old young man who looks like Martin Mystere – dead. The other two henchmen are holding the 10 year-old boy (CIGALE), who looks terrified.

Corona: Kill the boy now, Alberto. Then you will take my boat and dump their bodies off Capri.

Alberto: Yes, Master.

The killer approaches the young boy with the bloody knife. The boy's eyes grow wider. One quick slash and it will all be over.

Suddenly, a voice comes from the other end of the garden: "Wait a minute, my doves. IT'S GETTING DARK!"

They turn. We see the Colonel and the Marchef walking towards them. The Colonel is using a cane.

Corona's eyes now grow wide, expressing doubt, fear even.

Corona: "Godfather? What is it?"

The Colonel: "Fate has a way of making fools of all of us, except perhaps me... Do you know who the boys are, Corona?"

Corona, puzzled: "No, Godfather. As I said, they were orphans from France..."

The Colonel: "If you had taken the time to do your homework, you'd have discovered that they weren't really orphans. Their parents died, true, but their identity wasn't hard to fathom... As I did... They are the grandchildren of Valentine d'Arx... But perhaps you knew this already, no?"

Corona: "So what... They're enemies of our Brotherhood... Interlopers... They won't be missed..."

The Colonel: "Neither will you, Corona... Marchef, CUT THE BRANCH!"

Then with a phenomenal display of swordsmanship, the Marchef pulls out a saber and, in a swift move, decapitates Corona and two of the other henchmen (including the one who had killed Cigale's brother). The last henchman runs away in terror.

The Colonel bends down to talk to the boy.

The Colonel: "What do they call you, boy?"

Cigale (managing to suppress his fear): "Cigale, Monsieur."

The Colonel: "I am sorry that I didn't arrive in time to save your brother, but I gave you revenge. Three of ours for one of yours. We are even now, you and I, aren't we?"

The boy looks at the three corpses, and that of his brother, then in a remarkably mature fashion, he tells the Colonel:

"Yes we are."

The Colonel looks into the boy's eyes, his very soul, to test his sincerity. He appears satisfied because he stands up and pets the boy on his cheek.

The Colonel: "Very good. I don't want any more enmity between the house of d'Arx and mine."

Cigale: "Why? Who are you, Monsieur?"

The Colonel: "I knew your grandmother. She was a funny woman... You take after her quite a bit... What am I going to do with you now? I can see in you that you will never become one of us... It is not in your blood..."

Cigale: "Let me go, Monsieur."

The Colonel considers. Then: "Yes... You are a resourceful lad... Still, if I were you, I would avoid these parts for a while... The late Count Corona had some powerful friends who might seek revenge..." He pulls out a purse full of gold. "Go to the Orient. There you will find your destiny... Here is enough to facilitate your journey... Good-bye, young Cigale..."

The boy runs away.

Saladin walks in. "Did you do the right thing, Godfather?" he asks.

The Colonel: "I think so, Saladin. The best treasure one can acquire is not gold and jewels, it is lives. Today, I made an investment. Only time will tell if it bears fruit... Now Saladin, my dove, take care of clearing up this mess. The Schlieman's affair is yours now. I'm getting tired. I think it will be my last affair..."

The Colonel pulls out the photo of the two boys and looks at it...

We end the sequence on a CLOSE-UP of the PHOTO

BACK TO NEW YORK. BLACKSPEAR TOWER. THE ROOF TERRACE.

And we open on the Colonel giving the same photo to Martin, who looks fairly awe-struck.

The Colonel: "I'm sure you know that that boy was your great-grandfather, Cigale Mystere, whose heroic life dwarfs even your own prodigious exploits, Dr. Mystere..."

After a while, Martin: "Did you ever...?"

The Colonel: "No, we never met again. His path never crossed ours, whether by fate or by design, I don't know. But you understand now why I sought your help. I saved Cigale's life. You owe me, Dr. Mystere."

Martin: "Yes..."

The Colonel (happy): "Very good. I'll give you the information you need to get my Scapular, my dove... Then let's get back inside... It's getting too cold for my poor old bones... I swear, this will be my last affair..."

A PRIVATE AIRFIELD IN NEW JERSEY

A gulfstream jet is waiting on a landing strip, near a hangar. Mechanics finish refueling it, etc. It's got the BlackSpear logo on its wings (A black circle crossed with a diagonal white line.).

A car approaches. It is Martin's. Martin, Java and Diana get out. They're now dressed in their "adventuring" clothes, jeans, leather jackets, shoulder bags, etc.

Martin: "This is the place..."

Diana: "Nice plane." She looks underneath. We see partially camouflaged small air missiles. "Not the usual commercial model, I guess."

L'Amitié and the Countess come out of the hangar. They, too, are dressed as ordinary back-packers.

L'Amitié (to Diana): "I see you've noticed our weapons. It is sometimes necessary to chase away intruders..." He kisses her hand. "I am Julien Lecoq, but you can call me L'Amitié, Mademoiselle Lombard."

Diana: "Madame Mystere."

L'Amitié: "Ah, my apologies. I didn't know." Then turning towards Martin. "Congratulations. Dr. Mystere, you are a most lucky man."

The Countess: "I am the Countess de Clare. I shall be doing the flying today. Are you carrying everything we shall need, Dr. Mystere?"

Martin taps his bag. "I think so. Enough to stop an army of Men in Black, at least. But Muller has been collecting artifacts for a long time. I hope it'll prove adequate. What is our destination?"

The Countess smiles. "The Colonel instructed us to not reveal it until we get there. I'm sorry."

L'Amitié slaps Martin's back and says, "Let's get going then, *mes vaillants camarades*!"

Martin doesn't like that familiarity and has to shush Java who otherwise might be tempted to hit the Frenchman, as they get into the plane.

We end this sequence with the plane taking off.

INSIDE THE JET.

Hours later.

It's very comfortable inside the jet, like in any top executive's plane. The portholes are closed.

Martin is looking through a notebook, occasionally scribbling something down. Diana is reading a book. Java... I'm not sure how Java spends his time when he is alone?

L'Amitié is playing solitaire with a card deck. He looks at his watch.

L'Amitié: "Thank you for being so accommodating, Dr. Mystere. You can open the portholes now. We're about to land."

Martin: "We've been trying to guess where your secret hide-out is... Where your Colonel would hide the treasure of the Black Coats..."

Diana: "I said, an island in the Caribbean."

Martin: "Some place in the Rockies? The New Mexico Desert? Superstition Mountains?"

Diana (joking): "Any place but Area 51!"

L'Amitié: "You're not so far off the mark, Madame Mystere. Look!"

They look through the porthole – and we switch to an outside view of...

LAS VEGAS, NEVADA. McCARRAN AIRPORT.

There are plenty of good aerial views of Las Vegas from various American TV series such as *CSI*.

The Blackspear Jet lands at McCarran Intl. Airport (Las Vegas' airport). They're used to millionaires' jets landing there. They have special landing strips.

L'Amitié, Martin, Diana, then Java descend from the plane.

A wide black stretch limousine with chauffeur is already waiting.

L'Amitié: "Welcome to Las Vegas, Dr. Mystere, Madame Mystere."

Martin: "I. don't. believe. it."

L'Amitié (smiling): "Why not? You know the saying: what happens in Vegas stays in Vegas." He stretches his arms out, loving every minute. "What better place could we have picked?"

Diana: "He's right, darling. Las Vegas was a creation of the Mob. Bugsy Siegel came here in 1946 and with backing from Meyer Lansky and other mob figures built The Flamingo..."

L'Amitié: "That was before my time, but the Colonel once told me that he was very fond of Mr. Siegel."

The Countess comes down the plane, and hands the key to a waiting mechanic, giving him instructions. Then:

L'Amitié: "We were waiting for you."

Countess: "I'm ready."

They walk towards the Limousine.

LAS VEGAS. THE STRIP.

The Limousine is driving along the famous "strip" where all the big hotel/casinos are.

L'Amitié: "There we are. Home sweet home."

LAS VEGAS. JACK-OF-SPADES HOTEL. OUTSIDE.

A gigantic, ultra-modern hotel: the Jack-of-Spades Hotel. Outside, there is a giant JACK-OF-SPADES neon figure.

The Limousine enters a "reserved" parking area behind a metal gate that opens and closes automatically.

Martin: "The Jack-of-Spades?"

Diana: "But I was here last year for the YearlyKos convention!"

L'Amitié: "We're quite proud of it. We had it completely pulled down and rebuilt in 1998."

Martin: "THIS is your secret hide-out? I don't understand."

L'Amitié: "You will, Dr. Mystere. Like all of us, you will come to admire the genius of the Colonel..."

The Limousine stops. They get out.

Countess: "Make sure you have all your hocus pocus ready, Dr. Mystere. This is where the fun really begins.

LAS VEGAS. JACK-OF-SPADES HOTEL. INSIDE.

They walk though service corridors, then arrive in a luxurious office. There, there is a man in a business suit: FRANCESCHI.

Franceshi: "Monsieur Lecoq. I have papers for you to sign."

L'Amitié: "Not now, Franceschi. Is the commando ready?"

Franceschi: "Yes, sir. They were awaiting your orders."

Six men enter, wearing black jumpsuits, utility belts, etc.

Franceschi (looking a bit worried): "So you won't need me anymore then?"

Countess: "You may go, Alberto."

Franceschi leaves the room in a hurry.

L'Amitié speaks aloud, his voice being picked up by an invisible microphone.

L'Amitié: "Activate Protocol Mercy. Authorization Code Lecoq. IL FAIT JOUR!

Suddenly, the entire office starts descending. It is a giant elevator!

THE CONVENT OF THE MERCY UNDERGROUND / OUTSIDE.

When the elevator stops, and an entire wall slides out, Martin and his companions behold an amazing sight: the CONVENT OF THE MERCY from Corsica stands before them in a huge underground cavern lit up by an array of powerful spotlights

Martin: "It can't be. It's—"

L'Amitié: "Yes, the old Convent of the Mercy. The Colonel had it carted out stone by stone in 1946 and reassembled here, in these natural caverns which were enlarged with dynamite. Not unlike what they did in Area 51."

They descend onto an esplanade that leads to the entrance of the Convent.

Lecoq bumps into an invisible wall, he then puts his arm forward to touch it like a mime pretending to be trapped behind a glass. They all do.

L'Amitié: "You see our predicament. Machefer and his men have been inside for almost 24 hours now. We're fast running out of time."

Martin touches it too.

Martin: "As I thought, an Easter Island Egg. This is even more dangerous than you think. If not removed, the vibrations might eventually cause this entire cavern to collapse."

Diana: "The hotel above. There must be... thousands of people...."

Martin: "Yes. It would be monstrous."

Countess: "Can you take it down?"

Martin: "I think so, yes. Java, the bag."

Java gives Martin one of the bags he's been carrying. Martin opens it and takes a stone needle that was kept inside a leather pouch.

He holds the needle like an orchestra conductor holds a baton and, with it, traces an elaborate pattern on the invisible wall, then WALKS THROUGH IT.

The others are still locked behind.

Martin gestures them to wait, then walks to the stone arch entrance and there, on the ground, hidden behind a stone, finds a small, ovoid, stone object.

When we see it in close-up, we see that the egg has been intricately carved to contain a smaller egg inside and another one inside it, etc.

Martin pokes inside delicately with the needle, making the spheres inside the egg rotate.

There is a shimmering in the air and the field disappears.

L'Amitié: "I'm impressed, Dr. Mystère. We need someone like you in our Brotherhood."

Martin: "I'm not the joining type. Where to?"

L'Amitié: "I know where the Treasure Vault is. Deep inside, beneath the Convent. But I don't know how to get the Scapular."

Martin: "Colonel Bozzo-Corona told me. Not to worry. Just get me there and I'll do the rest."

Countess (amazed): "He... He entrusted you with that information!"

Diana (sarcastic): "Yes, it's astonishing that he wouldn't trust you two, isn't it?"

L'Amitié says nothing but makes a hand gesture of the "this way follow me" type and leads the Commando inside the Convent.

THE CONVENT OF THE MERCY UNDERGROUND / MAZE.

There is a maze of stone corridors, doors opening onto barren monk cells, a vast prayer hall, etc.

As the group keeps taking flights of stone stairs going further and further down, they are ambushed by another COMMANDO (Ohisver's Muller's men) dressed differently (so that we can tell them apart).

There is traditional thriller action, each side shooting at the other. More Black Coats men are hit than Muller's men.

Martin notices that the Black Coats seem to miss Muller's men more than usual. He then tells them to shoot a little more to the right, because he has realized that Muller's men wear a Tibetan silver pendant that causes people to see you slightly displaced in space.

This realization by Martin helps the Black Coats to re-establish parity.

There are DEATH TRAPS inside the Maze. The usual kind: spikes coming out of the walls on springs, trapdoors in the floors that open on pits with spikes; also secret passages where you have to move a statue, etc.

This sequence can be as long as short as required by the pacing of the story.

Because L'Amitié knows the Maze and its secrets, they can proceed far more quickly than Muller's men, so even though Muller's men were there before, the Black Coats commando reaches the lowest level first.

THE CONVENT OF THE MERCY UNDERGROUND / TREASURE VAULTS.

The Lowest Level is another maze – of canals. Dark waters with things inside. They have to take flat-bottomed barges which they propel with poles.

They finally reach the Treasure Room.

It is a massive, elevated square room, in the center of the water maze, that can be reached through stairs on each side. It looks a bit like a Temple; it is surrounded by large, square pillars.

Inside: the description of the Treasure of the Black Coats was given by Feval in one of his books: "gold bars... jewels... chalices stolen from the Church... columns made of gold coins... three thousand coins in each pile, twenty-five piles per column... four columns... ten million francs in gold... Paper money... one fifty thousand pound sterling note, especially printed by the Bank of England, twelve twenty-five thousand pound notes, two twenty thousand pound notes, forty-three fifteen thousand pound notes, one hundred and three ten thousand pound notes, two hundred and sixty five thousand pound notes... Four million pounds sterling in total... A hundred million francs in notes... Plus investments... Loans... In a safe, IOUs in amounts high enough to bankrupt Europe and America... More money than the three houses of Rothschild combined..."

In the center of all this is a case containing the SCAPULAR!

Martin, Diana, Java etc. disembark, climb the stairs and wander like Ali-Baba in this incredible place.

Both L'Amitié and the Countess's facial expressions reveal their naked greed as they discover the thing they covet most.

As Martin walks the amongst the treasures he sees the GOLDEN APPLE OF TROY. It's not really part of the story but I thought it would be nice to show it there.

The Treasure Vault is where the last chassé-croisé battle between the Black Coats and Machefer's men, who have arrived from another direction just as Martin was about to start trying to extract the Scapular from its booby-trapped case, take place.

The victory is secured by Martin and Java in typical style. Again, depending on the visual approach, I would use props such as ancient jewel-incrusted swords, etc.

At the end of this sequence, MACHEFER himself disappears in a mysterious, unexplained fashion. He is not killed. We don't see him run away. He might have fled through a secret passage or he might have used an artifact to teleport away. This should remain a mystery.

Then, Martin is able to open the case, and uses a gold metal glove to grab the Scapular from inside the case. Any other reactive substance, flesh, iron, etc. would trigger some kind of hostile response.

He then holds the Scapular.

L'Amitié: "What's in it?"

Martin: "Nothing."

L'Amitié: "Nothing? I don't understand. What do you mean. Is it empty?"

Martin: "The universe is mostly made of NOTHING, Monsieur Lecoq. That is what is inside. Pure NOTHING. You would be well advised to let it rest at that."

Their mission a success, they leave.

THE CONVENT OF THE MERCY UNDERGROUND / OUTSIDE.

The five protagonists emerge from the Convent.

That is the moment when L'Amitié pulls a gun on Martin.

L'Amitié: Give me the Scapular, Dr. Mystère.

Martin obeys.

L'Amitié: I'm sorry. You have been very helpful. Without your help, I never could have gotten my hands on it. It was too well-protected.

Martin: You planned this from the start, I imagine?

L'Amitié: Yes. I leaked information to Ohisver Muller, that I knew would lead to this moment. And now, with the Scapular in my possession and my men in New York ready to strike, I am the new Master of the Black Coats!

Martin: You're a fool, Lecoq.

L'Amitié: I'm going to have to kill all of you, of course... Perhaps not you, Countess. Choose your allegiance well, and I might let you live.

The Countess falls to her feet and begs: "Please..."

Lecoq points the gun at Martin, ready to shoot: "Well then, it's your turn Dr. Mystère."

Suddenly, a voice shouts: "MARCHEF! CUT THE BRANCH!"

It is Colonel Bozzo-Corona!

The Marchef steps out of the shadows of the Convent – and with a swift move, he decapitates Lecoq.

He then walks towards the Countess.

Countess: "Godfather! I swear! I'd never betray you!"

The Colonel pets her: "Of course, my dove, of course. Now go. I've got some unfinished business to attend to..."

She runs away towards the elevator.

The Colonel taps Lecoq's body with his cane.

Colonel: "He wasn't the first and won't be the last in my Council to try to betray me... What a shame I can never be surrounded by men like you, Dr. Mystere. *Sangodemi*! What wonders might we not accomplish together..."

Martin: "It was your plan all along, wasn't it?"

Colonel: "You've guessed of course. Yes, I knew there was a traitor in the High Council of the Brotherhood. What better way of flushing him out?"

Martin: "And Ohisver Muller?"

Colonel: "I reached an arrangement with Mr. Muller. His passion for collecting artifacts will now be exercised with greater caution when it comes to our Brotherhood."

Martin picks up the Scapular from where it lie, near Lecoq's dead hand..

Martin: "This was a fake, of course. Merely bait."

Colonel (laughing): "Is there anything you haven't divined, Dr. Mystere? Yes. The real one is hidden where none can find it. Decidedly, you are a man full of surprises..."

Martin: "I still have one more for you...."

Martin pulls out the Easter Island Egg and manipulates it.

There is a RUMBLING SOUND behind them – and the Convent collapses.

Colonel: "I see. Hmm. I might have expected something like that."

Martin (a bit taken back): "Is that all you're going to say? Your treasure is buried under tons of rubble..."

The Colonel takes them towards the Elevator.

Colonel: "As I told someone long ago, the most valuable treasure is not gold and jewels... These will be excavated in a couple of years... Less than a heartbeat to me... No, the greatest treasure is human lives. You owe me your life, Mrs. Mystere, and yours too, Dr. Mystere..."

<u>OUTSIDE – LAS VEGAS.</u>

The Colonel: "Someday, maybe far in the future, you, your children, one of his descendents maybe, will still owe a debt to the Black Coats, helping them in some affair we can only imagine – and that day, be assured that I will still be here to collect it!"

ARTICLE

Introduction to "The Avenging Saint"

The book you hold in your hands changed my life.

I know that sounds rather overblown, but it's still true. Without it, I might never have become a writer. Maybe I would have been a teacher, a lawyer, or (Heaven forbid!) a banker, but not a writer,

Because I owe it all to Leslie Charteris—and the Saint.

But not quite in the way you may think.

A bit of context is necessary before I go any further. Please bear with me while I acquaint you with the basics of the publication of the Saint in France.

Simon made his first appearance in a mystery imprint put out by publisher Gallimard in 1935, but it was the competing Editions Fayard which, from 1938 to 1968, popularized the character in France.

Since I wasn't born until 1954, you might well ask how this is relevant. It's like this:

Due to contractual obligations, Gallimard had reserved the rights to the two novels it published, *Meet the Tiger* and *The Last Hero*, so Fayard was obliged to start their own Saint imprint with *The Saint in New York* as #1, then *Knight Templar* (aka *The Avenging Saint*) as #2. The latter was released under the title *The Heroic Adventure*.

When I discovered, and began collecting, Saint books in 1967, at age 13, they were one of the cheapest and most entertaining series of paperbacks available on the market, endlessly reprinted since the 1940s.

They were virtually everywhere, on the newsstands and in the bookstores, given a boost by Roger Moore's television series, which was then playing on our small screens.

Graced by colorful, high design covers by the gifted Regino Bernad, most of the later volumes were loose adaptations of the American radio-plays or the *New York Herald-Tribune* comic strips, ably rendered into French by Madeleine Michel-Tyl, whose husband, Edmond (who passed away in 1949), was himself an author of popular novels. Edmond had not only translated the first Saint books, but also Rex Stout's Nero Wolfe mysteries for Fayard.

For the record, my very first Saint books were No. 48, *Le Saint exige la tête*, and No 18, *La Marque du Saint,* which contained such Charteris classics as *The Man Who Was Clever* and *The Logical Adventure.*

Being the kind of person I am, I immediately decided to collect them all, and read them in what I thought was their proper, numbered order. Unfortunately, as is often the case with series, No. 1 (*The Saint in New York*) was hard to find. In fact I never found a Fayard edition until much, much later, and I eventually had to satisfy myself with a Livre de poche reprint.

So I began the series with No. 2, *The Avenging Saint.*

The problem was — one couldn't very well follow *The Avenging Saint* without having first read *The Last Hero*!

There was no internet back then, no wikipedia, no books or articles where I could have looked up a complete bibliography of Leslie Charteris. And Fayard wasn't obliging enough to list *The Last Hero* (and *Meet the Tiger*) in their back pages, since they had been published by one of their competitors. In fact, Fayard didn't get to publish *The Last Hero* in its own imprint until No. 72!

So, there I was, stuck with *The Avenging Saint,* without a copy of *The Last Hero.* While I could plainly see that something was being kept hidden from me, I couldn't tell what. I had no clue that *The Last Hero* existed, only hints about the fairly cataclysmic events that had pit Simon against Rayt Marius (Marus in the French edition because the name "Marius" is associated with the happy go-lucky popular character in Marseilles fiction), Prince Rudolf and Professor Vargan, and that it had resulted in the death of the Saint's dearest friend, Norman Kent.

You might say, that's really all one needs to know to tackle *The Avenging Saint*, but it was still a very annoying feeling to realize that half of the story had somehow already occurred before I turned page 1.

Feeling very frustrated over that state of things, I did what any teenager in my place would have done.

No, I didn't discard the book; I decided to write my own prequel.

I promptly embarked upon writing my own version of *The Last Hero* and, with the touching hubris that only a 14-year-old can muster, I grabbed first credit by signing it "by Jean-Marc Lofficier & Leslie Charteris."

As William Goldman discovered when he abridged S. Morgenstern's immortal classic *The Princess Bride*, the problem with prose fiction is that one spends a lot of time with descriptions and other boring background stuff, and that we don't get quickly enough to the "best bits."

So, after a couple of pages, I switched to doing it in the comic book format, using an avant-garde artistic technique referred to by ignoramuses as "stick figures." If there is one character, after all, whose story can be told through stick figures, isn't it the Saint?

Story-wise, that worked rather well. In the space of a couple of months, I filled well over a hundred notebook-sized pages with small panels telling my own version of the Saint's adventure. If I recall correctly, in my version, Marius and Vargan belonged to a secret organization called "Shadow" led by a villain named Doctor (or was it Professor?) Skull. The story involved thuggees and idols made of a strange kind of unmelting ice and daggers that spat electron fire, and all kinds of outlandish elements.

Through it all, the little stick figure of Simon fought bravely through countless perils, dispatching villains with his unique brand of wit and determination.

When I was eventually lucky enough to talk to Mr. Charteris himself, in 1974, an experience which was not unlike that of a small village priest meeting the Pope, I conspicuously refrained from mentioning *The Last Hero* or Doctor Skull.

But for all its faults, its naiveté and outrageous pulpishness, its shameless "borrowings" from other sources and overmelodramatic plot, this was my first long-distance narrative, with proper dialogue and plot. It was an invaluable teaching tool that later enabled me to tackle more serious works, and eventually write real books and real comics.

If I had read *The Last Hero* before *The Avenging Saint*, would have I embarked upon such a Quixotic task? Who can tell? But I can't help feel that, if I became a writer, I owe it all to this odd case of the two books being published out of order.

Understandably, in light of what I've just written, *The Avenging Saint* remains, to this day, my favorite Saint book— in fact, the only one which I have in both its French and English editions. I would argue it may well be the best Saint novel of all. There are so many things to like about it, from Simon's ground-breaking triangular relationship with Sonia and Pat, with the shadow of Norman Kent's death looming over his head, to the return of Inspector Carn, from the callous villainy of Marius (a proto-Bondian villain who surely must have inspired Fleming!) to the smooth deadliness of Prince Rudolf, and, of course, the best ending ever!

But before you embark upon reading this thrilling novel, let me offer a word of caution:

Make sure you read *The Last Hero* first.

Because, otherwise, who knows, you might become a writer too.

First publication:
The Avenging Saint, 2013.